Roulette of Redemption

VIOLA HERMAN

Book Cover by GetCovers

Editing by Donna Marie West

Beta reading and editing by Aneta Muszczynski

First edition [2024]

Paperback ISBN 978-83-970252-3-3

Hardback ISBN 978-83-970252-5-7

Dedication

To every woman who wasn't afraid to fight for her happiness. This is for you.

TRIGGERS

"Roulette of Redemption" is a romantic suspense book. The story includes elements that might not be suitable for some readers. Mentioned kidnapping, abuse, torture, murder, death, obsessive partners, gun violence, are present in that novel. It includes also explicit sexual content and coarse language. Readers who may be sensitive to these elements, please take note.

Table of contents

PROLOGUE

I ran as hard as I could. My strength diminished with each step, but I couldn't give up if I wanted to survive. Even though I felt like falling to my knees and crying, I knew it was impossible to do so.

I was getting slower and slower, my movements becoming more and more chaotic.

"Come on—you—can't—give up—now—" I wheezed between breaths.

Thinking about all the cuts on my body didn't help, so I tried not to. Most of the time, I succeeded. My bare feet were on fire. The branches, cones, and stones I ran on caused hundreds of bloody scratches. My legs were marked, as I only wore shorts and a T-shirt.

These weren't my only injuries. I could still feel the punches to my stomach, the kicks to my back, the painful bruises on my arms. From beneath my hair, a trickle of blood ran down my forehead. However, that wasn't the worst part. There was no cure for the wounds that formed in a person's soul. The things I endured were beyond repair.

Despite everything, I continued to run. I was out of breath, my lungs burning. I could hear my heart beating in my ears so loudly that it gave me a migraine. Maybe it wasn't my heart at all.

Eventually, my legs disobeyed, and I fell forward. To lessen the impact of the fall, I reached out with my hands, yet my arms were too feeble to sustain me. As I closed my eyes, I felt my head hit the root of a large tree.

For a moment, I didn't realize what was happening. I was stunned. Then it all came back, and I pictured my mother's smile in my mind. She was saying something to me, but I couldn't understand or even hear her. She reached out her always warm hand to caress my cheek.

"Get up and keep going," I finally heard her whisper. *"You're not that far away now."*

An animal-like whimper came out of my chest as I picked myself up from the ground. I don't know how I found the strength. I was nearly dead.

Somewhere in the distance, I heard the snap of a breaking branch. That was a warning sign for me. He was getting closer and closer, and I didn't have a single second to waste. One second could mean life or death for me.

Without another sound, I rose from the ground to my knees and then stood up on wobbly legs. As fast as my strength allowed me, I started running again.

Inside the thick forest, the night became even darker. Towering trees hid the color of the sky. Maybe it was just my imagination, but it seemed like the temperature had dropped dangerously.

I kept running and running until the trees thinned out a bit. Grass covered the ground, and the moisture beneath my feet felt soothing.

A dark path emerged between the trees. It took me some time to realize there was a road in front of me. A black-paved road.

You were right, Mom.

I heard another branch snap in the distance. I had never been so close and yet so far from my goal.

Twenty more steps! Run! Go, go, go! Run!

I took steps, ran past trees, and reached the road. As if magically arriving at the finish line, I stopped. The blinding light instantly pierced my eyes with pain.

A car was speeding toward me. When the driver saw an obstacle in his path, they immediately hit the brakes. But I only saw the car's lights. Another wave of fear paralyzed my body. Had I fought for my life just to be killed by a car? What an irony...

I closed my eyes and started to pray. At least I tried, because I couldn't remember how it went. All the lines of the prayer blended together, and nothing made sense.

The tires screeched, then abruptly stopped. I took a deep breath and brought my prayer to a halt. I slowly opened my eyes. A pickup truck was stopped twenty feet from me. The driver's side door opened with a creak, and an older man stepped out.

His voice raspy, he said, "What in the world?"

I had appeared like a character from a horror film. The most crucial aspect was our limited time to leave. I had only minutes to convince him I needed help to survive.

I stumbled toward him.

CHAPTER 1

CASTRIEL

At this point, I was almost certain that the move was an excellent idea. Granted, I hadn't even landed on American soil yet, but I was already in heaven. Literally and figuratively.

Some turbulence rocked the plane, but not enough to make me take my hands off the blonde's head. My posture remained unwavering.

Opening my eyes, I saw an angel kneeling before me. She couldn't have been very comfortable in the plane's small bathroom, but it was what it was. She was here for just one reason.

Dressed in a flight attendant's uniform, with the buttons of her white shirt undone and her makeup smeared, she gave me a blow job. She wasn't a pro at it, so I snaked my fingers into her hair and forced myself deeper into her throat when I came. She was pretty, but a pretty face wasn't enough to hold my attention for long. I was an asshole, and I was well aware of it. I had made no promises to anyone that I would be a knight in shining armor.

My focus was on the sounds of her choking. It was music to my ears. I was rough, and I loved it. Once again, there was no promise of anything else.

I sped up the movements of the blonde's head when I sensed I was about to explode. The tingling sensation in my balls increased in intensity and my breathing became deeper and deeper. Concentrating only on my pleasure, I closed my eyes again.

In three powerful movements, I reached my climax. I was disappointed to see that the orgasm didn't engulf my whole body. On the contrary, it was like a flash of lightning, disappearing as quickly as it appeared. A real disappointment. Before my cum even had time to run down the girl's throat, I had already closed my zipper.

The stewardess opened her glassy blue eyes, and I saw hope in them. What was she hoping for? I had no idea. That I would fuck her? Ask her out on a date? Both options were likely, but neither was going to happen.

As an accomplished asshole who valued every spoken word like gold coins, I didn't even say thank you before I turned and opened the cabin door. I glanced over my shoulder at her. With a look of astonishment and maybe even some resentment in her eyes, she took in my actions. Still on her knees on the floor, she opened her mouth but before she could utter a word, I was no longer with her.

I walked over to where I had been sitting in First Class. The last thing I wanted was to chat with fellow passengers, so I immediately opened my laptop. I had a backlog of work that I needed to get done. As always, I had urgent matters to take care of.

"Would you like a drink?" The melodious voice belonged to a flight attendant; not the same one who had been in the bathroom with me, of course. I ripped my eyes away from the computer screen and saw a brunette in an identical uniform. She was smiling so broadly that it must have hurt her cheeks. The smile also said that she was completely unaware of my alone time with her co-worker—not that I had any desire to discover a new land on a flight that would last another hour.

I shook my head as a sign that I needed nothing. That was all she could expect from me. I was telling the truth when I said that I valued every word. If I didn't have a strong need, I remained silent. Absolutely nothing. I was the silent observer. It often made people in my company uncomfortable. They wondered what kind of crazy person had been appointed director of the American branch of the company.

To get rid of the uninvited company, I immediately went back to work on my laptop. My fingers raced over the keys at express speed, and I got carried away for good.

By the end of the flight, no one dared disturb me.

***

The apartment was only six miles from La Guardia Airport. The position of director entailed a mandatory relocation, which in turn entailed providing a new apartment. This would impress me if I were a sensitive motherfucker. Two thousand square feet, three bedrooms, four bathrooms, a large living room, and an extravagant kitchen—all unnecessary. Why did I need such an enormous apartment when I was going to spend most of my time in the office anyway? If anyone had asked, it was money unnecessarily wasted.

Everything was already furnished with taste and to the highest standard. I didn't pay much attention to such small details. It would be annoying if I had to take care of the furniture myself, so I appreciated the efforts. Even the refrigerator was stocked. It saved me time.

The only thing that attracted me to this apartment was the view. It was spectacular. Typically, that's the view of New York you see from up high. It was truly amazing. The view of the city stopped me in my tracks for a full three minutes, and I guess that meant something. Or maybe it didn't.

I had time to unpack and freshen up before my phone started vibrating on my nightstand. I buttoned my shirt with one hand and answered the call.

"Yes?"

I heard my boss's voice. "I hear you're in a good mood, boy."

Takashi Saurii was a hell of a smart man. Not just about the business he ran, but about life itself. He took me under his wing a long time ago, when I was in my twenties. I owed most of my knowledge to him. And my debt to him was much greater.

Even though a decade had passed, he still saw me as a boy. God knew I hadn't been one for a long time. Life itself had taken care of that.

"Hello, Mr. Saurii. Is everything okay?" My voice was indifferent, as always.

"Sure, sure. I just wanted to see if you were okay. Does the apartment suit you?"

"It would be a dream for a family of five. For one person who won't have time to enjoy its charms, it's an unnecessary expense."

The sound of Saurii's deep laughter reached my ears. My lips didn't even twitch, because I saw nothing funny in it.

"Only you, boy, would complain about the goodness that destiny brings to your door. Only you." He sighed loudly, still amused.

Perhaps he had a minor point. I was a flesh-and-blood minimalist. An unreformed one, I might add. Not that I didn't appreciate what I had. I appreciated it. I just didn't need a lot of it.

I muttered under my breath, not wanting to argue.

"Castriel…" Another sigh from him. "You need to take advantage of the life you've been given. There is a time for everything. There is a time for work. There is a time for fun. There is a time for being alone, and there is a time for love."

Work, I understood perfectly.

Fun? I was aware of how to enjoy myself. I really knew how. Perhaps in a less traditional way, but still.

Loneliness? Did anyone know more about that than I did?

Love? What the hell was he talking about? The only love I needed right now was my work. I didn't need any complications from a woman. My life was complicated enough.

No, no, and no… Absolutely not. No way.

"I know what you're thinking, boy. Despite the significant distance separating us, I'm fully aware of it. I also know that the day will come when you will change your mind."

I was the last person to talk nonsense. "Yes, Mr. Saurii," I agreed, but we both knew I wasn't thinking that.

I put my jacket back on and held the phone back to my ear. "I have to go to the office now, Mr. Saurii. I'll call you back soon."

"Absolutely not. You just landed. You'll start tomorrow; today, you'll relax. And for God's sake, I've already told you to call me by my first name."

"The conquest of a new continent is in store for us. It can't wait. I have a lot of work to do," I insisted.

"I've already called Meghan. I informed her you will be at work tomorrow. It's a work order," he said just as firmly.

I wanted to snarl and curse him. How dare he! I deserved independence as the head of an American branch office, but he was treating me like a subordinate.

"Ahh... And Castriel... Calling Mason or Emma to make some contacts might be worthwhile at first. You'll also need multiple marketing efforts. This will help you grasp the market and identify worthy cooperation partners."

I gritted my teeth because I was losing my cool. I understood what the hell I was doing, and I didn't require hand-holding. I was just over thirty years old, but in business, I had things most businessmen lacked: balls of steel and a brain the size of the solar system.

Saurii, on the other hand, had a weakness for Emma Lincoln. Not in the romantic sense, but he had a strange sense of protectiveness toward her. He believed they shared a connection at the level of the soul. I didn't believe in such nonsense.

"I believe I'm quite capable of finding companies with which Papilio will be able to establish a partnership," I said roughly.

"I didn't say you weren't, Castriel. You're the head of this branch, and of all the people I know, you're the most qualified for this position. I just wanted to help. Know that you're not alone, and that you don't have to face everything by yourself. You have my full support."

Shit. The old man meant well.

I was overcome with a pang of guilt.

Shaking my head, I closed my eyes. I didn't want to disappoint him and, at the same time, I knew I had to draw a line.

Even though Takashi didn't see it, I opened my eyes and took off my jacket again in a gesture of surrender. "I know that and I thank you. I'll call Emma and arrange a meeting. It wouldn't hurt to talk to her."

"Good, good..." He sounded pleased. "Whatever you decide, I trust you."

"Thank you, Takashi."

"You're welcome, boy."

A few minutes later, I hung up.

Looking around the master bedroom, I wondered what I was going to do with myself.

Takashi said no work, but not no working. I picked up the phone again and dialed the number for my assistant.

Meghan was a woman in her thirties, not tall, but feisty as hell. She was one of the best candidates we had recruited for the job. At the first interview, she was the sole candidate who could arrange a flight from Tokyo to London within ten minutes in front of our eyes. She spoke fluent Japanese, French, German, and Russian. English, of course, was her first language. I had no idea why she needed to use Russian, and, frankly, I didn't give a shit. The fact that she was the only person to pass this task convinced us that she was perfect for the position of my assistant.

"Good morning, Mr. Russell. I hope you had a pleasant flight!" Her sonorous voice irritated me immediately.

"Hello, Meghan. The flight was long, but at least I found some entertainment on it. Thank you for asking."

"Mr. Saurii warned me you would call and tried to convince me you're indispensable for work. I shouldn't believe your rantings."

To keep from spitting out a series of curses, I clenched my teeth.

This is the second time today. If this keeps up, I'll have to go to the gym twice a day to get rid of this negative energy. Or I'll find a much more pleasant way to release it. As long as it's not as mediocre as the one from the airline.

With a deep breath, I said, "I have no intention of coming to the company today. Please send reports on the results of the Media Linc campaign surveys for Papilio and the sales results for the quarter to my email."

"Sure. The results will be in your inbox within fifteen minutes."

"Excellent."

"Is there anything else I can help you with, Mr. Russell?"

"No, Meghan. That's all." Hopefully, she wasn't expecting a parting word from me. I put the phone in my pocket and headed for the exit.

Before I got caught up in the whirlwind of work, I had one more thing to do. Like oxygen, I needed that one thing in my life. The one thing that allowed me to experience freedom, if only briefly.

CHAPTER 2

IZZY

The job at Media Linc wasn't very demanding. All it required was a nice appearance, the ability to make phone calls, and knowing everyone in the company well enough. The rest came by itself.

But more and more, I felt that something was missing. The feeling of inadequacy grew stronger with each passing week.

When I moved to New York, all I had dreamed about was finding some job and supporting myself, having something with which to pay the horrendous rent for my tiny apartment, and something to put in my mouth. Survival was the priority.

Many jobs later, an employment agency got me in the hiring process for Media Linc. It was a job that didn't require me to sit down after hours or use up too many of my brain cells. Plus, the salary was great.

So why was I feeling anxious? Somewhere deep inside, I felt I had to do something with my life; change it, change my destiny. Being a receptionist for life wasn't my aspiration. I wanted to give my life a new meaning.

I read once that it's a natural human drive to want more. The issue isn't appreciating what we have. Everyone should want more so they can grow, change, and create.

I had reached that point. I wanted more. There was a hunger within me that couldn't be quenched by food or material possessions.

When I was halfway through my shift, my phone rang. The number was blocked.

Strange.

"Hello?" I said in a friendly tone.

Silence filled the receiver. But the silence wasn't absolute. I could hear someone breathing. Somebody was on the other end.

"Hello? Is someone there?"

As if that would help, I pressed the receiver closer to my ear. I threw in another "hello" and when all I heard was a broken breath, I hung up.

This was the third call this week where I hadn't heard from anyone. It sent shivers down my spine.

"Hi, girl."

I tore my eyes from the phone and raised my head. Standing in front of the desk was my best friend. It had only been a year since I met Emma. When she showed up at Media Linc she caused a lot of commotion, even though she didn't mean to. Her desire for invisibility was futile. Within five minutes, she had attracted the interest of numerous men, including her current husband, Mason Lincoln. That's a long story.

Emma was magnetic. I was the first to realize that she wasn't her twin sister Lena, who she was pretending to be. Anyway, a thread of friendship connected us. As soon as I started noticing details that made her different from her sister, I knew that one day we would be friends for the rest of our lives.

At that moment, I couldn't imagine a day without exchanging even one message with her. She was like the sister I'd never had, and I loved her deeply.

"Hi, Em." With a smile on my face, I leaned over the desk for a kiss on her cheek. "You're early."

"I know, I know." She raised her hands in a gesture of surrender. "You can't blame me. I've missed you and I'm sick of the male vibes in the house."

"I told you he was an Alpha through and through," I said with a laugh.

"Yeah, but this is a whole new level."

"Oh, shut up. You love that asshole, and you love that he's so possessive."

Her face displayed indignation, but I saw through her facade. "You know nothing about my life, young lady. Now, get off that sweet ass of yours and let's go get some coffee. I crave female company."

"Of course, before your predator figures out you're here and hauls you back to your den."

Em winked at me and a big smile appeared on her face. She was beaming, her happiness contagious to everyone around her.

Five minutes later, we left the Media Linc building and walked to the coffee shop where we usually took our coffee breaks.

"So tell me," I encouraged her as soon as we sat down at a table.

"Don't worry, everything's fine," she assured me. "It's just... Sometimes I have such strange moods. Yesterday, for example, I was in the shower and just like that, I cried. I don't know what's wrong with me."

I looked at her. She seemed paler than usual, but her hair had gotten even shinier. She was thin when we met, but now she had become even slimmer.

"You're not sick, are you?"

"No, not really," she replied. "I mean, I just don't feel like myself. Maybe it's some kind of food poisoning or virus, because I threw up my breakfast the other day. Do you think I should see a doctor?"

"You should," I confirmed. Smiling from ear to ear, I waited for her to catch the suspicion forming in my mind.

She scanned my face, seeking an answer in my eyes.

"Do you think it's something serious?"

"No, no... It will pass soon."

Without interrupting her observations, she grabbed a cup and took a sip of her favorite coffee. Almost immediately, she grimaced. She looked at the coffee with disgust, and my smile grew even wider.

"Have they changed the beans? This coffee tastes strange today," she commented.

"It tastes normal to me."

"Really? Maybe it's some new syrup they added to my coffee."

Wondering how my Em could be so oblivious to what was going on, I shook my head.

She pushed her cup away and leaned in.

"What's so funny, Izzy?" she growled in annoyance.

I raised my hands in a gesture of surrender. "Maybe we could try a different approach. Has anything else tasted funny lately, Em?"

She rolled her eyes. "Don't play psychoanalyst with me; just say what's on your mind."

"Please answer the question," I pressed her.

"Gee, I don't know. Mason bought stale shrimp a few days ago."

"Oh. What about sex? Don't you feel the need to jump on your husband a little more than usual?"

Em giggled and her cheeks turned pink. "You have no idea, girl. I thought things would change after we got married, but our sex has only gotten hotter. And I think it's all his fault. He made me addicted to him."

I nodded at her thoughts, but I still knew my own.

"I have another question, Em. When was the last time you had your period?"

The laughter that Em burst out with was so thunderous that the other customers looked at us with interest. I wasn't worried. I waited patiently for her to calm down while I sipped my coffee. After a minute, the air escaped her. The laughter faded and the smile disappeared from her face. When tears appeared in her eyes, my eyebrows rose.

"What the hell?" she whispered. "It's impossible."

"Are you one hundred percent sure?"

"Yeah, we only got carried away once when—"

"Yeah?"

"Oh, Izzy... What am I going to do now? Fuck, fuck, fuck... I'm supposed to go back to work, you know. This winter, we're supposed to fly to the Alps. Oh, God..." Em's head dropped, and she hid her face in her hands.

I stroked her hand. Women's first reactions to an unplanned pregnancy were different. There was no blueprint for how to do it. I was sure that once the initial shock was over, everything would settle down.

"Emma, before you panic for good, you should take a test and talk to Mason about it," I said.

"It's too late. I'm already panicking."

"Em, listen to me..." I grabbed her hand and pulled it away from her face. "No matter what happens, I'm here for you. So is Mason. He can't see anything beyond you. If, and I emphasize *if*, you're pregnant, he's going to get down on his knees before you with joy. I'm absolutely sure of it."

"You think so?"

"I would never lie to you. You're married, you love each other, you're crazy about each other. It's natural that eventually a child would appear in your family. Having it come a little earlier will not change anything. It will only complete your happiness."

"Oh, Izzy. What would I do without you? You're the best."

She wiped her forehead with her hand, then took three deep breaths.

"Okay, okay," she said. "It's going to be okay."

"Of course it will," I assured her. "Pregnancy test and Mason. In whatever order. Do you want me to be there when you take the test?"

"That would be wonderful, but you're right, I should talk to Mason first. I think I'd like us to do it together."

Smiling, I nodded. Her approach was understandable, but somewhere inside, I felt the sting of rejection. It could have been a sense of loneliness instead.

Em was already much calmer. She even tried to smile.

"Tell me about going back to work." I rattled off the first better topic to take her mind off the likely pregnancy for a while.

"I considered working for Takashi at first. He tried to recruit me in every way, even despite Mason's growing annoyance." She giggled. "My possessive husband would rather pack up the entire company and move it to Japan than let me leave him here alone. From what I understood between a lot of cursing, I'd have to do it over his dead body, and even if I killed him, I shouldn't expect any peace from him, whatever that means."

"Don't worry. We both know how possessive he is of you. Whatever you decide, it will be fine. Now you don't want to work for Takashi anymore?"

"I don't know," she admitted, looking out the window.

"Okay. If you had unlimited opportunities and resources, Em, what would you do? What would give you the most joy?" I asked.

Emma pondered, but the moment I saw the sparkle in her eyes, I knew she already had an answer.

"I would want to work with children. I love children. Starting a foundation or supporting disadvantaged children would be my likely course of action. I don't know. I've never thought about it that much."

"Maybe this is the time to think about it. I don't mean that you have a rich husband and don't have to work, although that's obvious. The world has given you the opportunity to help people without worrying about tomorrow, so you'd better take advantage of it."

Emma's eyes lit up even more. Just the prospect of this made her happy.

"This is work; hard work. It won't be easy, and your heart will probably break more than once. But the reward for such work is the sweetest of all."

"I don't even know where to begin," she whispered.

"By identifying who you want to help and how you want to help them. We'll take it from there and find ways and means step by step."

A smile broke out on Em's face that soon made her whole. It brought me joy to see my friend so happy.

Seconds later, Em's phone vibrated on the coffee table. A picture of her newlywed husband appeared on the screen.

"Speak of the devil..." she said, lifting the phone to her ear. "Hello, sweetheart. I'm currently with Izzy..."

My mind wandered back to the advice I had just given. I should take it to heart myself and start by setting some kind of goal in my life. Sooner rather than later, I had to change something before this need exploded inside me.

Em interrupted my thoughts. "I'm sorry, Izzy. Mason couldn't bear not to ask when I was coming home. I'm telling you. That guy is going to drive me crazy one day!" She laughed.

"It's no big deal," I said. A lump rose in my throat. Our meeting was already ending.

Remorse appeared on Em's face, but I didn't want her to feel that. I smiled as broadly as I could and said, "You should go see your husband now. You need to have a serious talk and after the sex marathon that Mason has in his repertoire, let me know if I'm going to be an aunt."

"No," she objected almost immediately. "We've spent so little time together lately. I need that time with you."

"I know, but you need Mason more now. You need to talk and take that test. We'll meet soon and then you'll tell me everything."

"Are you sure?" she asked with sadness but also hope in her voice.

"Absolutely. Go ahead."

"I love you, Izzy. I'll get back to you as soon as I take the test," she assured me, standing up and giving me a hug.

Before I knew it, I was sitting all alone at the table. "I love you too," I whispered to no one.

***

Working at Media Linc was a big part of my life. However, when I had the desire or need to feel truly free, I transformed into someone different. My need to escape was something I didn't share with anyone. I never uttered a word about my need to feel when adrenaline coursed through my veins.

It's not that I was ashamed of my second personality, filled with tension and risk. There was no reason for me to feel ashamed. I was rather possessive of the part of me that belonged only to me. How come I never mentioned this to Emma? I didn't know the answer.

After meeting with Em, I went straight home. I took a quick shower and got ready. I put on a leather outfit, protectors, gloves, and high boots. With my bright green helmet tucked under my arm, I grabbed my keys and walked out. I went down to the underground garage in my building. It had cost me a lot to buy a space in this place. I couldn't leave my Bird on the sidewalk, and the garage was protected with no public access. A special app that scanned irises was required to access the garage door.

Inside the garage, I walked to the left and after a few steps, I saw my Honda CBR 1100XX Super Blackbird. My Bird was the same bright green color as the helmet. The bike was beautiful and dangerous as hell. She had layers of power that sometimes scared me. More than once, I felt like I was taming a dragon. This fierce machine was perfect for me.

No one would have guessed that I could drive such a beast. If a man drove her, he would sit in a semi-upright position. With my small size, I was tightly fitted to her like a glove on my hand. As a result, I could feel her every breath, every gust of wind.

As I approached the motorcycle, I tenderly ran my hand over her tank. Sitting down, I turned on the ignition. A low rumble echoed through the space. Between my thighs, I felt the vibrating power of the beast and a shiver ran through my entire body—a feeling of awe experienced only by those who shared my deep love for these machines.

I clipped my phone into the handlebars, put on my helmet, and tucked my leg in. I turned the throttle slightly and slowly drove to the garage door, opening it with the app. Riding out onto the street, I experienced a rush of adrenaline as I pressed my knees into the machine. Even though I had felt this way before, it never truly fizzled out for me.

Without hurrying, I made my way through the jammed streets of the city. It took me almost twenty minutes to get to Bronxville, and from there I drove to White Plains. Then north.

I cranked the throttle and felt the true power of the Blackbird beneath me. As I shot forward, hugging the machine, I felt another shiver run down my spine. Even during sex, I had never felt anything like this. The adrenaline amplified the excitement. It increased as I gained speed.

Only then did the stress and intrusive thoughts that kept me awake at night leave my body. My head cleared. Nothing existed but this moment. This overwhelming feeling of total freedom, with no yesterday and no tomorrow.

I rode forward, concentrating on the road and freedom. The machine underneath me purred, and it was only a moment before another engine roar reached my ears. Surprised by my disconnection from reality, I looked in the mirror. A biker rode a few yards behind me. He matched my speed, staying on my tail.

Before I knew it, the driver jumped out from behind me and caught up with me, riding in the opposite lane. He wore a black leather outfit and a black helmet with a white ghost pattern on the side. Judging by his physique, he was a man, a tall man. I was more interested in what he was riding. The black Suzuki Hayabusa had gold inserts and a gray Japanese sign glued to the body. The wheels, of course, were also gold.

The Hayabusa whined under the control of its driver. I looked ahead and froze because a truck was coming from the opposite direction. A drop of sweat ran down my forehead and I licked my lips. I looked again at the madman, who was about to play a very dangerous game of chicken, but could see nothing through the darkened glass of the helmet.

I turned my eyes back to the road ahead. If he wanted to kill himself, let him. I wasn't the enemy.

Seconds later, his machine roared, and he was suddenly several yards ahead of me. When his helmet turned, I knew he was watching me out of the corner of his eye.

Obviously, he liked the fact that I was behind him; I liked it a little less. As soon as the truck passed me, I mindlessly jumped into the opposite lane and leveled off with the Hayabusa.

Another shot of adrenaline pumped through my veins. Every cell in my body buzzed with joy. The energy flowing through me was electric. I twisted the throttle again. The Blackbird went even faster, and then I drifted back into my lane.

Like the Hayabusa driver before, I turned and looked back. I wasn't naive to think that I could meet him one-on-one. With the power of his wild beast, I wouldn't stand a chance in a speed race. But that wasn't the point here. It was a game of cat and mouse for him. He was provoking me.

The road in front of me narrowed a bit, and the turns began. This was a route I had driven several times before. If one of us got too competitive, it could be tragic. But often the adrenaline rush is so addictive that it blocks logical thinking and the expectation of what lies ahead.

Before I made the first sharp turn, my opponent sped up again. He caught up with me and, as I looked at him, he suddenly lifted the front wheel of his bike. He looked like a wild black horse. I blinked once, a second time, and his bike was in front of me again.

I had to admit, the guy had skills. He knew what he was doing on his wild machine. The corners were getting sharper and sharper, and he was leaning on the bike more to get through them. His knee guards were touching the pavement, just like mine. At that speed, there was no other way to get out of the turns and survive.

Aside from the guy's skill, what pissed me off was that he turned a relaxing ride into a peeing contest. This wasn't how it was supposed to be, but the devil in me couldn't let him go. He whispered in my ear to show him his place, to hit him, to teach him respect.

This devil was sneaky because he whispered for so long until I changed lanes on one of the curves and, like in sync, we both took the turn, almost glued to the asphalt.

That was stupid on my part. At that speed, a small rock on the road would have been enough to put the bike out from under me. The Hayabusa was behind me again, the only good thing. Now I led us through a serpentine of curves.

The man quickly copied my move, ending my brief victory. The difference between the situations was that I was much luckier. When we came out of the corner, a pickup truck was heading in his direction at high speed.

In those moments, quick and instinctive decisions based on the circumstances were essential. If the driver took a second to think, it would mean the cross for him. I didn't know if the circumstances paralyzed the Hayabusa driver or if he had a death wish, but he didn't swerve into my lane. He drove straight into the car. He had no chance.

I felt heat flooding through my body. Fear kicked in. I took my foot off the gas and dropped a gear to let the engine slow down. Sudden braking would have resulted in a skid at the speed I was going.

The Blackbird reacted, and I fell behind. With enough room, the Hayabusa driver could get away from the speeding pickup. Yet he didn't do it right away. He kept barreling toward the truck. My eyes, like my mouth, opened wide in surprise and horror. A lump formed in my throat, growing with each passing second. Frozen blood coursed harder through my body. I couldn't believe what I was seeing. This guy was either trying to kill himself or he was a complete idiot.

There was nothing I could do to save this asshole if he didn't want it. Time slowed down as he dodged the pickup at the last possible second. Okay, he was on the right side of the road.

I followed him for a few more minutes before there was a spot on the side of the road where the Hayabusa could pull over. The driver came to a sudden stop, causing dust to come up from under the tires.

I did the same. Suddenly, everything was back in place. Time flowed at a reasonable speed. The blood in my veins boiled. A headache hit me. My heart was pounding in my chest and wanted to jump out of its prison. I clenched my shaking hands into fists.

I reached the biker and stood within a few feet of his parked bike. He was staring straight ahead as if he were somewhere else. It was beyond my comprehension.

I just lifted the visor on my helmet before I said what I had to say. "Are you crazy? What the hell was that? Do you believe you're unstoppable like a ghost? What you did was stupid and dangerous not only for you, you idiot!" My voice rose with every word. I almost shouted at the stranger, who hadn't moved from his spot. "Is this your way of playing games with fate? Do me a favor: the next time you're about to roll out of this world, don't show up on the same highway as me. Okay? I'll be forever grateful if I don't have to watch your ass get splattered all over the place! You asshole!"

It felt like I was yelling at a statue. This guy completely ignored me throughout my speech. He didn't even turn his head in my direction.

Only when the last word came out of my mouth did the helmet turn in my direction. A hand rose from the cuff and lifted the black windshield. Eyes the color of warm chocolate looked directly at me. They were motionless as if hidden behind a wall. There was no sign of emotion and absolutely no reaction to anything I had said. The man didn't even blink.

"You spent a lot of time thinking about my ass," he said in a low voice. "Are you done?"

Another shiver ran through my body, whether it was from his intense gaze or his deep voice.

I nodded. He simply closed his helmet window, accelerated, and took off. Moments later, he was nothing but dust.

CHAPTER 3

I got into a rusty Ford. It was old and in terrible shape, but I didn't need a better pickup. This one was good enough for my needs. Mechanically, it was in very good shape. So what if the gray paint was peeling off the wheel arches or the trunk and it had a few dents?

Half an hour later, I arrived at my destination. I parked in front of a three-story brick building, similar to all the others on the street. They were all built the same way. A staircase, twelve steps to be exact, led to the entrance. Above the entrance was a small window. On the left side, there was a semi-circular bay window, with three windows on each floor. The buildings were connected, so there was no way around, yet I knew that under the stairs was a small window that the owner of this particular house always kept open for ventilation.

The clock on the dashboard said one a.m. Most buildings were cloaked in darkness in this area. In this one, the light was on in the bedroom on the top floor. I knew the layout of the house like the back of my hand and was familiar with the owner's routine.

For a moment he appeared at the window, walking, presumably, from the bathroom to the bedroom. He had no shirt on, and his hair was wet after a shower. A moment later, the light in the window went out.

Now I had to wait for him to fall into a deep sleep. So, I looked around the neighborhood, which was completely frozen at that hour. No one was on the sidewalk; no cars drove by.

I opened the glove compartment and took out a brown manilla envelope. I laid it on my lap and opened it. The streetlights were dim, and the car's windows were even darker.

I went through the contents of the envelope again because with this task, I left nothing to chance. I already knew Leo's daily routines by heart, his medical records, and even his educational and professional history. I even knew the location of the scars on his body and the bones that had been broken in the past.

I closed the folder and put it away, picking up a bundle of photos. I looked through them all like I had done this a thousand times before. In front of a huge building, four young men stood accompanied by girls. Each one of them wore a college T-shirt. They all wore big smiles. With their hands on each other's shoulders, they appeared as if they were about to dance the Cancan. They were friends, or maybe it was just a superficial layer of real relationships between them.

The girls were happy and laughing—except for the one who hid her face behind her hands.

I glanced at Leo, positioned near the center. He was a dark-skinned boy with short hair, which he had shaved completely now. He didn't look very impressive then. It was evident that he had invested time in the gym to develop his physique.

He looked neither threatening nor overconfident. He looked like an average student.

I grabbed a black marker from the armrest and pulled off the cap. Enjoying the moment, I circled Leo's face, leaving a black mark. When the perfect circle was complete, I drew a line to the right and another to the left, making a letter X.

Without giving it any more of my attention, I put the marker and the photos back in their place. After another quick sweep of the area, I concealed myself by pulling down my baseball cap. The cap covered most of my face in case a camera registered my presence. Even though I was familiar with the camera placement, caution was always necessary. I tucked the balaclava into my pocket and pulled gloves over my hands. The special metal box was placed into the pocket of my black sweatshirt. Behind the waistband of my pants, I still had my gun and under the leg of my pants, I had a hunting knife.

Stepping out of the pickup, I headed toward one of the houses. Acting casual as if I had stopped by for an evening drink, I walked behind the stairs instead of going up to the front door. Total darkness enveloped me.

I took a deep breath and slowed my heartbeat. I stood still for exactly five minutes before taking my next step. Crouching down in front of the ajar window, I put my hand through the crack. The moment I encountered the first resistance, because the crack was too narrow for my hand, I clenched my teeth. Ignoring the burning pain, I pushed my hand deeper until I felt the handle of the adjacent window. I flicked my wrist and the window latch released. Step one was over.

Even though the window was small, I squeezed through. I slipped to the floor and locked the latch again, this time on both windows.

Leo had no pets, which made my task easier. Knowing the house's layout made it simple to enter his bedroom. I knew every obstacle, every dresser, every corner, even every squeaky board in the house. How did I know? Well, this wasn't my first time here.

So, I went straight to Leo's bedroom. In a central position, against the wall, stood the bed. Leo was sleeping there on his stomach, one hand tucked under the pillow and the other resting along his torso. His face was buried in the soft pillow. He slept without a blanket, wearing only gray sweatpants.

I didn't have time to play cat and mouse now. Even though my beast wanted to get out and play, it had to wait for the right moment.

I took the metal box out of my pocket, opened it, and withdrew a syringe with a needle that I had prepared earlier. Inside was a drug that would allow good old Leo to relax, but not so much that he would be unconscious. When he woke up, he would be extra friendly for a while afterward.

It's amazing what you can learn from Eastern cultures if you're interested in chemistry.

Syringe in hand, I approached the bed and plunged the needle directly into Leo's upper arm. He only twitched a few times before the entire contents had been injected into his system.

"What the fuck?" Leo turned onto his back, his eyes filled with terror as he peered at me. By the time his consciousness processed that he was facing an unknown predator, the drug had already taken effect. It took only fifteen seconds for the first signs to show.

Leo smiled at me, his expression changing from surprised to friendly. He lazily stretched his arms over his head like a little child.

"Hi... How are you?" he mumbled.

"Come on, we need to leave," I replied, putting the syringe away.

"Really? Can't we just relax here? It's so nice here..."

His own words made him laugh like it was the best joke under the sun. There was a tiny possibility that I had overdone it a bit.

"Yeah, but maybe next time, okay?"

His lips curled into a horseshoe.

I leaned over him, grabbed his arm, and pulled him to the edge of the bed. He shifted and let me help him. At least for the moment, he cooperated.

Once he was stable on his feet, I had one more thing to do. I pulled a pouch out of my pocket, opened it, and pulled out a bullet. It was pristine. I had taken care of every detail. I placed it on the pillow, hid the pouch, and turned to the wobbly Leo.

Without bothering with his shoes, we left the bedroom and went downstairs. Every now and then, he giggled as if he was having a great time.

When we reached the front door, I had him turn the lock and push the handle. The only and last prints on it would be his own.

The air outside was fresh and invigorating. I took another look around the sleeping neighborhood. Not even a rat scurried across the street. The distant sound of a police siren reached my ears.

I threw my arm over Leo's shoulder to make it look like a college outing, in case anyone noticed us. Granted, he was shirtless and barefoot, but he didn't care, and I didn't care either. He kept giggling quietly, like a teenager after his first beer.

We walked down the twelve steps to my Ford. When we stood next to the rusty machine, he looked at it carefully and whistled. From his reaction, someone would think I was driving at least a Ferrari.

I opened the passenger door for him. "Get in," I commanded, and he obeyed.

I walked around the car and got in as well.

"Fasten your seat belt and go to sleep for a while. I'll wake you when we get there."

"Are you sure?" he asked, his lids already drooping from their own weight.

"Yeah, buddy, I'm sure."

The belt made a click and Leo fell asleep immediately.

Only then did I take a deep breath. It was too easy. Once the drug subsided, his awakening would bring the harsh truth of his limited time in this world. But it would be too late. I needed a name, and he knew it, so he would either give it to me or die for it.

CHAPTER 4

CASTRIEL

Life has moments when boredom destroys our last brain cells. No. In fact, if I could, I would kick my brain cells in the ass. If only I didn't have to go through this tedious torture...

As the head of the department in charge of recruiting and assigning models, Miles offered to let me take part in the first casting. I looked to my left, where he was sitting. This was the face of a man who would never convince me of anything again in my life. His positive approach to reality was matched by his overly poor taste in female beauty.

Why did I accept his invitation? God only knows. I regretted that decision within the first fifteen minutes of this masquerade.

Miles seemed oblivious to my death stares. He was gazing at another girl not worth our time as if she were the most beautiful toy of the season.

"What motivates you to pose for us?" Miles asked.

I peeked at the blonde. She smiled sweetly at him, yet her eyes occasionally wandered to me. Like many faces in this profession, she was completely fake. A fake smile, fake eyelashes, fake white teeth, fake body... Nothing that would make her stand out from the crowd, which was what I expected from our brand.

"And who wouldn't want to be a Victoria's Secret model? That's the top of my dreams." She chuckled, pleased with who knows what. Maybe at her own intelligence, which she didn't have in abundance, in my opinion.

I kept a stone face, even though I wanted to throw her out. I let the idiot next to me lead the way and said nothing.

"But this isn't an audition for Victoria's Secret, sweetheart."

"Really? The girls said so before I came in..." She thought for a moment, opened her eyes wide in surprise, and then showed a row of snowy teeth again. "Well, you can't have everything. I still want the job."

Yeah... No!

"Wonderful." Miles beamed. He was thinking with his dick and not with his head. "The photographer, Jason, will capture your image before we proceed."

God, I'm in hell.

"Okay, but I hope those pictures don't end up on some porn site."

I was almost certain that my blood pressure was reaching the peak of my endurance, and I was approaching an inevitable pre-cardiac state. I couldn't believe my luck.

"I assure you, sweetheart, nothing like that will happen," Miles reassured her.

Jason placed the girl in the correct position and asked her to act natural. I was afraid that she and natural were a million years apart.

"She's not that bad, is she?" Miles leaned over and said in a hushed voice. I gave a cold stare to the idiot I had come across in this cursed city. "That angelic face and sinful body, those legs..."

I gazed again at the girl whose name I didn't remember. None of the assets Miles presented were obvious to me. None of what he said was visible to my eye. The model was making bizarre poses and grinning, her gigantic eyes staring into the lens, looking like a stupid doll.

Before I knew it, I stood up and headed for the exit. I remained deaf to Miles's calls behind me because I couldn't stand another five minutes in his presence.

There were three other girls waiting outside the room, which I eliminated within seconds. Today's casting was a total bust.

The girls whispered to each other, ignoring my presence when I stood in front of them. I crossed my arms and waited for them to stop chatting. When the dark-haired girl raised her eyes and fell silent, their fascinating conversation about Hermes handbags came to an end.

My eyes swept over each of them. "You can go home now. Today's casting has just ended."

They all stared at me as if I had revealed a third nipple. Their surprise almost amused me, but as they processed my words, their dying hope confronted me.

One by one, they spoke.

"But how?"

"Who was chosen?"

"That's not fair!"

"Why don't you at least give me a chance?"

"Do you even know who I am?"

I think this is some kind of fucking joke.

I completely ignored them and went to the bathroom. My irritation with the day was turning into aggression. It flowed through my veins and fed my body. I had two choices that could keep me from exploding. Either I would find someone and fuck them, nice and hard, or I would kill someone.

The first option swirled in my thoughts as the bathroom door opened mid-handwashing. I ignored my surroundings in my usual style, but I still heard, "I was told you're the decision-maker on this job."

In the mirror, I saw the reflection of the empty-headed doll Jason had photographed a few minutes earlier. I rolled my eyes and concentrated on wiping my hands on a paper towel, but the girl was either too dumb for signals or she was determined.

"I think," she continued, "that in a few minutes I'll be able to help you make the right decision regarding my person." The sound of tapping filled the bathroom, and I turned in her direction. In the middle of the bathroom, on the dirty floor, she was kneeling and smiling flirtatiously.

My eyes ran over her tiny figure. I knew her purpose for coming here. Trying to get the job through sexual favors was nothing new in this business.

When my gaze returned to her eyes, her hands were on the floor and, with slow movements, she started crawling toward me. Her dress was up on her hips and if someone had entered the bathroom at that moment, they would have had a good view of her ass. I stiffened, but not out of excitement, although not more than a few minutes ago, I'd had an unearthly desire to fuck someone.

Before she made it to my feet, I reached out to stop her. To no avail, she crawled even closer. Looking at me from under her squinted eyelids, she got up on her knees and placed her cool hands on my thighs. Even that gesture didn't work on me, because my cock didn't even twitch. Nothing. Zero.

The whole situation was pathetic. I took a step back and headed for the exit, bypassing her. "You were right. But it only took me half a minute to decide about you. You're skilled," I growled.

I stopped understanding myself. I had missed the opportunity to release built-up tension. Why on earth? She was easy, she was willing, she was already on her knees, and yet...

"Fuck!" I growled under my breath and walked across the hall. I reached into my pocket and pulled out my phone. "Yes?"

Meghan's voice filled the phone. "Mr. Russell, let me remind you of an upcoming meeting at Media Linc in less than an hour."

"I remember," I told her and hung up. Of course I didn't remember, but it didn't matter either way.

Meghan was good at what she did. She was like a walking calendar, reminding me of everything I shouldn't forget, no matter how much I wanted to. The stack of cash she was paid each month was worth it.

Less than an hour later, I walked into the Media Linc building. As courtesy dictated, which also irritated me, I approached the reception desk to announce my arrival.

Behind the desk stood a woman whose red curls made it impossible for her to go unnoticed in the crowd. Their color was unusual, more copper than red. Her front strands were pinned up, while the back strands flowed down behind her shoulders. Her perfect skin was pale, although it looked nice and soft. My fingers twitched, letting me know they would love to touch her skin.

Most redheads had thousands of freckles, but not her. She was different. Her skin was alluring. For a moment, I had an image of sinking my teeth into her and marking that perfect skin. It was a moment of weakness that I quickly locked away in a dark corner of my personality. It should have stayed there.

Meanwhile, my eyes traveled to the rest of her body. Her slender neck and petite shoulders, her round breasts hidden behind the fabric of her white dress, her small waist were all I could see without leaning over the counter. She wasn't a tall woman. She probably wore high heels every day to give her a little height but compared to me, she was still very short.

When I was a child, I was small. In school I was a little shorter than my classmates. Then, in puberty, I became taller than most of my peers and even my teachers. In the years that followed, I gained mass, developed muscles, and became the motherfucker I am today. Thanks to my sense of my awkwardness, I had plenty of time to do it.

I brought my thoughts back to the present moment and noticed with annoyance that the woman's green eyes were staring at me. No, I was wrong. They weren't green; they were emerald, intense. I saw a glint in them but didn't know what it could mean. Her lips parted in a smile. Her lips moved, but I didn't hear a word. My attention was focused on their shape, texture, softness. They were rosy in a natural way, without lipstick, just a gloss.

"Excuse me. Are you all right, sir?" Her soft voice reached me at last.

I returned my gaze to her eyes, even though I didn't want to. I really should get laid soon.

"Yeah," I growled. "I have a meeting with Mason and Emma Lincoln."

"Of course. Please take the elevator to the top floor. The person who will direct you next will be expecting you."

Without waiting for me to leave, she grabbed the phone, punched in three digits, and waited for the call. Rearranging some documents on her desk, she gave each sheet a little attention. She did this by reflex, which meant that she had been working for Media Linc for some time. Interesting, because I hadn't noticed her the last time I was here with Takashi.

"Toria, there's already a person for Mr. Lincoln's three p.m. meeting."

Isabelle, said a badge pinned to the girl's left breast. She hung up the phone and continued to work. Only after a while did she notice I was still standing in the same place, staring at her. Like a freak.

"Are you sure you're okay?" she asked with a gasp. Her emerald eyes widened in fear.

Interesting...

Apparently, I wasn't the only one who thought I was a freak. It was high time to stop this nonsense. I nodded and forced my legs to cooperate. Step by step, I reached the elevator. As I was going up, I felt relieved. On the one hand, because this strange moment was behind me, on the other, because I didn't even look back.

***

"I don't quite understand what you mean when you say it's crap," Mason's words echoed through the conference room. He glanced at his wife, Emma, who sat next to him, and for a moment they communicated without words.

Mason had become CEO of Media Linc a few months ago, after his cousin killed his father. Supposedly, he had intended to kill him himself, but life had mocked him. While it's easy to find a dysfunctional family these days, theirs beat out ninety percent of the others.

Mason himself was an intimidating bastard. Not to me, of course, but probably to many. He was like a hawk watching everything and everyone, just like me. We had that in common, only I was much more reserved in my words and gestures. For example, at that moment when he was communicating with Emma in a silent way, his hand involuntarily went to her hand lying on the glass table. It was certainly unconscious on his part, but he wanted to communicate clearly to the world where his territory lay. As if it wasn't clear that she was his wife, he stroked the shining gold band on her finger with his little finger.

Emma smiled at him and then turned her attention to me. She wasn't as messed up as Mason. After all, she had only pretended to be her twin sister. Hers paled in comparison to his actions.

She was a pretty blonde but her beauty was too popular for me. Not my taste, so Mason's possessive gestures were pointless. For the sake of entertainment, I didn't want to mention it.

"Most marketing efforts are crap. Template, learned, under-critical shams," I started. "One is similar to the other. Only the faces change, but even that gets mixed up over time."

"The campaign for Takashi was innovative," Emma interjected. "It wasn't cookie-cutter. That's why it was so successful."

That campaign had just been created by Mason and Emma, so her defensiveness didn't surprise me. It was their baby.

"Yes, it was," I agreed. "That's why you have the clients you have, for the money you collect, because it's worth it. All I'm saying is that most of the professionals in this city suck."

"That's because we hire the best ones," Mason pointed out.

"I need a breath of fresh air and creativity for Papilio. I came back from a casting call for the face of the brand and I'm deeply disappointed. I don't want someone famous. I've seen models from Italy, France, some exotic places. It's still not like that. The modeling agencies are spreading their hands. I need the best of the best."

"If you expect unconventional, we have to look in unconventional places," Emma chimed in. "We can give you the leads to the best agencies in the world, but that won't be enough."

"Look for an ordinary girl on the street," Mason challenged.

All of a sudden, Emma's hand was on her lips. Her face turned gray and green and her eyes glazed with tears, her nostrils flaring with each breath.

"Excuse me for a moment." Her hand almost drowned her words out.

She rose from her chair and walked out of the conference room with a quick stride.

A worried Mason looked behind his wife, and I knew he was fighting with himself not to run after her. He considered his options for a moment before turning to me in a gesture of surrender. "It's okay. We're pregnant, and Emma's taking this first trimester a little hard."

No kidding. We're pregnant? Maybe you could take care of her morning sickness too?

"Congratulations," I said, though I doubted there was anything to congratulate. In my thirty years of life, I had never considered fatherhood. Driven by other priorities, I knew it wasn't in my cards.

"Castriel, we'll have to cut our meeting short. If you would like, we can continue our search in finding a suitable candidate to be the face of the Papilio brand. You're opening a branch, you probably have a million things on your mind, and this is one problem you can get rid of. But unless my intuition is incorrect, you don't trust anyone and you won't even give up a little control over to a stranger. Is that right?"

I stared at him. He couldn't read anything from my face, I was sure of it. I was good at hiding my thoughts. I didn't nod, didn't even blink.

"Relax." Mason raised his hands in a gesture of surrender, and a mischievous smile appeared on his face. "I know that because I'm the same."

Doubt it.

Still, I didn't say a word, so he continued. "I think you know exactly what you're looking for. If you don't want something ordinary, then look for it in non-standard places. Additionally, I believe that the best option for the brand would be someone who hasn't been trained as a model—a natural, normal girl from the street. But like I said, I think you know what you're looking for and you're wasting your time."

What Mason meant to say was that I was wasting his time. Of course, I was wasting his time. Unfortunately, my own as well. I had no intention of being here. I only did it to get Takashi off my back and let him sleep peacefully while I built this brand.

I stood up and walked over to Mason. A mischievous smile appeared on my lips. Maybe we had something in common after all. I respected his insight.

We shook hands, and I left the conference room without another word.

On the ground floor, from the moment the elevator doors opened, I immediately noticed the copper-haired woman at her desk. Without a second thought, I walked over to Isabelle. God knows why, because I was on autopilot. I stopped in front of her desk and stared at her like an idiot. Once again.

At first, she didn't even notice me standing there. She was working; this time, she was sorting the mail. She also answered two phone calls and switched to a certain department without even raising her eyes. I was still a ghost to her.

A few minutes later, she raised her emerald eyes to me and she jumped, letting out a muffled squeal. Her eyes widened and her hand landed flat on her chest. I could see a throbbing artery under the skin of her delicate neck.

"God, you scared me," she whispered, then tried to soften her reaction with a mask of nervous laughter.

Of course, I didn't apologize. I didn't speak. There was an awkward silence all around. It was fine with me, but apparently not with her. Her gaze swept across the lobby and then back to me. The more I stared at her, the more her curiosity grew.

She gazed first at my face, then at my suit, my chest, my bulky arms, and finally at my hands. I had one hand tucked into my pants pocket while the other dangled carelessly, holding a motorcycle helmet with my elbow.

And on that, for a long moment, Isabelle focused her attention. She looked shocked, as if she had just noticed this and had overlooked the detail before. A minute later, a frosty green found my eyes.

"Venus rotates in the opposite direction around the sun, and a day on Venus is almost as long as a year on Earth."

As soon as these words came out of her mouth like a machine gun, her hand was immediately on her lips, as if she wanted to close them. It was a little too late for that, but who was I to tell her that?

The big eyes got even bigger. It really was possible.

"What the fuck?" These words were only supposed to appear in my head, but now they were out. Confused, I didn't know what she was talking about.

Let's go back. Did she say something about Venus? About Venus, the planet?

My eyebrows went up, and I could only assume that my eyes were just as big as hers. What was that about?

Isabelle's hands found their way to her face, and she rubbed it in a nervous gesture. A red blush appeared on her cheeks, and soon it flooded her neck and cleavage.

Delicious.

"Ah... Nothing, Mr. Russell. I just remembered something."

I peeked at her with suspicion, not believing a word she said. Instinct told me she was trying to hide something. Not that I had any right to demand the truth. I didn't know this woman, and yet I stood there like a madman. Because I was a fucked up lunatic.

I shook my head as a sign that there was nothing she could do for me.

My heart beat faster. For the first time in years, I felt its rhythm. For the first time in many years, I felt something resembling fear.

This was the ultimate proof that I should stay as far away from this woman as possible. Even though this was the first time I had seen her, I hoped it would be the last too.

I turned and walked out of Media Linc, erasing all my thoughts and memories of this day.

Chapter 5

IZZY

Walking home I twice took a wrong turn. I scolded myself mentally for my stupidity, then realized I had turned the wrong way once more.

I was in a bad mood for several reasons. Before day's end, another call came in. Like the previous times, no one said anything. I knew someone was there. I could hear them breathing again. Him or her. I felt someone's presence as if I was being watched and goose bumps appeared all over my body.

I had bad feelings. I couldn't shake this state until I entered the building where I lived. My thoughts were interrupted just a moment later, when I waited for the elevator.

"Isabelle? Izzy?"

Standing in front of me was a tall, stocky blond man with golden skin. His smile was so bright that his energy could light up half the neighborhood. Dark jeans clung to his lower body and a white polo shirt to his upper body. His biceps, triceps, and whatever else on his shoulders were highlighted as soon as he put his arms on his chest. The guy knew that I was scrutinizing his body and knew his physical assets. He wasn't a man who would catch my eye, but I could admit that he was handsome.

He noticed my consternation and added after a moment. "Brad. Bradley Donovan. We went to college together."

Gears turned in my head. Memories of him emerged. To be frank, there were only a few.

Brad had changed since then. His features had taken on a masculine edge. His body was more developed and, if possible, he had grown even more.

The situation was getting more awkward. "Brad! Of course," I greeted him. "Sorry, I've had a rough day and I don't know where my head is."

"Don't worry, it happens to all of us." He laughed. "I'm glad you remember me. I didn't know you lived here."

Brad and I hadn't been part of the same crowd. We had our own circles, though we all rotated in the same orbit. A few times we might have been at the same party, talked two or three times. And that was it.

"Actually, I've been here for some time now. Isn't that strange?"

"More like a coincidence. You've changed, Izzy," he announced, moving his eyes up and down my body. "You've grown up and you look gorgeous."

Would it be rude of me to suggest you get your eyes checked?

I was tired, jumpy, and sleep deprived. Whenever I tried to fall asleep, I ended up rolling from side to side. The past few nights had been like that. It was taking its toll on my appearance and my mood.

"Thank you, Brad. You've changed too. For the better, I might add."

He smiled even wider at that and took a step toward me.

"Thank you. I work in modeling now. My body is my tool to make money." He shrugged and looked confused, as if he wasn't quite ready to admit it.

"Seriously? Cool. I never would have guessed, but in my defense, I'm pretty ignorant of this industry. I don't watch commercials, I don't know the names. I'm obviously an exceptional type of woman."

"That's who you are," he admitted, amused. "You've always been exceptional. Don't get me wrong; that's your advantage. I always knew that about you."

"That's interesting, because I always thought I was rather invisible to those around me." At least that was my intention.

My words amused him even more, as he let out a laugh and shook his head. He never diverted his gaze from my face.

"Impossible. You're not, and never have been, a woman easily overlooked," he complimented.

Behind me, I heard the elevator doors slide open. I was surprised to find that this moment in Brad's company had completely taken me out of reality. Talking to him was easy, relaxed.

As I stepped into the elevator, a hand touched my lower back. Brad's hand, to be exact. I tensed all over for a moment because I wasn't used to gestures like that. Even when I was dating, no man had ever made such a gesture. The warmth of his hand went through my dress. It was a pleasant feeling. Not overwhelming, but nice.

I pushed the button on my floor and Brad was standing in front of me, just smiling. He had a carefree charm about him, the charm of the boy next door, despite his manly face and body.

"Aren't you pushing your floor?" I asked in surprise.

"What are you doing these days, Izzy?"

"I work at Media Linc as a receptionist."

"Nice."

"Probably," I joked. "Hardly a challenging job, but the important thing is that it pays the bills on time and allows me to live in relative comfort."

"That's true." Brad's eyes traveled to my hand for a moment. "No husband?"

Is he fishing for information? Is he flirting with me?

"No husband," I admitted. "No wife either. And you?"

"No wife, nor any husband." He laughed. "I'm satisfied with that for now."

The elevator stopped, and the doors opened. We were on my floor. I stepped out into the main hallway and turned to face Brad. I was sure this was the end of our conversation, but he surprised me by getting off as well.

I was about to ask him about why, but he beat me to it. "You don't know how happy I am to run into you. And we're neighbors, no less. Sometimes I wondered how your life turned out after you graduated college, but you're like a ghost. I couldn't find you on any social media."

Brad revealed more than I expected. Was he wondering about me? Was he searching for me on social media? I didn't exist online, of course not. I wasn't stupid. I was careful at every turn.

"Really?"

"Yes, really," he said as we stood outside my apartment door. He looked at it and added, pleased with himself, "At least now I know where to find you."

All the pieces of the puzzle fell into place. "Clever," I complimented him. "And what apartment do you live in?"

"Twelve C. Right below you."

"I can't believe I'm going over your head."

Brad's laughter filled the silent hallway. It was warm and deep. I liked it. The laughter, of course.

"In more ways than one," he replied with satisfaction. "In more ways than one... See you later, Izzy." He leaned over and planted a quick kiss on my cheek.

Turning around, he walked a few quick steps to the elevator. Before the elevator doors opened, he sent another seductive smile in my direction.

I touched my hand to the spot where his lips had been seconds before. It was pleasurable, although it didn't trigger any desire in me. I didn't feel butterflies in my stomach. But then again, did they always have to be present? The unexpected encounter with Brad was definitely what I needed this day. However, not wanting to get too excited, I pulled my hand away from my cheek and entered the apartment.

***

For the next few hours, I tried meticulously to control my thoughts. I didn't want to think about Brad too much, because that was life playing a trick on me. Another man—dark-haired and dark-eyed—entered my mind.

The last thing I needed was for my mind to return to the situation at work. I was embarrassed. When Castriel Russell stood in front of me like that, something inside me opened up.

His huge figure filled a suit that obviously cost several thousand dollars, and my eyes wandered over his body. I've always had a weakness for tall, stocky men. He was damn tall and damn stocky.

To remove Castriel's large hands and arms from my imagination was nothing short of miraculous. I've always had a well-developed imagination, so I knew with little effort what he could do with those hands. I could imagine what it would feel like to have them on my body, what they would taste like. That alone made me feel a tingle in the pit of my stomach.

Without much effort, Brad disappeared from my mind, but Castriel was another matter entirely. When his silhouette in that expensive suit entered my consciousness, it refused to be pushed away. I tossed and turned, trying to think about the future, about work, even about the damn manicurist. Nothing had any effect or gave me any relief.

Restless and sweaty, I finally gave up. It would be more accurate to say that my subconscious defeated me, because when I realized the situation, my fingers were already under the elastic band of my panties.

Fingertips found my clit and rubbed it. In my imagination, I saw Castriel's fingers replace mine. They were large, rough, and they filled the lips of my pussy. A moan came out of my mouth, immediately followed by a sigh. Which one of us was sighing and which one was moaning? It was impossible to distinguish between the two of us. Everything was blurred. I felt his person towering over my writhing body.

"Open wider for me," he whispered in a low voice, and I listened to it like a spell. My legs opened wider, giving him access to my most intimate places. The fingers of his right hand stroked my clit faster and faster, while his left hand slipped under the material of my shirt and squeezed one of my breasts. Again and again, but it still wasn't enough. To the point of pain, I grabbed a hard nipple and twisted it. Immediately, my back arched as if it craved more stimulation. So I gave my body exactly what it needed.

I squeezed the same nipple twice more time, then let my hand play with the other breast. My fingers between my thighs worked to bring my body to the peak of pleasure. They rubbed the swollen clit up and down, but as soon as they drew circles on its surface, it was over.

Drenched in sweat, my body bucked even harder, a loud moan escaping my dry lips. A hot and lazy wave of orgasm swept through my entire body. My chest rose and fell at a rapid pace, my lungs working hard to draw breath.

Although the shock of the orgasm was tremendous, it ended all too quickly. My limp body sank to the bedding. I slipped my fingers out of my panties. They were all wet and sticky.

Castriel disappeared from my mind as quickly as he had appeared.

My breathing slowly returned to a normal rhythm and my heart calmed. Still, my body hadn't yet experienced complete relaxation. I had never experienced this with a man before, and now I disappointed myself.

Castriel Russell slowly faded from my memory, but only for a moment. After a few minutes of peace and hope that I would finally fall asleep, I was reminded of the worst moment of the past day.

Venus rotates in the opposite direction around the sun, and a day on Venus is almost as long as a year on Earth. Seriously? I couldn't have made a worse idiot of myself?

The mere thought of it made me want to laugh at myself, and my cheeks grew hot. I was ashamed, I was embarrassed by the whole situation, and in the end I was just plain pissed.

The fact that he was so silent, distant yet present, focused on me like no one else in my life didn't make me feel better at all. His mesmerizing gaze followed me around all day. It was frightening and exciting at the same time.

To top it off, Castriel was carrying a helmet under his arm. Not just any helmet. It was a motorcycle helmet. A nice black one with a ghost painted on it!

He didn't recognize me, which didn't surprise me at all. But I recognized him without a problem. That damned asshole with whom I had raced a few days ago, who had almost lost his life because of his own arrogance, whose pride was bigger than the surface of Central Park, was standing in front of me in the flesh. Castriel was that biker.

I sighed and rolled back to the other side. A vibrating cell phone interrupted my thoughts. I opened my eyes and reached for the nightstand.

The clock showed two in the morning. I had three hours of sleep before I should get up for work.

A picture of Emma appeared on the screen.

"Hi, girl," my friend's soft voice greeted me.

"Hi. Is something wrong?" The panic in my voice was obvious.

"No, no... I'm fine. I just couldn't sleep. I felt you were still awake."

"You weren't wrong. I can't sleep either. If I turn around a few more times, I'll make a hole in my mattress."

Emma chuckled softly.

"Mason isn't sleeping either?"

"Oh, he's finally asleep. Every time I tried to get out of our bed, he woke up right away. I swear the guy has some kind of motion detector built in. Anyway, he announced in that innocent voice of his that I needed to rest for the baby's sake. He's insufferable now, so I'm sure he'll drive me crazy when my belly grows."

Mason and Emma were proof that two different worlds could coexist and be happy together.

"I thought that after a few days, when the initial emotions wore off, life would return to normal," I said.

"And that's where you were wrong, Izzy. It's only getting worse! He really went crazy with the baby, with me being pregnant and being responsible for us all. It used to be unbearable, but now it's, like, running through his veins," she joked.

"How are you feeling?"

"Everything is normal. It's just a pregnancy. You know, every morning you vomit your guts out and wonder how you can kill your husband and hide his body. Then you think about the bean growing inside you and feel hopeful. Finally, in the evening, you can fuck your husband a thousand ways and blame it all on the hormones without being suspected of nymphomania."

My laughter was so loud that Em shushed me. For a moment, I couldn't calm myself as I imagined poor Mason having to endure her bouts of sexual hunger.

"So it's safe to say that the blessed state is serving you well," I commented when I calmed down and wiped a tear from my cheek. "I'm so happy I'm going to be an aunt."

"You won't be happy when I get cravings and you feel stupid refusing a pregnant woman's request for ice cream at midnight."

"It won't be that bad. Those cravings are stereotypes; not every woman experiences them."

"Um... We'll come back to that," an amused Emma threatened.

"So tell me, why are you awake? Are you worried about something?"

"I don't know, Izzy. Sure, I'm worried, but not so much that it keeps me from sleeping. I think about the future, about the past, about Lena—"

"Oh, Em."

"I know, I know... I just miss her so much. I wondered what it would be like if she were with us now. Is my happiness something she would enjoy? Could she have become as crazy as Mason? Despite all this time having passed, would she still be a bitch?"

It was hard for me to lie to my best friend and assure her that Lena would be a different person now. Probably not much would have changed in her life, or maybe I was wrong. We would probably never know.

"What if—"

"Lena loved you. She made mistakes in her life because she was human. We have to forgive her now, because it will change absolutely nothing. But I'm sure she looks up to you and misses you just as much."

For a moment, there was silence, and then a gasp.

"You're right, Izzy. Thank you. You're my family and I love you. Remember that."

"I know, silly. I feel it and I know it. I love you too."

In the blink of an eye, Emma's mood improved. She cheered up and changed the subject to something lighter. Until she dropped a bomb.

"One of Mason's clients needs a model for a photo shoot. I think you'd be perfect."

I was taking a sip of water, and before she could get the last word out, I choked. Single drops spilled from my mouth directly onto the bedding as I coughed uncontrollably. My throat burned and tears streamed into my eyes.

It took about two minutes for the coughing to subside until it stopped completely. I took a deep breath, wiped my wet cheeks, and picked up the phone.

"If you were planning on killing me, know that you failed, although you were close," I said.

"I'm so sorry, Izzy," Emma huffed. "I really didn't mean to. How could I have known you would react like that?"

"You couldn't." I took a few more breaths to calm my heart. "What were you even thinking? Are you crazy? Me? A model?"

"No, I'm not crazy. And why wouldn't you be able to be a model?"

"Because I don't have a model's figure?"

"What nonsense. You have a great figure. Perfect for the job."

"I'm far from the standards of this industry."

"And that's the point. Platinum blondes abound. You have a unique beauty and that's what we need."

"We? You mean who?"

"I told you, it's Mason's client. I'm just helping."

"Em, I appreciate your suggestion, but it's not for me. I'm not a teenager, I can't walk the runway, and I can't handle the fame."

"I know, I know, but listen to me, okay? It's not about age or walking the runway. The client wants to conquer the women's lingerie market. It's not what you think, I promise. The lingerie is unique. It's for mature, confident women who know what they want. And it's for very rich women. Each piece of lingerie has unique embellishments, such as gold thread, pearls, diamonds, emeralds—"

"Wait, wait," I interrupted her. "Are you telling me that there are women who will pay thousands to wear damn diamonds between their buttocks? Or worse—"

"There are such women, and I think they'll gladly pay any price for a piece of that lingerie. And you know why? One, they can afford it, or their husbands can afford it. Same difference. Two, it will increase their value in the eyes of men, and that's their actual power."

I shook my head and sat up higher on the bed, leaning against the headboard.

"I understand what you're trying to tell me, Em, but this is absurd. It's not even funny. I'm a modest girl, not a model."

"I think you're just what they need. You're new, fresh, and you're a rare, uncut diamond. You have a wonderful figure, an unusual face, and beautiful hair. In addition, you radiate something that makes a person cling to you. The customers of this company will see you as a confidante, a friend from the heart who can advise on the choice of lingerie for a husband or lover."

"You're not helping," I growled, irritated. "If this lingerie is going to cause women to cheat on their husbands, I'm not going to be responsible for that."

"And who cares, Izzy? This is just your image, and if they want to cheat on their husbands, they'll do it anyway. You have no control over it, so there is no question of responsibility. Please, Izzy, at least consider this. Meet with the person in charge."

"Em, like I said, I appreciate your suggestion, but it's a waste of both parties' time."

"I would also like to mention that we're talking about a six-figure salary," she announced with hope in her voice.

I drew in the air with a sigh. Well, okay, the six-figure offer got my attention. I could put it aside and invest it in opening something of my own. If, of course, I had a definite direction.

There was still the problem that I hated publicity. I avoided it like a hell fire.

"Do it for me, please, please, please..." Emma whined. "Just do the casting. If you feel uncomfortable, you can leave. I won't hold a grudge. But try. Live a little. Go crazy. Think about it, okay?"

There was a moment of silence, and when I sighed, defeated, Em squealed with joy into the phone. I had a soft spot for my best friend. She was the sister I never had.

Not much later, we hung up. When I put the phone back on the nightstand, I noticed I had an unread message from an unknown number. I opened it and froze. It was only a few words, but they shattered my peace of mind.

"I'LL FIND YOU."

That night was another night where I didn't sleep for five minutes.

CHAPTER 6

IZZY

As soon as dawn broke and it wasn't too early, I grabbed my phone. With a business card in my trembling hand, I dialed the number. I lived hoping I would never have to use it. I guess life had a different plan for me.

My breathing got faster and shallower. When I heard a slow beep on the phone, everything around me spun. I sat down on the sofa in case I passed out. Getting a bump on the head the size of an avocado was the last thing I needed.

I counted the slow signals, and only on the sixth ring did I hear a low, hoarse voice. No doubt I woke him up.

"Yes?"

"Morning. This is Isabelle Knox."

"Isabelle." The man sighed, and I gave him a moment to remember who I was. "I was hoping you would never call my private number."

"Me too. I'm sorry to call at this hour, but it's an emergency."

"That's all right, Isabelle. That's why you have this number. Please give me a moment to leave the bedroom without waking my wife."

"I'm very sorry. I didn't know what to do. I panicked," I gasped, shaking my head.

"Don't apologize. It's obviously important if you've called me." I heard a rustling in the background, followed by a man moving and a lock clicking on the door. "Talk to me, Izzy. What's going on?"

I took a deep breath before explaining the events of the past few days. "I've been getting calls, deaf calls. Once a day, but at different times. I don't hear anyone, I just hear someone breathing on the other end. At first, I thought it was just phone problems. Anyway, it's happening regularly now. It's made me more vigilant."

"I see. Do we have a phone number?"

"No. It's unknown."

"Yes. What else, Isabelle, because I feel that's not everything?"

"No, it's not. I received a text message. It said, 'I'll find you.'" My voice faltered at the end.

Closing my eyes, I returned to the worst memories of my life. Real screams broke into my consciousness, broken breaths and curses, almost inhuman growls. Fear that overflows and overwhelms a person to the point of dictating every step.

I couldn't allow this nightmare to exist in my life again. Never again. Tears came to my eyes and flowed freely down my cheeks. I brushed them off with my fingertips, then heard the voice on the phone.

"Izzy, are you there?"

"Yeah, sorry," I grunted. "The memories came back."

"Listen to me carefully, girl. I remember what kind of nightmare you went through in your life and I will not let it happen again. Do you understand me? I will not allow it. If necessary, you'll change your name and location. You will even live with me, but I won't let anything happen to you." His voice was reassuring.

"I believe you," I said, despite my doubts.

"Good. Now I find it impossible to believe that the two cases are connected. I should have been informed of any unfavorable decisions regarding you. No one has contacted me. I don't think they screwed it up that badly but honestly, nothing will surprise me anymore. Maybe it's all just a fucking coincidence. I'll have to make calls and ask, as I'm currently on vacation."

"Damn, sorry, Detective Burk. I'd appreciate it if you'd make those calls."

"Stop apologizing. I made you a promise and I'm going to keep it. As soon as I find out something, I'll get back to you, okay? And then we'll decide what to do next."

"Okay. Thanks for everything, Detective. I appreciate your help." My voice was much calmer.

"I know. Call me right away if you need anything else."

"I will."

A moment later, I hung up. Talking to the detective had calmed me enough that the room stopped spinning and my breathing returned to normal. My heart no longer wanted to jump out of my chest. My hands stopped shaking. The tears dried up.

I found a small spark of hope. I wouldn't let the past destroy everything I had built over the years. And if he tried to come back into my life, I still had a gun. I had gotten a license long time ago and bought a CZ Shadow 2 pistol. The item had sat neglected in a closet corner for a while. It ended up there when one day I felt freedom from constant fear. I stopped sleeping with the gun under my pillow then.

***

For the first time in a long time, I called my supervisor and asked for a day off. This was new on my part, so I heard the concern in her voice. I should have felt remorse for lying, but I didn't have the strength.

After calling the detective, I finally got some sleep. Even during those few hours, I slept and woke up several times.

I was filled with gratitude as I finally got the rest I so desperately needed.

The sun was high when I got out of bed. It was after noon and a message from Emma was waiting for me on my phone with information about the casting. On the same day, in three hours.

"Fuck," I cursed and hurried to the bathroom.

Fifteen minutes later, after a quick shower, I was standing there wrapped in a towel. I didn't give myself a moment to think about this whole crazy idea. If I had analyzed it, I would have done anything to avoid going there.

However, I couldn't break my promise. It cost little to try something new, even if it seemed absurd. Besides, I had been feeling like I wanted a change in my life, hadn't I?

Maybe that was what I needed. I was a cheerful person, full of enthusiasm and smiles. I needed to feel like myself again.

The makeup took a few more minutes, but I didn't overdo it. If I was going to be in photos, I wanted to look like the real me, not a fake doll.

The biggest problem was finding something appropriate in the closet. When half of it was on the bedroom floor, I found what I was looking for. The white dress was perfect for me. It reached almost to my knees, and the neckline was V-shaped with elbow-length sleeves. The white lining had small hand-embroidered flowers and was decorated with white tulle. The tailor had sewn lace under the breasts and at the waist.

When I put on the dress and silver sandals with heels that were tied just above the ankle, I felt light and special.

Maybe it's too much, Izzy...

Before I could change my mind about the outfit, however, I grabbed my purse and left the apartment.

It took me a half hour to reach the place. The buildings weren't much different in this part of New York. Each of them was impressive, intimidating. A blue sheet of glass filled dozens of floors of the skyscraper. At the entrance was a sign in white letters that screamed *PAPILIO*. I was unfamiliar with the brand but had little interest in it either.

As I entered the lobby of the building, the noise of the city was quickly replaced by a comforting silence. The floor had a lining of black tiles with glowing dots. When I took two steps, I thought it was like stepping on a starry night sky.

Not bad!

The effect was electrifying. I had never seen anything like it before.

There were a few couches in the lobby for waiting people, but nobody sat there. To the left was a white counter, and behind it was a beautiful, black-haired woman. Her soft curls fell over her shoulders. A peach dress accentuated her golden tan. She didn't wear heavy makeup, but with her natural beauty and delicate face, it wasn't necessary.

I felt immediate sympathy for the girl, having been in her position and knowing the sacrifice required for such work.

"Welcome to Papilio..." Her melodious voice filled the hall. "How can I help you?"

"Hi, Rachel." I read her name from a pinned badge. "My name is Isabelle Knox. I have an audition with—"

"Miles." She interrupted me, smiling. "He's waiting for you in the room behind that door. The person before you just left."

"Oh…" I hesitated. "Sorry, I'm nervous. I don't know how it works exactly. I don't know what to do."

Rachel laughed and shook her head. "You'll figure it out. You're so beautiful, Isabelle. I hope you'll have more luck than the previous ones. If Miles had the sole decision, he would choose the first blonde. The final vote belongs to the CEO, and he's a tough nut to crack."

"Is that so?"

"Yes. I think he's looking for something in the candidate that he himself can't quite define. But please keep that to yourself." She chuckled. "I'm crossing my fingers for your success. Knock 'em dead."

I nodded thoughtfully and moved in the direction she showed. I took a few breaths to control the nervous fluttering in my stomach.

What the hell am I doing here? This isn't my world!

My promise to Em came to mind. That was why I was doing this. Afterward, I could tell her I tried, but it didn't work out.

Standing before the door, I knocked and heard a faint, "Come in." I did it without further hesitation.

My expectations weren't met by what I witnessed. The room wasn't large. There was a conference table facing the entrance and a man sitting behind it. He had on a gray suit, white shirt, and no tie. A handsome man with tousled blond hair. His blue eyes lit up at the sight of me and his lips curved into a dazzling smile. At that moment, he looked like he was advertising some miracle toothpaste.

Next to him was another man dressed in jeans and a black T-shirt. He had a camera in his hand.

I glanced around the room. There was another chair in front of the table, presumably waiting for me. On the left side was a platform, and that was all. Vertical blinds covered the glass wall.

"Good morning," Miles said, getting up from the table. He circled the other man and approached me with his hand outstretched. I shook it, staring at his smile.

"Good morning. My name is Isabelle."

"Yes, yes. I received information at the last minute that someone from Media Linc's recommendation would show up. It's a surprise no one was expecting." Miles let go of my hand and wrapped his eyes around me. All of me. From my toenails to the top of my head.

"Hence the term surprise," the other man added in a low, serious tone.

Miles turned to him, as if he had just remembered he was there. "Indeed."

Miles's eyes returned to me. "You are..."

"She is," the photographer added.

I shifted my eyes from one to the other, not understanding what they were talking about. They were obviously reading each other's minds.

"Please, let's sit down," Miles said. He pointed to a chair for me. I smiled, embarrassed, when Miles had already returned to his seat. "I have to admit that I don't have any information about you. I don't have your portfolio. I have no dates or dimensions. Just nothing."

"That's because I'm not a model. I mean... I'm gonna be honest. I have no experience as a model. I'm here at the request of a friend whose overactive imagination told me I'm up to it and that I should try it. I think the opposite. I have no experience. I don't know the industry. I'm not known. I haven't even had time to google the brand."

The surprise on Miles's face was clear. His gaze rested for a second on the photographer, who was now grinning like a cat chasing a mouse.

The discomfort I felt made me stand up from my chair. "This was a mistake. I won't waste your time."

"Please stay!" Miles chuckled softly. "Don't misunderstand us. This is an unusual situation for us. Usually women vie for this job. We've met no one who wouldn't do anything to be the face of this brand."

"I understand." It wasn't true. I understood nothing. I was eager to depart.

"An unusual situation calls for an unusual approach," he continued. "Maybe we should start by talking about you, what you do for a living, where you come from..."

After a few minutes, the nerves left my body. Both men listened as I briefly shared about my work and life.

Miles then told me about the Papilio brand, which was new to the American market, although it had already gained a certain following. The company was based in Asia, where the unconventional lingerie had become an icon of exquisiteness. Expanding into new markets was a natural progression.

"This is a unique product that we want to highlight with a unique face. A face that, to be honest, we haven't seen yet. I will not promise you the fame that other brands bring with a contract. At least not at this stage. But you will earn a handsome sum of money if everything goes well."

"I don't care about fame," I added quickly. "I don't know anything about shows, catwalks, or whatever you do. I think it's going to be more inconvenient than helpful for you."

Another laugh filled the room. Both men smiled at me, as if captivated. I didn't know what they saw in me, but the situation was hilarious.

"Let's focus on the photo shoot for now. The next lingerie show won't be until next summer. We have plenty of time to prepare. With small steps, we can achieve this."

"What amount did you mean?"

Miles tore a piece of paper out of his notebook and wrote something on it with a pen. With a boyish smile, he flipped it over to me and slid it across the table.

I tore my eyes away from him, looked down, and froze. My breath caught in my throat. I felt breathless and hot altogether.

"It's also unconventional, like this whole meeting. We rarely discuss finances before we take pictures. But I have a feeling about you. This is what you'll earn for a one-year representation contract."

A one-year contract to represent the company? I wasn't making small money at Media Linc, but the amount written was, at a quick count, three times my income!

I glanced around to make sure they weren't mocking me. Their faces were deadly serious. This money could open doors for me I had only dreamed of. After a year, I could start my business, grow, travel, and change my life.

"All this for pictures of me in my underwear? No nudity?"

"No nudity," Miles assured. "Except maybe your ass."

"And you're offering me that kind of money when you haven't even seen my body? What if I have scars or tattoos?"

"Do you have any? Anyway, that's the job for the magician next door. He can correct some imperfections with a few clicks of the keyboard."

"I don't have a tattoo." I deliberately left out information about imperfections. The traces of scars were already almost invisible and easy to hide with foundation. No one needed to know about them; they would only raise unnecessary questions.

"Perfect!" The photographer clapped. "Then may I see your beauty through the lens of the camera?"

"Please forgive Jason. He's extremely anxious around you," Miles joked.

This was the moment I had to decide. On the one hand, I wanted to avoid publicity at all costs. I don't know what I had expected, maybe a local lingerie company and wrestling to break through in a tough market. But this was a different level. This was just the beginning for this brand, and building awareness would take time. The first year of the brand may not be a threat to me, but the money offered would bring new opportunities.

My hesitation was clear to both men, but they waited with patience for my decision. I shouldn't have made that decision until I heard something specific from the detective. However, the dream brought me back to some rational thinking, and I dismissed the reality of the threat.

"Let's do it." My whisper broke the silence.

Everything happened quickly after that. Jason grabbed my hand and pulled me toward the platform. Standing there, he instructed me on what to do and how to express emotions. The emotion clues were the most helpful to me, and according to Jason, my face conveyed them perfectly.

I kept hearing *click click click*, along with praise coming out of Jason's mouth. He said how great I was doing, how perfect I was for the job, how beautiful. I was flattered, and when I relaxed completely, I felt fantastic.

Miles watched us work, leaning against the conference table with his arms crossed over his chest and a gentle smile on his face.

Everything was going perfectly until the door to the room opened and a man walked in.

Castriel Russell.

The door closed softly behind him and he stood, stunned, when he saw me at the podium. Motionless as a statue, he stared at me with wide eyes, chocolate irises darkening. His face remained impassive, devoid of emotion. Not surprise, not sympathy, not even annoyance. He didn't even blink. After a moment, however, I noticed that a single muscle in his jaw twitched in sync with his heartbeat.

Miles began, "Mr. Russell—" but a raised hand silenced him.

Castriel's gaze sent shivers down my spine. Everything else froze. I stopped breathing for a moment. When my lungs started burning, I quickly regained composure and took a deep breath.

Jason's eyes jumped with curiosity from me to Castriel and back again.

"What the fuck is the meaning of this?" Castriel spat out the words and shot an angry look at Miles.

"We're just finishing a trial session with a candidate. This is Isabelle—"

"I'm not blind. I asked what this means," he growled. "This isn't the candidate we're looking for. She's not a model."

"She's not, but Mr. Russell—"

"Get rid of her," he growled.

"But—"

"Didn't I make myself clear? She's not the model we're looking for! My answer to that is no. Find someone else in her place. Anyone!"

There was absolute silence in the room. Miles didn't dare say another word. Instead, he looked confused. His face flushed and his eyes dropped to the floor.

Jason turned his attention to the camera instead. He gazed at the photos he had taken and acted as if the situation from seconds ago had never happened.

My legs shook, but I forced them to cooperate anyway. Anger slowly filled my veins. Who the hell was this man who treated other people like this? Who was this man who humiliated a subordinate? Who was this asshole that fate had once again put in my path?

I stepped down from the platform, and this brought Castriel's attention back to me. I pasted a mask of indifference on my face, not wanting him to enjoy my humiliation. I straightened up, raised my chin, and approached the bastard.

His huge figure towered over me, and yet I refused to show fear. I looked into his dark eyes. If only circumstances and his behavior hadn't been so awful, those captivating eyes could have been my downfall. I loathed Castriel Russell, yet something in me was drawn to him too. Maybe it was his mysterious aura, maybe it was his arrogant attitude, or maybe I was just a magnet for psychopaths. Either way, I suppressed any human impulse toward this asshole.

We continued this battle of gazes. Neither I nor he looked away. I already had some cutting retort on the tip of my tongue, anything that would move this devil, at least sting him, when different words came out of my mouth. "Male dolphins have a reputation for being incorrigible rapists."

In that one second, I hoped the earth would part and swallow me, along with my curse.

Castriel's eyes twitched, and I saw fire in them. Before he could utter more curses or foolish questions, I swiftly walked around him and exited the room. I hurried down the hall, then dashed into the street.

Once again, I had made a complete fool of myself in his company. Only I knew that this was stronger than me and what it meant. To them, I was just crazy.

CHAPTER 7

The air carried the characteristic smell of dampness, common in old, abandoned basements. It smelled of mustiness and rotting corpses, as if something had fallen dead here. Well, that wasn't far from the truth.

A normal person would find this place creepy enough to send shivers down their spine. I wasn't normal, so I didn't even feel a tingle.

The dark room was lit by a bulb hanging from the ceiling. In the far corner, rats were crawling around, unafraid of our presence. They were either used to humans or desperate. Or both.

My eyes found the silhouette of my new friend, hanging from the ceiling by metal chains. While unconscious, he was damn heavy, I must admit. It took some strength and time to hang him. The effort was worth it, though. The result was a masterpiece.

"Wake up, sleepyhead," I growled.

The taut chains rattled when Leo tried to move. He raised his head slowly and looked up, trying to understand his situation. With his wrists locked together, he couldn't support his weight, and tense muscles must have been on fire by now.

Then Leo looked at the rest of his naked body, his feet bound just as tightly. Finally, he graced me with his gaze.

"Who the hell are you?" he asked.

The drugs had just finished their journey through his body. He shook his head a few times, as if to clear his mind.

"What do you want, you fucker? I'll kill you at the first opportunity!" he spat out threatening words.

"Tsk tsk... That's not a nice way to talk to a friend, Leo," I scoffed. "Is that how you treat all your friends?"

"We're not friends. I don't know you. What do you want from me?"

"You're right, we're not. I have some questions for you, and if you answer them correctly, our paths will never cross again. If you answer them wrong or refuse to answer, we'll have some fun here."

"I'm not afraid of you." He laughed, thinking it was a joke to talk to me.

I shook my head. I hated people underestimating my intelligence. I hated people who underestimated my abilities even more.

Turning my back on him, I took off my jacket. I threw it on a nearby chair and rolled up the sleeves of my shirt.

The sound of the chains echoed through the basement walls again. I smiled to myself because Leo's behavior was so predictable.

When I looked at him, fear was reflected in his pupils. A series of curses followed a moment's hesitation in my direction. That didn't impress me. I was a cold-hearted bastard, and it was time he knew how cold I was.

Before I could take two breaths, I was standing right in front of him. In the next two breaths, my fist landed on his face four times.

Anger filled my veins. Soon this feeling turned to rage and my only outlet was my fists. I saw red. Anger or Leo's blood; it made no difference. It was only red.

I breathed deeply, my lungs burning with a living fire. Stepping back, I looked at my creation. Leo was hanging and moaning like a slaughtered lamb. His left eye was so swollen he couldn't open it. The right eye was in slightly better condition, and it was in that eye that I saw Leo's realization that this was no joke. Thin traces of bright red blood oozed from his nose and from his mouth, where I had knocked out several teeth. He was breathing as hard as I was.

This is all for you, Little I.

"Let me share how this story can continue, now that we know each other better." I lowered my voice. "As I said, I need some answers from you, my friend. You can help me and this will all be over quickly. If you refuse to cooperate—"

"Then what? You'll kill me?"

"The smell of blood dripping from your mouth, nose, and eyelid is already reaching the rats partying in that corner. Do you know a hungry rat can attack a human when it smells blood? Yes, it's possible. Did you know a rat can throw itself at a man nearly sixty inches high? Not bad, huh?"

"The rats can bite my ass!"

"Don't give them any ideas about what they can do to you or where they can get in. You're all alone here. You can scream and no one will hear you while they're eating you alive. Three rats won't kill you, though, will they? I guess not. But if we add new wounds to your body every day, fresh cuts, we'll have quite a party here within a week."

"You're fucked up, dude!" he exclaimed.

"That's partly thanks to you, you know? But let's get to the point, because I'm getting bored." I pulled a picture out of my pocket and showed it to him.

His first instinct was not to look, but curiosity won out. Leo was easy to read. His eyes widened in surprise and then closed.

He shook his head.

"I want the name of this person," I growled.

"Fuck you. I don't know that person."

"You know…"

"I don't remember," he hissed.

Before he had time to open his eyes again, I pulled a knife from my pocket. The skin on his chest opened immediately as I sliced a large "X" across it. Blood flowed in a stream down his abdomen and even lower.

The sound of moaning was like a melody to my ears.

"Want to play this game with me? Memory problems will not help you. Look closely."

The squealing of the rats, smelling fresh blood, grew louder. Out of the corner of my eye, I noticed they were starting to move in our direction. These bastards had no fear at all. Leo's eyes suddenly opened, and he looked in that direction as well.

Fear was visible on his face. Interesting… He was more afraid of them than me, even though I was the apex predator in this underworld.

"Look again, Leo, I don't have all day to play with you," I said, demanding his concentration.

"Who the hell are you?" he asked again.

"What is this person's name?"

"I can't…"

"You can, Leo; you have a choice."

Leo's eyes fell on the photo again and he trembled. His breathing became ragged, and I almost lost my temper completely. I didn't have much time left.

"Name!" I shouted in his face.

"I don't remember!"

Leo shook his head before letting it fall forward against his chest. The screeching of the rats grew louder, drawing his attention. I saw perfectly when fear took over his life.

Leo's eyes darted from me to the rats and back again. Paranoia set in and he looked around. His body was working fast and hard.

"Who is that person?" I felt a trickle of cold sweat run down my neck.

"No, no, no..." he groaned.

"Leo, focus! This is your only chance to survive!"

"G— G—" Leo's voice trailed off, even though he evidently wanted to say something else. I watched expectantly until he said the name, but within the next few seconds, he choked on his own breath.

I sighed and put the knife and photo in my pocket again. I had expected a little more from our conversation, but what the hell? Turning, I headed for the door.

But before I reached the exit, Leo let out a wheezing gasp and a last choked breath, and then there was silence. Motherfucker had a heart attack before I had time to warm up.

CHAPTER 8

CASTRIEL

From the very morning I was annoyed. The mission to get to my office was interrupted now and then:

"Good morning, Mr. Russell."

"Nice to see you."

"Morning, sir."

Did the people I met along the way, to whom I had no intention of returning their greeting, not see that there was nothing good about this day?

Thoughts of yesterday's casting didn't give me a break. When I entered the audition room, Isabelle was the last person I expected to see.

Not only had she been popping up in my thoughts at random times over the past few days, like an unwanted clown out of a box, but I found her in my professional space too. What a fucking disaster.

It was like a strike of lightning when I saw her posing for Jason. I was taken over by shock. I couldn't move. All I could see was her: her pale skin inviting me to touch it, her seductive form ready to be explored, her hair I longed for in disarray.

None of this was my style. I had never noticed such things.

There's nothing more annoying and mood-killing than an unwanted woman stalking you. She hadn't done it on purpose. I knew that. How hard was it to stop thinking about someone? Shit, it was the first time I realized it could be a problem. I had never before experienced such a lack of control, and I despised it.

Going back to this morning, Isabelle was in my thoughts before I woke up. In my dream, she got down on her knees and begged me not to fire her. *Ha! In your dreams, baby!* Or rather, in mine. Anyway, she was kneeling in front of me, begging, and all I could see was her tear-stained face. Black mascara ran down her rosy cheeks, leaving trails. She was so beautiful in this tragic picture. I couldn't control myself and with my thumb I caught one of the black tears and smeared it on her creamy skin.

When I woke up, I was hard as a rock. Blindly, my hand went under the covers, succumbing to temptation.

I came fast and instead of relief, I felt growing frustration. What the hell was happening to me? What the fuck was wrong with her?

That's why the people I met on my way today got exactly what they got.

I wanted to punch Miles in the face for this mess. Maybe I should do that at today's meeting. In a few minutes, I would fine an outlet for my negative energy.

Like a thunder, I took the elevator to the twelfth floor and directed my steps toward the conference room assigned to Miles's department. My posture and stride clearly showed a man on a mission, so no one else dared to speak to me.

Crossing the doorstep, I saw Miles and Jason leaning over a conference table. Pictures covered the length of the table. They were conversing in hushed tones, Jason's hand pointing to one photo.

Behind my back, the door slammed shut with a loud bang. They both jumped up and turned to face me. Miles's eyes went round, and I saw fear in them. And rightly so, because he had been on very thin ice since the incident with Isabelle.

"Good morning, Mr. Russell. Jason and I were just talking…"

I walked around the table and faced them, then looked at the photo they had just discussed. In an instant, I identified the person because of her unique appearance.

"What have you got for me, Jason?" I raised my eyes to him.

"We've chosen a few girls we think are perfect to be the brand's face."

"You don't understand. I'm asking what you have for me. I desire a brand-appropriate diamond, not just anyone. I want to see this diamond sparkle from a photo such that it will light up the darkness in Miles's ass. Do you have anything like that for me?"

Miles's face reddened and Jason burst into a loud laugh.

"Poetic," Jason howled between rounds of laughter. "I've got something perfect for you."

"Show me," I demanded.

His hand dropped to the photo of the girl, and he turned it to me.

"This is what you're looking for."

Miles shifted from foot to foot. One peek was enough to understand where his uncertainty was coming from.

"No," I growled in a low voice. Despite my warning tone, I couldn't take my eyes off the photo. A magnetic force prevented me from doing so.

The girl stood on spread legs, leaning forward. Her pale skin was silky, inviting. She was flawless. Slender calves gave way to shapely thighs. The white dress reached to her knees, the V-shaped neckline stressing her round and perfect breasts. The dress wasn't as revealing as many models had worn. The cut might be deemed conservative by some, but to me, it was simply delicate and feminine. I had the impression that the narrow waist invited me to lay my hands on her, while her delicate neck asked to be bitten. I couldn't accept my emotions upon seeing the girl's face.

"Abso-fucking-lutely no way," I growled again and was met with silence.

Meanwhile, Isabelle's intense, shining eyes didn't surprise me, but it stirred up a desire within me to reclaim all the pictures Jason had taken of her. The rosy cheeks matched the ones in my dream. The seductive smile promised something a man couldn't buy for all the money in this world.

"Keep looking," I snapped, finally tearing my eyes away. "That's not what we're looking for. I made myself clear enough."

Why does it sound like I'm trying to convince myself more than them?

I took two steps toward the door. It felt like the room had suddenly lost all oxygen. Miles said nothing, but Jason replaced him. "Castriel, wait a minute. Why do you think this is such a terrible choice?"

My arguments were unnecessary.

"Jason, my time is a specific number with a dollar sign. I would advise you to keep that in mind. Find me another candidate."

"You're not thinking clearly. Let me show you something."

"I don't have time for this nonsense. My answer is 'not her.' " Still, I stood there.

"You didn't even look at the other pictures," said Miles, gaining some confidence.

I rolled my eyes, my nostrils flaring, but I did my job. I walked over to Jason and let him show me the other candidates. As if we were at an exhibition, he introduced them to me. One was similar to the other. They differed in face, clothes, poses, but nothing else.

"And this is Stacy…" Jason went on. "Which one do you like best?"

"None." The word fell out of my mouth, and it was unnecessary to develop this thought.

"Why is that?"

My eyebrows shot up, but I kept my words to myself. Who was this idiot that I had to explain myself to?

"Okay, let me show you something else." He raised his hands in a gesture of surrender and laughed.

He placed a photo of each candidate next to him. My eyes were captivated by the red-haired beauty and refused to avert. Once again.

What a shitty day.

Objectively speaking, Isabelle had natural talent. The camera loved her. She was perfect in every way and unique, sexy, and…

"I know what you're trying to do, Jason, but my answer is still no."

"There's no one quite like her. She's both a mystery and a solution. She demands your attention and has no intention of apologizing. Castriel, I know you can see that." His words were met with silence from me, so he added at the end, "She won't adorn Papilio; instead, Papilio will enhance her beauty. Isabelle is as unique as this lingerie. This is exactly what we've been searching for. This is the face of the brand that cannot be missed. This is our diamond."

I was known for my tenacity and speed of decision-making. This was probably the first time I didn't understand what my instincts were telling me.

Jason was right. Even though I didn't want to say it out loud, the asshole saw it in my eyes. Staring at the photo for a second, I let my guard down, and that's when he saw it. But he had enough of an instinct for self-preservation that he didn't say so outright.

I left him with Miles and their pile of photos.

***

My annoyance with the entire world grew with each passing hour. I took a deep breath when my butt touched the seat of my motorcycle.

I rode aimlessly, gripping the handlebars tightly. The growl of the engine between my knees excited and calmed me at the same time. Speed, feared by some, was my drug.

I was an aggressive rider. I wasn't afraid of speed and I knew my skills or the capabilities of my bike, loved lying down on the turns, passing more obstacles at breakneck speed, and feeling complete freedom. I was a grumpy motherfucker, but in those rare moments, I allowed myself to smile.

In the midst of speeding past cars, the intercom alerted me to an incoming call. Slowing down, I answered with a touch on my helmet.

"Hello?" A female voice filled the space of my helmet.

"Hi, Emma."

"Hi. Mason asked me to contact you. Am I interrupting?"

"No." A snarky remark was on the tip of my tongue, but I held it back for the sake of the matter. "I need Isabelle's address."

"Why do you need her address?"

"Because I need to talk to her."

"She's not answering her phone? What's so urgent? How did she do at the audition?"

Seriously? I had to get through talking with her friend to reach the feisty little creature? Fuck my luck.

"Emma, can you give me her address, or should I find her another way?"

A burst of laughter rang through the intercom. I clenched my jaw to keep from saying more than I had to. How Mason got along with her was beyond me.

"Hold your horses, cowboy. I didn't say I wouldn't help you. I'm just worried because she's been shutting down since the phone calls started." Emma let out a loud breath and groaned. "Shit! Stupid hormones do whatever they want to me. I didn't say anything," she growled.

My curiosity came alive. "Phone calls?"

"Forget I mentioned it. It's probably nothing and I'm being oversensitive."

There was no way I could forget it, but I left the subject for later. In the meantime, I took advantage of Emma's remorse. I took a longer pause before attacking again. "So, how about this address?"

"I'll send it to you right away."

Couldn't you have done that before?

I ended the call before she could say anything else. I turned back. This time, I had a destination for my fast ride.

I was near the city when a motorcycle suddenly appeared in front of me. It was impossible to confuse it with anyone else, as I already knew this blatantly green beast. A mischievous grin appeared on my lips.

"Hello again," I whispered to myself.

The last time we played together, I'd had fun. Me maybe a little more than her, but still...

I felt the excitement.

I added speed and within a second I was next to my new companion. She didn't notice me at first, but then her helmet turned slightly in my direction. She watched me out of the corner of her eye, and I was sure she rolled her eyes and cursed me.

My mischief bared its fangs and chanted that it wanted to play. I didn't have to wait long.

The bike whined and she shot forward.

I laughed because it was too easy. Every biker should learn how not to get roused by another rider. I knew I was a hypocrite. This thought made me laugh even more.

In the blink of an eye, I found myself on the tail of the green monster, clinging to it. The more she wanted to get away from me, the more I wanted to subdue it. My heart beat faster.

We drove into the city. She went first, and I followed. Did she feel my breath on the back of her neck? Was she like a rat trapped in a maze with no way out? I was fucked up, no question.

She turned left, then right, then into another alley. I was her shadow. It turned me on like hell.

We slowed down before the intersection, where a red light had already jumped in. What I didn't expect, however, was my friend stepping on the gas and taking off. Immediately, angry drivers honked. I hadn't anticipated such a move, and it cost me. As soon as I entered the intersection, a truck pulled out to my left. I was forced to brake or I would have been a bloodstain on a New York street.

When I had a clear view again, the green beast was gone. "Fuck!"

All good things come to an end.

Another game awaited me—much less exciting, but necessary. I punched Isabelle's address into the navigation, and it turned out that I wasn't that far from her apartment after all. I drove the rest of the way at a snail's pace.

CHAPTER 9

IZZY

My breathing calmed down only when I parked my Bird in the underground garage. Relief washed over me as I finally felt secure.

I had gone out that afternoon because I needed to clear my head from tormenting thoughts. I felt the walls of my life suffocating me. Memories of my childhood, phone calls, my behavior around Castriel... I couldn't stop thinking about them.

I would rather not ponder what the presence of Castriel Russell did to me. The embarrassment overshadowed everything else. It crept uninvited into my thoughts several times during the day, so that each time the shame grew stronger.

A throaty sound broke from my mouth at the mere memory. I was exhausted. Even the ride that was supposed to be my liberation had turned out to be a failure because of him.

My blissful mood vanished the moment I saw him beside me on the road. The ghost helmet stood out so it couldn't be mistaken for anyone else's. Rolling my eyes, I cursed, even though no one could hear me.

With every mile I drove, he annoyed me more, following in my path. If I turned left, he was right behind me. When I turned right, he followed in the same direction. And then I saw an opportunity and took a chance. It was a foolish move that could have ended with a visit to the hospital or the morgue, and yet it was successful.

I got rid of him once and for all, and I hoped I would never have to face him again.

With my helmet under my arm, I made my way to the elevator. I pushed the button for my floor and leaned against the opposite wall.

In a second, the elevator stopped at the first floor; the doors swung open, and there stood Brad. When he saw me, a seductive smile appeared on his face.

"Hi, gorgeous," he said in a low voice. He got on the elevator and leaned over to kiss my cheek. "I'm glad to see you."

I smiled back. "Hi. How have you been doing?"

"Good. Work, work, and work. I didn't know you rode a motorcycle."

"Yes. I'm addicted to my baby. I don't know a better way to relieve tension."

Brad's eyes lit up and his smile became even wider. "I don't think I can agree with you. I could try to show you other ways to get rid of that tension, though."

"Oh my God, did you just suggest what I think?" This time, I burst out laughing.

The elevator doors opened again, and just like last time, we both got off at my floor. At my door, I turned to Brad.

He looked amused, but also a little confused.

"That sounded ambiguous," he announced. "In my defense, I meant to have dinner in brilliant company, with dancing and laughter all evening."

"Yes?"

"Yes, but I also like your train of thought." He laughed.

I felt a blush creep up my cheeks. "Now I'm petrified. I'm sorry, Brad."

"You have nothing to be sorry about. It's normal to think about sex with me twenty hours a day! I assume you dream about me the other four."

We were grinning at each other like two teenagers when a grunt sounded in the hallway. I glanced over Brad's shoulder at the source and the smile melted from my face.

Standing at the exit of the stairwell was Castriel, dressed in his black motorcycle outfit with his helmet under his arm.

Did he just come all the way up here by stairs when all normal people used the elevator?

His clouded gaze lingered on Brad's back until he turned to face the newcomer. His posture straightened and seemed to take up space. They stared at each other like two warriors.

"Do you know each other?" I asked, not knowing what this was all about.

"No," Brad replied, while Castriel remained silent and continued to stare at him.

A minute passed, and they continued this silent battle. Castriel's gaze became cold and hateful. Usually aloof and silent, he was suddenly very expressive. This was awkward.

"Okay," I said to break the silence. "Brad, it was nice to catch up with you. See you around."

Brad turned to me then and his eyes were soft again. They just weren't as happy as before.

"Back to dinner with dancing and laughter... Are you interested?"

I smiled and was about to open my mouth to answer when I heard a low growl. A real deep, manly growl.

My eyes found Castriel, who took two steps toward us and stopped. Now he looked like a wild animal ready to pounce on Brad.

"She's not interested," Castriel answered for me.

"Excuse me?" Brad asked with surprise when I started say, "And you are...?"

Again, silence filled the heavy atmosphere. I rolled my eyes in annoyance.

"If you knew anything about women, you'd be able to tell when she's interested. For example..." Castriel suddenly stood a foot in front of me. Like a switch, my mind operated on a different frequency, aware of his presence and every movement. My body temperature jumped, and the room suddenly felt like there was no oxygen left. I felt the rhythm of my heart quicken. "If you lifted a woman's head with your thumb so that she could met your gaze, would her lips part slightly like Isabelle's lips?"

Castriel's warm thumb found its way under my chin and lifted my head. I parted my lips but didn't notice that until a moment later. The man's eyes framed my gaze.

"If you move her hair back over her shoulder or a strand away from her face, will it cause goosebumps on her perfect skin?" His thumb moved down my neck, leaving a hot trail. Now it was official. I couldn't breathe as his finger pushed my hair from my shoulder. I knew the goosebumps had appeared.

Castriel's chocolate eyes followed his thumb and returned to my eyes with satisfaction.

"And if you lean in a little—" From under half-closed eyelids, I saw Castriel's face lean in, and I felt his cool nose on the skin. He dragged it along my neck and I was ready to melt. "Can you feel the growing excitement on her skin?"

That's what I felt: a growing excitement. It started with a gentle flutter in my stomach and went lower and lower. It placed itself right between my thighs, which I clenched. At that moment, our helmets collided. This caught Castriel's attention, as he looked at my green helmet for a moment. Understanding suddenly appeared in his eyes.

"That's the interest you won't find in Isabelle when it comes to you." His words sizzled and he took a step back.

I looked at Brad and my excitement was obvious. My whole body vibrated just below the surface of my skin.

"Now go away. Isabelle and I have some things to... undress."

Brad shifted from foot to foot. Whatever was going through his mind was causing him to back away, both mentally and physically. He took two steps back and rubbed his neck with his hand. "Izzy, are you okay with this guy?"

I nodded several times because I couldn't find my voice.

"I'll see you soon then, and we'll get back to that dinner. And interest."

I heard and physically felt another warning growl from Castriel. His displeasure was clear.

After another nod, Brad turned on his heel and headed for the stairs.

It was just Castriel and me. It was beyond my comprehension what had just happened. We didn't even like each other, so why the hell was he playing the role of a possessive asshole? And why the hell did my body react like that?

When we were alone, I found Castriel with my eyes. His dark eyes were watching me again. They bored into me as if they wanted to bite into my soul and find what they were looking for there. I couldn't let that happen.

I snapped out of my trance. "What are you doing here?"

When my question was met with his silence, I was a bit taken aback. My eyebrows went up. I couldn't believe that the man who had so much to say a few moments ago was now silent again.

"What the hell are you doing here?" My tone was sharper this time.

I'd had enough of his silence for a lifetime. "Listen. If you want something from me, you need to talk to me. I'm not a psychic. I don't read minds or pupil movements. I respect your mysterious and silent aura, but I need words to understand you."

"You're the one," he started to say with a deep, menacing voice. "You're the biker I met the other day. And also today."

An answer wasn't necessary since it wasn't a question. I shrugged as if it didn't matter.

"If you thought girls can't ride motorcycles, I have to disappoint you," I said.

"You're not surprised. You knew it was me out there on the road." He crossed his arms.

"I didn't know it right away. I figured it out when you came to Media Linc, and I saw your helmet."

"And you said nothing."

"What would be the point? You didn't answer my question. What are you doing here?"

Silence surrounded us again. His chocolate eyes moved over my body from top to bottom and back again. Every inch of my body tickled, as if thousands of needles were piercing my skin. Meanwhile, the excitement returned with renewed force.

I shook my head, took the keys to my apartment out of my pocket, and put them in the lock. I wanted to open the door, walk in, slam it behind me, and forget the whole day. But he had other plans.

As soon as I crossed the doorway, satisfied that I had left Castriel on the other side, I pushed the door with all my strength. I waited for the big bang, but it didn't happen.

In an instant, surprise replaced my satisfaction. A firm hand grabbed my shoulder, then the expected bang occurred. I was turned around and found myself pushed against the door.

I could feel the heat radiating from Castriel's body even through our outfits. Helmets were rolling around on the floor somewhere, but I didn't care. Finding myself trapped once again by his gaze and his proximity, I almost moaned.

What the hell is happening to me?

There was no space between us. Castriel's whole body was in contact with mine. With my head tilted, I stared at him. My pulse quickened, as did my breathing.

Castriel's eyes lit up when he realized how close we were. For the first time, I saw a small smile appear on his lips. If I hadn't been concentrating on them, I wouldn't have noticed it. It was barely visible. There was something mesmerizing about his lips. I wanted to lick them just to taste their taste.

Then another wave of arousal flooded my insides, stronger than the previous one. Heat rushed explicitly through my insides, melting every bit of resistance.

Our breaths mingled. I couldn't believe I was reacting to him this way. At the very least, he could drive a woman crazy.

I should get my purple vibrator out from under my pillow tonight.

"If you want to keep your clothes on, I suggest you stop looking at me like that." Castriel's whisper brought me to the edge of my sanity.

"I'm not looking at you *like that* at all," I denied, shaking my head.

"Are you sure?" I felt the touch of a finger on my thigh. It was close. Too close to where I wanted him most, but still too far away. "I'm willing to keep checking. I wonder how you'll react when I prove you to be a liar."

"Castriel, stop it," I said. A moment later, my true nature revealed itself. "The vibrator predates electricity. The first vibrators were powered by a hand crank and were used in medicine to reduce female hysteria."

Castriel's big eyes darkened, and he tilted his head to get a better look at me. I couldn't believe I had done it again. How many times did a woman have to make a fool of herself before she died of shame? I wanted to run and cry at the same time. I was so fucking ashamed.

"What did you just say, Isabelle?"

I pursed my lips and pressed my hand to my lips to stop the damn nonsense.

Castriel's gaze became even more intense. I could see his mind racing, trying to find a logical answer for my behavior.

I sighed in disappointment. "Get out, Castriel."

"Oh, no, no, no. Not this time, Isabelle."

"Why do you call me Isabelle and not Izzy, like most people do?"

"As far as I know, Isabelle is your name, and I'm not like most people."

"No, you're not." Putting my hands on his chest, I pushed him. Not hard enough to make him lose his balance, but enough to make him take a step back. His firm muscles jerked, and I felt them through the clothes.

Oh God, what would have happened if I'd touched his hot skin in that place without restraint?

"Don't think I didn't notice the attempt to change the subject. It wasn't very effective, but I appreciate the effort. You could have said you didn't want to talk about it."

"I don't want to talk about it." I rolled my eyes.

"That's too bad, because I feel like I need to know that about you. Before you talk back, you should know that it's unusual for me to be interested in someone."

I rolled my eyes again. I couldn't believe I had let myself get caught up in something like this.

"What do you want from me? Why are you here?"

"Why are you saying all these weird things? Jesus, a crank vibrator?"

"I get like that sometimes." I let out a sigh, but when I saw Castriel wasn't satisfied with my answer, I continued. At least my arousal decreased drastically when I wasn't thinking about his hard chest, lips, hands… "I'm a person who hates not knowing. If I have an unanswered question, you'll find a phone in my hand. I won't find peace until I know the answer. Most of this random information is stored in my head. Sometimes it finds its way out through my mouth. Satisfied?"

"Hardly," he replied, losing concentration for a moment to look at my mouth. "I think you know very well when and why you say them. For some reason, you don't want to tell me."

"Really? I don't know where that assumption comes from. Look, Castriel, we're not friends and we don't even know each other. You ask me things that are private and you're surprised I don't feel like answering. Guess what? None of your business, asshole!"

Anger replaced the curiosity in Castriel's eyes. He took a step toward me, closing the distance between us again.

But before he questioned me further, my phone rang.

I unzipped my motorcycle jacket and reached into the inside pocket. On the screen I saw that the number was unknown. All the anxiety I had shed during the ride returned.

My hands shook, and I closed my eyes for a moment. When I opened them again, I realized I had piqued Castriel's interest even more.

"Aren't you going to answer?"

I just shook my head. The phone went silent and the 3 Doors Down ringtone started playing again. Before I could decide whether to answer this time, Castriel grabbed the phone and pressed the green icon.

"Hello," he growled.

Hungry for details, his eyes never left mine.

For a moment, Castriel didn't speak, just listened. When he said another "hello," I already knew it was my stalker on the other end.

Finally, Castriel ended the call and put the phone back in its place. He put his hand under the lapels of my jacket, rubbing his fingers along my chest in the process. Shivers ran down the surface of my skin.

"Is there something you want to tell me, Isabelle?"

CHAPTER 10

CASTRIEL

She looked at me with wide, surprised eyes and shook her head. But when I pushed back the layer of surprise, I saw a dim glimmer in them. She knew exactly what I was talking about.

"No, absolutely not," she gasped, trying to convince me.

My eyes saw every detail and my mind soaked them up. Isabelle Knox was clearly hiding something. I felt it in my dark soul. Maybe that was what was calling me to her.

"There was someone on the other end. I could hear them breathing."

Fear appeared on her face. Her emerald eyes shone with terror and the muscle just above her left eye jumped. Isabelle was trying to breathe steadily— with mediocre results, if anyone asked me.

"Maybe it was a wrong number or a telemarketer. You know how persistent they can be."

"Probably. Maybe he was overwhelmed with fear and couldn't get a word out."

Isabelle nodded briskly in support of the story. In return, she received my grimace.

"Who was that, Isabelle?"

"What is this, some kind of interrogation? Why don't you hook me up to a lie detector?"

That was the idea. I stared at her without saying a word until she squirmed in discomfort. It gave me pleasure; a lot of fucking pleasure.

Isabelle was a beautiful woman. It wasn't hard to admit that. I had met a lot of beautiful women in my life. Women who, with little effort on my part, fell to their knees before me. Women who would have intimidated the biggest tough guy with their beauty. Yet only this one could get through my hard shell of insolence and indifference.

I felt myself grow hard at the sight of her discomfort. Why did I get aroused by that?

"We will return to this subject. I promise. In the meantime, I would appreciate the answer to my previous question. Why do you say these random things?"

"This is not your—"

"Don't say those words if you're not ready for the consequences that might await you. I'm damn interested in the answer to that question, and that means I'm going to pursue the subject long enough and hard enough to get an answer."

Isabelle raised her head cockily, and I wanted to smile. I never smiled. The fire that made Isabelle who she was attracted me like no one else.

I leaned even closer to her so she could see in my eyes that I wasn't joking. She had no idea.

"Castriel, please stop."

Oh, firecracker, I'm just starting to play with you.

"Although I find pleasure in your begging, the answer remains 'no.'"

"I'm not begging," she scoffed.

"That remains to be seen."

The pink blush on her cheeks caught my attention. The flawless skin looked so soft. The tingling in my fingers was annoyingly tempting to draw my fingertip across its surface.

"Why are you saying all these things?" I growled, staring into her emerald eyes.

"Castriel—"

"Why?"

"I don't—"

"Why, Isabelle?" I raised my voice, and it only made a tiny crack in her stubbornness.

"Because I'm nervous! Okay?"

"You say all those things when you're nervous?"

"Yes," she whispered.

"Interesting. My presence makes you nervous... Why do you feel like that, Isabelle?"

Her eyes widened further, resembling those of a trapped animal, yet she remained silent. She didn't even breathe. "Do you feel on edge when I'm near? Does it start here?" My forefinger touched her temple. "Here?" Down her neck, I traced a path between her breasts, where her heart was. "Or rather, here?"

My hand found her warm abdomen and only then did she take a greedy gulp of air. Isabelle's eyes sparkled and the throbbing in the artery in her neck accelerated. I was captivated and couldn't look away from her. It might have been seconds, maybe minutes, before Isabelle jumped aside as if my touch had burned her.

She took a few steps, leaving a space between us I didn't like.

"Stop touching me," she growled, glaring at me.

That's when I realized for the first time that her fire was addictive. *I'm afraid it won't be that easy.*

"Why did you come here?" She changed the subject by lifting her helmet from the floor to find its place on the hanger hanging by the door.

"I came to discuss your cooperation with Papilio."

Like an obedient dog, I followed Isabelle to the kitchen, where she poured two glasses of water. She placed one in front of me on the kitchen island and drank the other, grasping the glass in a stranglehold.

"I'm not working for Papilio. Listen, I came to the audition by accident. I promised Em that I would try it. It was her idea. I thought it wouldn't be the worst thing, but I was mistaken. It's not for me, so you don't have to worry about me showing up there again."

"Jason and Miles think you're the best candidate to be the face of the brand this season."

"Then it's fortunate that you're the CEO and have a say in this," she replied, not holding back her sarcasm.

"For the sake of the company, I can turn a blind eye to my dislike of you."

"How comforting. You really know how to make a woman feel good."

"You need me to make you feel good?" My eyebrows rose as I leaned over the island that separated us.

"Don't flatter yourself, Castriel. Men. You all behave like barking dogs."

"What does that mean?"

"Nothing."

Isabelle was arousing more curiosity in me, and if that wasn't what she wanted, she was out of luck. She had to learn to control her tongue.

"Just say the word if you desire to witness my persuasive abilities again. I'll be more than happy to oblige."

She rolled her eyes in return.

"It just means that men like you talk a lot, but when it comes to keeping a promise, the fairy tale ends. Don't flatter yourself that you can make me feel good. That's all."

Her words left me stunned. The pieces of the puzzle fell into place in my mind and I couldn't believe my ears. This woman believed that no man could physically satisfy her.

I grabbed the counter with both hands, holding myself back from seizing her and proving right there and then how wrong she was.

"Are you saying that none of the guys you've fucked have been able to make you feel good?"

"Of course not. I felt good."

"But not enough to see the fucking stars. Not enough to melt like ice cream on a sunny day. Not good enough to have a cosmic fucking orgasm," I guessed.

The woman just shrugged. The annoyance and relief hit me like a tsunami. None of her previous lovers had brought her to the orgasm she deserved. It was embarrassing for every man out there. The challenge flowed through my veins.

"It is what it is," was her response, minimizing the problem. "Not every woman can come during sex."

If she had grown a second head, I would have been less surprised. I couldn't help but burst out laughing, which was even more unnatural. The strange, deep sound of my laughter echoed through Isabelle's small apartment. She watched me closely, first with intrigue and then simple annoyance. She assumed I was laughing at her, when in fact the target was her stupidity and her belief in what other men were trying to tell her.

Slowly, the laughter died on my lips. I couldn't believe that she had achieved something as great as my laughter. I looked at her in fascination.

"Isabelle, you're not a stupid woman, although what you're saying might question that truth. You let lame guys with limp dicks make you think there's something wrong with you?" I thundered.

"Shhh..."

"Don't shush me, woman. Maybe this is just what you need to wake up Sleeping Beauty. When your fingers fuck your cunt, massage your clit, do you have trouble coming?"

"Oh my God." Isabelle's hand slapped her forehead. The crimson of her cheeks grew in intensity. "I don't feel comfortable talking to you about this. There are things you don't discuss with a potential employer."

"A while ago, you said it was a mistake. Let's get back to that, just to get the subject of your orgasm out of the way. Answer my question."

The hand that had been on her forehead fell to the tabletop of the island with a thud. Angry eyes found mine.

"Of course I have absolutely no problem with that, you nosy asshole!"

There was only a few inches of space between us when my reply wrapped around her face. "There you go. You alone know which side is at fault. You're capable of a mind-blowing orgasm. It's they who have failed to rise to the challenge and bring you to such pleasure that you feel like tearing your own skin. It's their lack of skill that has never made you scream in relief by jumping off the edge."

After these last words, my eyes went to her mouth, from which a muffled, agonized sound escaped. I was sure my words had aroused her and she was now wet, even drenched. I was hard at the thought of what I could do to her; what I would like to do to her.

My eyes followed the trail of pink tongue that moistened her chapped lips. I had the urge to bite them. This was a first. Kissing a woman never interested me. Fucking her mouth, yes, but not kissing her.

From outside the window came the sound of a car horn and the moment between us was interrupted. Isabelle moved away. She looked to the side.

"Whatever you might think"—another shrug—"life isn't an erotic affair and we're not the heroes of it. The men who always bring women to orgasm only exist in books. And orgasms and sex itself are often overrated."

Did she not know how challenging she was to me? Did she really not understand that she was provoking me? I wanted to shake her world to its foundations.

"No, we're not heroes. You may not always make it, but you never did. It's not the same. Orgasms and sex *are not* overrated. It's fuckers like the ones you slept with that make women think the big O is a myth."

What was happening to me? I wasn't myself. I was also the motherfucker. Most of the time, I didn't even care about a woman's orgasm. The most important thing was my release. I was always sincere in my intentions to give the woman a free choice, though I wanted Isabelle's faith to match my confidence.

Isabelle's eyes fell to the floor as she brooded over something. "You should leave now, Castriel," she said.

"We have one more thing to discuss: cooperating on Papilio."

She muttered something under her breath.

"I would ask you to translate that into a language I know with the right pitch."

"You're such an ass! Was that loud enough in a language you know?"

"I can definitely hear you better now. While it's necessary to improve our communication, I must admit that I also like to see you with the sound muted."

Annoying her was becoming one of the few activities that evoked any emotion in me. Her cheeks puffed out and her teeth bit into her lower lip.

The internal battle that was going on inside her made me even more eager. Common sense suppressed the urge to show aggression.

"It was a mistake." She sighed and began pacing the small room called the kitchen. "I won't model for Papilio."

"Why not?"

"Let's see. Maybe because you and I make a spectacular drama at every contact."

"Absurd. When the situation calls for it, we're both capable of behaving professionally. Give me another reason."

"Okay. I'm not a model. I have no experience; I don't know what I'm doing in front of the lens."

"It was about reasons against, not for. What you brought up is in your favor in this case."

"I don't understand. The name Knox doesn't benefit anyone."

"It doesn't matter. When I see the perfect model for a job, I'm not interested in her details."

Isabelle finally stopped. As her green eyes focused on me, I took a deep breath. "So you admit that I'm what the company is looking for, expecting, and needing?"

"It's not proper for you to ask for praise, but if you're so eager to hear it from my lips... You're the person Papilio is looking for; you're perfect for the job. Here you are and you're welcome." It wasn't my job to boost anyone's ego.

For a moment, Isabelle considered my words. "Despite everything... In spite of everything, I must thank you for this proposal," she said.

"What is the breaking point not to make the opposite decision?"

"I don't want to be famous. I don't want people to recognize my face."

Most of the women I knew would have thanked me for the opportunity, without even asking how much would go into their account. Why did this one have to cause problems?

"I don't want to spoil the vision in your head, but if you think you're going to become Kaia Gerber or Gigi Hadid overnight, you're wrong. It's more than likely that we'll get to that level of model in the next five years, but not yet. The fame talked about in the gossip magazines doesn't threaten you yet."

"Who?"

I lied. Of course I was lying. If I had anything to say about developing our company, its shares would explode like a balloon full of helium. It wouldn't happen in a month, but my six-month plan included a more ambitious goal than anyone had dared to imagine.

For now, though, Isabelle didn't have to worry. All in good time.

"Kaia and Gigi are world-famous models," I explained.

"I have no idea who you're talking about."

"Anything else in the way?"

"I have a job at Media Linc. I'm not just going to leave it. Miles presented me with the amount of the fee, but that doesn't mean—"

Fucking Miles.

"You can keep working for Mason. I don't care. Do we have a contract?"

Isabelle's eyes still showed indecision. I had to steer her subtly onto the correct path.

I pushed off the countertop, straightened up, and looked at Isabelle as if she were my prey. I slowly circled the kitchen island, approaching her step by step.

By the time I stopped, perhaps half a foot separated us. The air filled with unfamiliar vibrations and tension. Images filled my mind of what I could do to this beauty.

She looked at me shyly, then with a fiery expression.

"What are you doing?"

"Is there anything else I should..." I paused for a moment, building up tension in her. I ran my eyes over her torso, still clad in the suit, down her neck, her face, until I saw goose bumps. Satisfied with her reaction, I continued. "Undress... I mean disarm, before you agree to become the face of the Papilio brand?"

I knew exactly how my charm worked on women. I could turn it into a weapon of mass destruction without breaking a sweat. Isabelle was different in many ways, but she wasn't immune to me.

"Say please." Her whisper was barely audible. "Maybe then I'll agree."

A small smile tugged at my lips. I leaned into her ear and whispered, "Please. This is the first and last time you'll hear it from me. The next time, it will be you begging me."

CHAPTER 11

The body of a young man lay on the bed in front of me. He was alive, but I was sure that if he saw himself through my eyes, he would want to die. His eyes were sunken, his complexion pale. The body had been stripped of most of its muscles. The man was as slim as a doll, a marionette. I suspected that years of lying in bed had done that to him.

Connected to the body were tubes that pumped oxygen into his lungs and food into his stomach. A catheter that removed urine. Electrodes that monitored his heartbeat and other vital signs. The sound of faint beeping alternated with the sound of the ventilator machine in the room.

Although we weren't in a hospital, the decor of the room was little different from one. The only additions were a comfortable couch and chairs, a dresser, and a few trinkets. The man in the bed needed nothing else anyway.

My eyes had never left his body for a moment since I arrived. His motionless posture fueled my anger. When I saw him, the monster inside me fought to get out, jerking and writhing, clawing and trying to tear me apart.

The thoughts in my head flowed faster and faster. Pictures from the past appeared, along with plans that had yet to come to fruition.

The blood rushed through my veins faster and faster. Even though the temperature in the room didn't increase by a single degree, my skin was getting hotter and hotter. Or maybe that was just my imagination.

When I'd had enough, I got up angrily. I closed my eyes and let the monster inside me take control. After a moment, I took one more look at the man lying there even though it was too much, turned around, and left the room. Avoiding people who might have seen me on the way, I slipped out of the building.

CHAPTER 12

IZZY

"**I**s something wrong, Isabelle?" Detective Burk asked as soon as he answered the call.

"Hi, Detective. Please call me Izzy. I'm supposed to call you when something concerns me. Did you hear the news about the young man's murder? Leo?"

"I can't say that I have. What happened?"

I took a deep breath and told him everything I knew about the case.

The police tried to keep as many details as possible to themselves, for the sake of the investigation. Nevertheless, certain details emerged. There will always be someone who wants to make a few bucks by revealing them.

Leo, a man about my age, had been kidnapped and murdered. The media said he was tortured. However, they didn't give a definitive cause of death. His butchered body was found in White Plains a few days ago. No one explained how he got there.

"In the city where you live, Izzy, this is nothing new. Murders are the order of the day. There's always something going on," he complained when I finished telling the story.

"You don't understand, Detective. I don't want you to think I'm crazy, but I think it has something to do with me."

"How so?"

"One witness who saw the body before the police arrived on the scene says he had an inscription cut into his chest with a sharp tool. The inscription said, 'I will find you.'"

"And you think this is the same person who sent you the message?" A hint of disbelief crept into his voice.

"We could consider it a coincidence..."

"But?"

"If it weren't because I know him," I admitted. "I mean, I knew him. I knew him back in the days when I was finishing school. We weren't close or anything. It's just that our paths crossed a few times in the past."

Silence filled the air. I looked around my small apartment, stopping at the window and then the door. I had recently taken great precautions for my safety. I locked the windows at night, checked the locks several times, and closed the curtains. I always had my phone and a folding knife with me. Almost always.

"I see," he choked out. "I haven't learned anything new since our last conversation. The person monitoring him while he serves his time is also on vacation. I've made several phone calls and no one will give me an answer, not even if there was a parole board. We have to wait until my man comes back to work. I'm sorry, Izzy."

I was sorry too. But I was more hopeful that by the time his guy got back, it wouldn't be too late. Before my own father finished what he started many years ago.

The image of his face with a trickle of blood running down it appeared in my mind. A grimace of annoyance turned to rage. Terror chilled my blood, but I knew at that moment that I had only one chance to survive.

I shook my head to get rid of it.

"Izzy, I'm almost certain you have nothing to worry about. If he got out of prison, the media would be all over it."

"Detective, I know this sounds like my paranoia. I'm not crazy, I'm not making this up. Someone is trying to scare me and it's not my ex or a jealous boyfriend. If that's what you think, please tell me, but please don't play it down, even at the expense of reassuring me."

"You're right. I apologize. I didn't mean to minimize what's going on. Under normal circumstances, I would suggest that you report this to the local police. They might find out who contacted you. Here, however, I'll pass the subject on to my colleague. I need you to send me all the details of this message and the calls you received on your phone. We'll see what we can do in that way."

"Fine, thank you."

"But Izzy, think about changing your phone number too."

"I've been thinking about it," I said. "I'll look into it and get back to you soon."

"Good. Be safe."

Icy chills ran through my body as I ended the call. Reason told me that Leo's death had nothing to do with me, but intuition told me otherwise. I had a feeling. Talking to the detective didn't calm it down.

Maybe I should listen to my gut?

And what? Run from the shadow of a man who might not even be free?

Maybe he is, maybe he isn't. If he is, then you will pack your life into a suitcase.

The internal struggle with myself gave me a headache. All this—the sleepless nights, the exhaustion, the constant worrying—provoked migraines. The pain increased at an alarming rate.

Waiting no longer, I found myself in the bathroom. In the cabinet were the medications prescribed by my doctor. I put one of them in my mouth, drank water from the tap, and looked at myself in the mirror.

I barely recognized the face looking back at me. I was pale and tired. Completely different from a month ago when Castriel offered to work with me. I hadn't seen him since that day. He didn't show up at Media Linc, didn't contact me, and I didn't meet him on the streets.

At first, I was relieved by his absence. His always appraising gaze, intense, stopped my heart for a moment. The blood in my body circulated faster than usual, my temperature rose, and anticipation crept under the surface of my skin. This, combined with his magnetic eyes, caused my irritation, and I talked about stupid things.

Why do I react to him this way?

I didn't know, but the question haunted my thoughts. Yes, it had happened to me several times in my life. But I had never been so affected by someone's presence before.

He almost forced the answer out of me. I didn't want to give him the satisfaction or boost his ego. Castriel was dangerous when supported by determination.

After the first few days of relief caused by his absence, something inside me changed. I killed any thoughts that went in that direction.

I have bigger problems, and he's my boss now.

Sometimes it took a reminder to get my thoughts back on track. The stakes were too high.

The shoot for Papilio was to start in an hour. I had to look my best, and I did everything in my power to do so. When I took the elevator to the company headquarters an hour later, I was relatively satisfied with the results.

I got off at the seventh floor. As the elevator doors closed behind me, the first thing I noticed was chaos.

They had prepared the entire floor to look like a set. On the right, the crew had prepared two sets, one with a white background and one with a black background. On the left were benches upholstered in green plush and hangers filled with lingerie. In front of them were three stands with mirrors, a preparation center for the makeup artist and hairdresser. Scattered about were some sort of tripods, extra lighting, some other items...

I didn't know that so many people were involved in taking a few pictures. Some people were handling the equipment, others were moving props, talking and gesticulating. Like I said, chaos.

"There she is! Our star! Isabelle, over here!" I heard my name through the noise.

I followed the voice with my eyes and found Miles waving his hand from the corner of the studio. Next to him was a smiling Jason.

I moved toward them when the man standing in front of them turned to face me. I froze.

"Brad?" My voice was full of disbelief. "What are you doing here?"

A shy smile appeared on his handsome face. He looked a little confused. He only answered when I took a step away from him, just after he leaned in to kiss my cheek. "Hi, Izzy. Looks like we're going to be working together. I didn't know you wanted to pose."

"Do you know each other?" The question came from Miles.

I smiled, although seeing all that made me nervous.

"I didn't plan to go down this road at all," I explained to Brad. "It just happened that way."

"And yes, we know each other. We're…" I answered Miles, searching for the right term for our acquaintance. "Neighbors."

"Old friends." It fell from Brad's lips and our eyes found each other.

This is awkward.

He didn't look offended; more like surprised.

"We're neighbors and we know each other from school," I finished.

"Wonderful." Miles clapped his hands, excited. "This will make things a lot easier for us."

I had no idea what he was talking about.

Jason remained silent, just watching our interaction.

Someone called out to Miles, who nodded. "It's time for me to go. Lyla will take care of you soon, Izzy."

He took a few steps away, and I followed. "Miles?" I stopped him and when he turned to me, I made sure no one could hear my words. "I know it's not my place to ask, but does your boss know you hired Brad for this job?"

"The boss has been in Japan for the past week and hasn't had a chance to meet Brad, but before he left, he gave me free rein to hire a co-model. Brad is a successful professional and a sought-after face these days."

"I don't doubt that, but we've already met and I think—"

"All the better!" His smile grew even wider. "Relax, Izzy. I know it's your first rodeo, but you'll be fine. Since Castriel gave me free hand, that means he trusts me. I trust my instincts. Lyla, please take care of our Izzy, because I have to do something."

The tall, brown-haired woman was standing in front of me when Miles was already walking away. All that remained was to hope that Miles's instincts wouldn't fail him and that Castriel's dislike for Brad wouldn't affect us all.

Lyla proved to be an extremely patient and understanding person. She immediately sensed my newcomer's anxiety but didn't criticize it. With a smile, she gave me some valuable tips on how to relax and forget that twenty people were watching my every move.

My makeup was taken care of first, again. My makeup wasn't bad, just inappropriate for the lighting, the seductive atmosphere, and apparently my aura. How Lyla saw my aura was beyond me. In the mirror, I saw a different version of myself, with smoky eyes, extended eyelashes, and flawless skin. I looked like a real model. Despite the makeup, I still looked natural. I liked what I saw.

The hairdresser took care of my hair, accentuating my curls, but in a more controlled way. The slightly straightened waves were longer and beautiful.

After the prep was finished, someone pointed me toward a dressing room behind a previously unnoticed door.

"Please start with this pearl set," Lyla said as she walked by.

I ducked into the dressing room, leaned against the door, closed my eyelids, and took a few deep breaths.

There's no point in getting nervous. Remember, you can always quit. Violating the contract will also violate your budget, but you'll get through it. As you always do. Now go, wear your big girl panties and demonstrate what Isabelle Knox is capable of.

I walked over to the hangers holding several sets of lingerie. The guys hadn't been lying when they told me each pair would cost a small fortune. I knew that right away. Each one was amazing, unique. One set had black diamonds, another had white diamonds, and another was embroidered with gold thread. I was sure it wasn't metallized thread from the haberdasher on the corner.

On one hanger, I found what Lyla had told me about.

"There's no way. That's not an option. Well…"

The front of the panties were cut in a "V." The tulle was embroidered with black-and-blue butterflies with gold elements. The tops of the "V" were connected by a string of small pearls, and from the center of this connection, another string ran down. With little effort, I saw that a row of beads went all the way to the back, connecting the side strings, and there was another beautiful butterfly on the connection.

The bra was made of a similar embroidered tulle fabric. Each breast in this bra was decorated with the same pearls, going from the center to the straps.

The whole thing was finished with a necklace of six rows of white pearls.

I couldn't believe what I was seeing. This set was beautiful, sexy, alluring. It covered the most intimate places. Despite that, I was going to go out and show my ass in front of all these people?

I began to retreat toward the door, as if the proximity of this lingerie set would burn me. Before I could grab the knob, the door swung open and Lyla appeared inside.

"Are you okay, Izzy?" she asked with concern when she saw the fear in my eyes. She came inside and closed the door. "What's wrong, honey?"

"I can't do it," I choked out through a clenched throat.

"What can't you do? Don't you like them?"

"No, it's not that. The lingerie is exquisite, but I can't go out in it in front of all those people."

Understanding appeared in her eyes. She came over and put her hands reassuringly on my shoulders.

"It's just nerves, Izzy, nerves because you've never done this before. Think of it like a bikini. You've probably worn one more than once."

"There's nothing bikini about this fickle little thing, and nobody stands out on the beach in a bikini," I said.

"You're right, but we have people working with us who have been in this business far more than a day. They're familiar with the many layers of modeling, even nude modeling. Your body is your working tool. You're supposed to show emotions through it that you can't express in words."

"I didn't think about it that way. All I had in mind was my bare butt with the light and the camera flash falling on it."

"It's much, much more than that. The body doesn't impress anyone in this profession, believe me. This job isn't about the perfect body. Minor imperfections can be retouched by any mediocre photographer. Capturing emotion, thought, chemistry is something not everyone can do and what we're all about."

I nodded a few times, regaining my confidence. "Thank you, Lyla."

"You're welcome. Now, jump into this treasure. Let me help you put the collar around your neck."

***

With each *click* of the camera, the nerves left my body. At a certain point, I stopped noticing other people. I was doing my thing, and they were doing theirs. When Jason finally decided that I had calmed down enough, he invited Brad onto the set.

They placed a lounge chair covered in black plush against a white background. Gold buttons decorated the back.

I sat on this lounge chair with my legs slightly apart, dressed in a fortune in lingerie. On my feet were stiletto sandals, golden straps encircling my ankles up to my calves. I felt... unbelievably sexy, beautiful, special. Only then did I understand what the whole thing was about.

"Brad, stand behind Izzy... Touch her neck... Lean in... Izzy, look over your shoulder... Brad, more affection. It's not you seducing her, it's her seducing you," Jason commented, gently giving orders. He knew exactly what he wanted to see in these photos. "Izzy, it's perfect, baby. Brad—"

It was a bit like theater. If you pull a string in one direction, the puppet goes that way. If you pull another string, it does something else.

Click, click, click...

At one point, I turned to the camera and stood as if someone had struck me. I was sure that all the blood had drained from my face. All the blood except for my cheeks.

Miles was standing nearby, explaining something to Castriel, whose eyes were on me. I could feel them on my body. They wandered over every piece of flesh to come to a final stop at my eyes.

When did he arrive? How long has he been here?

I felt a tickle in my stomach, which was just nerves. At least, that's what I had been telling myself for the last few weeks. Something else appeared inside me. A need?

Seeing my frozen expression, Jason stopped his camera and there was silence.

Without taking his eyes off me, Castriel said, "Miles, you're fired. By the end of the day, get your stuff out of the office and go straight to Human Resources."

I felt sorry for the poor guy. I had tried to warn him earlier, but he wouldn't listen. He lowered his eyes to the floor and headed for the exit.

"Show's over. Move on," Castriel growled into the room.

I rolled my eyes as I saw his subjects immediately obey the order. Meanwhile, Castriel approached Jason, folded his hands on his chest, and waited for us to continue our work.

I had to admit that he looked sexy in his black suit. The pose he had adopted accentuated his biceps. The slightly spread legs, especially the solid thighs, drew my eye. His face revealed nothing. He was like a rock that no one or nothing could move.

A wave of heat swept through my body, exposed to such an intense gaze. He was judging us. He was judging *me*.

"Brad, show me how much you desire this woman. Yes. Even more affection. Look at her like a hungry wolf. Brad... Izzy..."

Now I was lying on the ottoman with Brad's silhouette hovering over me. Impatience was in the air. I was doing my best to live up to Jason's expectations, but it still wasn't enough.

I looked at Brad and saw something was missing. I liked my partner as a man, but I didn't feel that special something that can burn your soul before a man's mouth even falls on yours. I couldn't wring out the chemistry between us.

"Enough!" Castriel yelled. "You're not in kindergarten. You're professionals, so start acting like it. What I see is pathetic."

In response to Castriel's sharp words, Brad straightened up and gave him an icy stare. "Pathetic?"

"So fucking pathetic. Show me what we're paying you so much money for, because all I see so far are shitty pictures from a low-grade erotic magazine."

"It's not pathetic at all," Brad said, but his voice was quieter now.

"We need passion, Brad. Give it to us," Jason added, causing Castriel to roll his eyes and mutter something under his breath. "Let's try again."

The atmosphere seemed to thicken to the extreme. How one man could do that with his mere presence was beyond me. But I felt it in my bones. Suddenly, I was aware of every move I made, every seductive smile, the gaze of every pair of eyes in the room.

Jason ordered me to lie on my back. Following my invention, I arched my back, one leg bent, and my hands moved of their own accord below the line of my breasts. I ran them down along my skin.

Heat spread through my body. I felt someone's eyes following the trail of my hands as they found my exposed breasts, the curve of every nook and cranny of my body. Not someone else's. I was sure they were Castriel's eyes.

Brad stood before me like a stone.

What the hell are you doing? Move, at least. Do something! Start breathing, damn it!

My screams stuck in my head, but it was too late anyway.

"Come on. He's like a dead fish," Castriel scoffed, and someone giggled in the background.

I got up and sat down. What the hell did he expect from Brad? That he would parade around with an obvious erection?

"Excuse me, what?" growled Brad, his face flushed with anger.

I could feel the battle in the air, the bloodlust, so I announced to no one in particular, pointing to the bathroom door, "I need to take a break." I got up and rushed toward the sanctuary. Thank God no one even looked at me, but as I passed Castriel, I felt the hairs on my body stand up as if by electric force.

"You heard me. You have no idea what you're doing. You don't know what to do with this woman." Castriel's deadly deep tone made my stomach turn.

"You think you know better? That you can do it better?"

What are you doing, Brad? Are you out of your mind?

"I know perfectly fucking well I can."

I didn't hear the rest of the conversation. I didn't want to hear it. It was a perfect recipe for disaster. This was supposed to be an exciting challenge, a new experience, but it wasn't.

I took my time in the bathroom. I washed my sweaty palms twice, combed my hair with my fingers, lifted my breasts. I pinched my cheeks for the effect of an extra blush, though it wasn't necessary.

When I came out of the bathroom, Brad was sitting in a chair right next to Jason. I walked over to them and saw how the others had gone about their business.

Castriel was sitting on the lounge chair. His legs were spread in that manly way. He had lost his jacket somewhere. He had rolled up the sleeves of his white shirt to his elbows. His chest rose and fell. His untied tie hung loosely under his collar, and the top button was unbuttoned. For the first time, I noticed how sexy his strong neck was. I wanted to run my tongue over it.

Wait a minute. What are you thinking, horny crazy girl?

His jaw was shaded with stubble, as if he hadn't had time to take care of it today. If I hadn't looked at him so closely, I wouldn't have noticed the small smile that appeared and disappeared a second later. And when I got to the eyes...

My God. His gaze can melt the panties off any woman within a few miles.

"What's going on?" I asked, tearing my eyes away from Castriel.

A confused Brad looked to the side without saying a word. Jason shrugged and, still looking into the camera, said, "Everyone could use a break. You can relax, play the role in your mind, whatever."

There was only one person who knew the answers to the questions that arose in my mind.

A magnetic force drew my eyes back to Castriel. From that moment on, I couldn't stop looking at him. Why in the world did he have such power over me?

"Come here," he said in a deep, hoarse voice.

CHAPTER 13

CASTRIEL

My voice seemed oddly low even to me. The woman in front of me was a witch who was changing me against my will.

I didn't need any complications in my life right now. I didn't need distractions either, but here we were.

She appeared in my thoughts more often than I cared to admit, as if she had found refuge in them. I seethed with anger toward her, craving to teach her a lesson. It didn't matter if it made sense or not.

I wanted to see my hand reflecting on the smooth skin of her ass. I wanted to see my hand squeeze her tender neck. I wanted to tie her up and make her my slave, doing my bidding until she got bored and left my thoughts alone.

"I said come here," I repeated. She had better not test my patience now, because the audience might witness a whole new kind of fun.

When she moved toward me as if hypnotized, I breathed a sigh of relief. Her every movement was graceful, seductive.

Before she stood between my open legs, I looked at her as if she were my last meal.

Isabelle's feet in those sandals were the fulfillment of wet dreams. She was all that. I wanted to run my tongue along her slender calves, kiss her thighs, and lick her pubic bone. Even her belly button was perfect. Her skin was smooth and gleaming. Higher up, her breasts curved, and I yearned to discover their weight. And that face... Shiny, puckered lips, rosy cheeks, sparkling eyes... I wanted to eat her whole.

Isabelle looked magical in our underwear. I had to clench my fists to keep myself from grabbing her and throwing her on the bed. The row of pearls between her buttocks was the highlight. Saliva filled my mouth as I thought about what I would do to her.

The sight of her and Brad drove me crazy. The guy had no idea what to do with her and in my soul, I understood the guy. A stunning phenomenon, Isabelle captivated the guy's mind and diverted his attention. I didn't like the way he looked at her. Gouging out the bastard's eyes wouldn't satisfy my thirst for blood.

When my patience was wearing thin, this person had to challenge me. Now everyone would suffer the consequences. My hard cock came first. Fuck.

Isabelle stood between my legs, her hands on her hips, and looked at me in a challenging way.

"What will you do now that I'm here?" she asked in a hushed tone that only I could hear.

A mischievous smile proved stronger and appeared on my lips. *If only you knew my intentions...*

My hands touched the back of her knees. I lifted myself slightly and looked into her face. I let her see in my eyes the effect she had on me. She sucked air into her lungs with a rush and goose bumps appeared on her skin.

"Are you ready to hear what I'm going to do to you? Or are you just playing hard to get?"

I ran my right hand down her tempting calf, and when I returned to her knee, I grabbed it, lifted it, and placed it bent over the seat. The knee was now so close to my balls and throbbing cock I could feel her heat.

"Put your hands on my shoulders," I ordered, and Isabelle's breathing sped up almost to match the flame in her eyes.

I was confident she would follow my words precisely. Her hands moved from my hips to my shoulders. She pushed me back until I slumped against the backrest. We were each playing by our own rules. Isabelle leaned against my shoulder with one hand, grabbed my loosened tie with the other, and pulled my face into hers. My hand from under her knee moved higher and found itself just below her ass.

As I tightened my hand, my fingers were inches from her pussy. We were both aware of it. A soft moan escaped Isabelle's lips and with my last ounce of strength, I stopped myself from pulling my fingers a little higher.

I looked into her eyes with a dark smile. "Isn't this an interesting turn of events?"

"Castriel... What are you doing?"

"I'm playing with fire that will soon burn us both. Heaven is for the rest of the world, but hell is reserved for us."

"Stop it."

"I wish I could."

The warmth of her breath wrapped around my lips, and when she looked at them, I almost bit hers.

God, this woman is going to be my undoing.

I hadn't been able to get our conversation out of my head since we last met. I had to test a theory born of experience.

Isabelle squealed in surprise as I grabbed her with both hands and before she knew what was happening, she was on her back. Under me. Exactly where I wanted her.

Her dilated pupils, the throbbing pulse in her neck, her rapid breathing, and her parted lips were proof that I was affecting her as much as she was affecting me.

I leaned my face against the base of her neck and traced a path with the tip of my nose up to her ear. She shivered beneath me and it satisfied me.

"What happened, baby? Cat got your tongue?"

"When Los Angeles was founded, the city was called 'El Pueblo de Nuestra Senora Reina de Los Angeles Sobre el Rio Porciuncula,' " she whispered.

The primitive element of my black soul growled with satisfaction, possessiveness, and excitement.

Mine...

I reached behind my neck with one hand and pulled my shirt over my head in one motion. I didn't have time to wonder why provoking her gave me so much satisfaction, but it was the truth.

"Mr. Russell, what are you doing?" she whispered, pushing her hand away.

"Now I'm Mr. Russell again? Is there something wrong with my given name?"

Bright eyes stared at me, not so much frightened as eager. I witnessed their struggle behind the wall and, as she succumbed, her eyes fixated on my chest. She licked her lips, and when a deep growl erupted from my throat in response to that slight gesture, she looked up into my face with all her might.

"We should be professional. I need distance between us."

"That's the last thing you want or need, Isabelle." My hand cupped her calf, slowly moving to under her knee, which I pulled up. I found a space between her thighs that barely fit my hips. But it had to be enough on the small seat.

A soft moan escaped her lips, and I was sure that if I had moved a little higher, I would have felt the wetness that marked the company's underwear.

"When Earth was created as a planet, a day on it lasted only six hours." The words that came out must have embarrassed her even more.

I leaned into her ear. "That's fascinating, but no more so than you. Share it later. You have a confession to make now."

"To what?" she gasped.

"That you want me." I could smell her overpowering aroma mingling with the scent of excitement. I had always thought it was nonsense to smell someone's arousal. With Isabelle, I realized I was mistaken. I could only describe it as the deep scent of summer coming from every part of her skin. "Before you dirty your mouth with lies, know that I have no doubts. You don't react this way to Jason, Brad, or any other man here. You just react this way to me."

"Stop it."

"Admit it, Isabelle." I trailed my nose along the curve of her neck again, and she arched her back as she moved her breasts toward me. She hid her emerald eyes behind her eyelids. "Admit it, baby..."

"Okay now, okay... It's all about you. Happy?"

"Not really. Admit that you want me and that you want me to give you what you haven't gotten from any other man."

"What? No way. Your inflated ego has trouble fitting in this room any-way."

I grabbed her hand with my left and lifted it above her head, then did the same with the other. Her moan reached my ear. She didn't even know how much that moan told me the truth.

"We'll work on your honesty. In the meantime, I suggest that we both stop fighting this attraction and work on your big O."

Her eyes opened. Big, round, and confused. "No way!"

I smiled mischievously. This woman had more fire in her than the burning forests of the Amazon. "Are you afraid?"

"I'm not afraid of anything." Defiance was painted on her face.

"Prove it."

"Do you think you can catch me in such manipulations? Provocations? I see what you're doing."

"That's okay. I have nothing to hide. And I understand you. You're just afraid of yourself, of your reaction, of your pleasure. You're afraid that someone will prove you wrong, that someone will shake up your world."

"Fuck off."

"Again, I wish I could."

"Again, I'm not afraid of anything," she hissed.

I lifted my body a little higher. I towered over her as my hips pressed against her pussy. Feeling the proof of my interest, she opened her mouth as if to say something.

I beat her to it. "I dare you. I dare you to prove me wrong. You and me. Let's race."

CHAPTER 14

Loneliness matters. It really does. If you lock someone in a dark room alone for an extended period, say weeks, they can go crazy quickly. Add to that combination restricting water and food, say every few days... God knows what will happen.

I once read a book that described methods of torturing prisoners during World War II. The secret police used this method every day; they perfected it. The physical side isn't always weaker.

"Where can I find this person?" I asked for the second time.

Tiredness and excitement danced under my skin.

"I don't know anything..."

"Bullshit. Recently, I saw a photo of the two of you on Instagram. You last saw each other a few months ago."

"I really—"

"Listen to me carefully, Maverick. I'm tired, I'm pissed, and I'm honestly horny." I pulled out a knife and held the blade to his throat. "I would appreciate your help. I don't want to leave you here alone for another few weeks."

"No... No... No..." He struggled like a wild animal in a cage.

His hands and feet were chained together with three-foot-long chains. It was impossible for him to move more than one step.

My words frightened him. He repeated the word "no" over and over, trying to break the restraining chains.

At one point, he pulled so hard on the chains that one of them rattled and broke free at the connecting mesh.

I would almost have been impressed, except that the broken chain gave Maverick a new range of motion and he collapsed on me. By the time I realized what was happening, it was too late. Blood was gushing from his throat. Maverick let out a weak shriek and then a throaty gurgle.

"Well, fuck me! You sure know how to ruin a party."

I looked down at my hand holding the knife in his throat and then back at him.

"This rebellious gesture means you're not going to tell me anything after all?"

Maverick's eyes fogged.

"Fuck."

CHAPTER 15

IZZY

When I got on my motorcycle, I knew I would win. Not because I was lucky, but because confidence would be Castriel's undoing.

When he challenged me to a fight the other day, I wanted to laugh in his face. Not only had he manipulated my body and turned its reactions against me, but he had also mocked me. Well, okay, maybe that's not exactly true, but that's how I felt.

He provoked me, aroused my ambitions, demanded that I prove how much I was worth as a biker. Maybe he just wanted to fuck me and get the tension out of his system once and for all. Maybe he played a game where he alone knew the rules.

Either way, he violated something that was sacred to me: my motorcycle and my skills as a rider. I didn't know many women who rode machines. In fact, I didn't know any. I was a lone wolf, and I liked it that way. Motorcycle clubs didn't interest me. Neither were meetings and parties from dawn to dusk. Besides, I didn't have time for that.

Many men thought that because a biker didn't have a dick between their legs, they weren't worthy of their machine. Castriel's approach wasn't sexist or demeaning to my gender, but it still irritated me.

I was good at riding my Blackbird. Very good. When he questioned that, fueling it with accusations of fear, I couldn't refuse his challenge. Annoyed, I accepted with my head held high in pride.

My pride will abandon me one day, but not before Castriel's self-confidence abandons him.

I patted my Bird as usual before I let myself feel the vibration of the engine between my legs. I loved that hum, that power hidden in a piece of metal, and how it made me feel liberated. I smiled and let myself be carried away.

Before noon, my phone rang. Castriel's deep male voice announced that we would meet an hour before sunset, and then he hung up. I felt like scratching his eyes out for his rudeness when I received another message with directions.

I had to do a series of breathing exercises several times, which was supposed to calm me down. Otherwise, I was ready to bite through his artery.

Half an hour later, after a calm ride, I found the marked spot. As I slowed down, the motorcycle purred more softly.

I parked on the side of the road right next to my rival, who, as usual, was wearing a black riding suit and black helmet. The visor of the helmet was raised. I did the same with mine.

Castriel fixed his eyes on the horizon at the sight of the setting sun. For a moment, he paid no attention to me, absent-minded in spirit.

"Cas," came out of my mouth.

Cas? Really? Since when did you and he get to the silly nickname stage?

He continued to ignore me. He didn't even seem to hear me.

"Castriel!"

The raised voice only caused his head to turn in my direction. He blinked once, a second time, and his chocolate eyes softened. He stared at me almost tenderly.

"Castriel? And what happened to Cas?" The smile I couldn't see on his face was reflected in the mirror of his eyes.

I felt a warm blush spread across my cheeks, and it was fortunate that he couldn't see it either.

"Don't get me wrong, baby. I'm glad you're looking for a way to shorten my name. It will come in handy when you find yourself below me, seeing the rain of shooting stars and screaming my name."

"You dickhead," I growled at him, rolling my eyes. "Don't rush to the prize phase before winning. Confident, huh?"

He shrugged. "What can I say? When something catches my attention and I want it, it's only a matter of time."

"I'm not your trophy. We're wasting time. Let's race."

I could see from his face that he was smiling even wider.

"Okay. Do you know this track?" He asked.

"I've driven it once or twice."

"Okay. We'll circle around and reach the same spot."

"How many times have you ridden this route?"

"Once or twice. Don't forget, I'm new to this city."

I didn't hide my suspicion, caused by his light, playful tone. He was right. He had just arrived, but something felt off to me.

"You're not going to chicken out right away, are you?" He was trying to provoke me.

If someone had measured the temperature of my gaze at this confident asshole, it would have probably exceeded that of the Arctic. My fingers clenched into a fist as he added, "I can wait a few seconds and give you the upper hand if that would help."

"The only thing that would help me right now is to teleport you to another space-time continuum. Preferably two hundred years back," I growled and started the engine.

I drove and then stopped in the left lane. I heard his thunderous laughter behind me. I liked the laugh, although I would have denied it even if they burned me at the stake. But below my belly button, something was swirling in my gut.

No. Absolutely not. Don't even think about it now.

Out of the corner of my eye, I saw Castriel standing right next to me as I closed the visor of my helmet. Right after winking, he repeated the action.

Don't let him distract you! He does it on purpose.

He stretched his left hand over the handle bar, showing three fingers, while he pressed the accelerator with his right hand. Once again, he was provoking me, trying to scare me, trying to knock me down. Literally and figuratively.

His hand showed two fingers, then one, and then I moved without waiting for his next sign. Was it cheating? Never. We hadn't agreed on anything. Let him smell my fumes.

As before, we raced at breakneck speed. Castriel quickly caught up with me and then swept past. In a moment, he slowed down a bit, and we rode side by side, only for him to pass me again in a moment.

He was playing with me, which annoyed me even more. I knew, however, that I had to keep my emotions in check, or I would only lose.

He didn't pass me because he had a better bike. Although there was that too. He won against me because he rode aggressively. He never slowed down at any curve.

I wonder how often he changes his knee sliders.

God. Focus, because you're losing!

I had a thought that maybe I didn't want to win against him. Maybe I was enjoying this cat-and-mouse game. I wondered if he was equally aggressive in bed. Like, outside of the company and outside of riding his motorcycle.

A shudder ran through my entire body, concentrating dangerously deep.

I dismissed the absurd thoughts, shaking my head and accelerating. I overtook Castriel in a second and was the first to pass the turning point on our route.

I bit my lip, regretting that I didn't have time to enjoy the beautiful sunset—orange mixed with purple across the sky.

Exiting the turn on our route, I made an error. A big mistake, one that almost cost me my life.

Eager over my new power manifested by riding as aggressively as Castriel, I was blinded by the lights of a car coming from the opposite direction.

I looked to my right, where Castriel was already staring at me. I couldn't see through his visor, but his helmet was facing me. I don't know why I thought he was afraid of the situation.

My heart threatened to escape as I glanced left. Beyond the road's metal protection was an embankment where death lurked. Death remembered me after long years.

The noise in my ears drowned out my own thoughts. I had a split second to decide correctly. My life depended on it.

Tires screeched, Castriel vanished from the right lane to make room for me.

At the last second, I avoided an encounter with God. It was only when I passed the car that I noticed the driver kept honking.

A trickle of sweat ran down my forehead, another down my neck. I couldn't feel my arms or legs; they were numb and heavy. As the adrenaline wore off, I felt my body twitch. I slowed down. I expected Castriel to use this against me right away, but he continued to follow me for a while.

I knew he wouldn't give up, regardless of the situation. He would wait for the perfect time to strike. I wasn't wrong. After a short while, he made an attack on the leader's position, so I boldly swerved in his way.

I had a déjà vu feeling because I knew this street dance from our first meeting on the highway.

At one point, the phone in my helmet receiver buzzed, but I hit the "Ignore" button. It rang a second time, then a third. By the fourth, I couldn't take it anymore and answered.

"Yes?" Although I tried not to sound like a mean bitch, I wasn't very successful.

"Hello, Izzy. This is Burk." I heard his deep voice and felt immediate tension.

"Hello, Detective. Can I call you back later? This isn't a good time."

"I need to tell you something, Izzy. It's important."

Fear crept under my skin. I believed there were no positive updates for me.

"Go ahead, Detective."

"The colleague I mentioned to you recently, who supervised your case, just returned from vacation. He called me back as soon as he got my message. He also checked in to see how things were going."

"And?"

"There was an oversight for which I don't even know how to apologize to you..." The detective's words were enough for me to know how the conversation would continue. I knew. I just knew. Like a fool, I had ignored my earlier feelings, ignored all the red flags. "That's why no one notified you."

I let my bike slow down. Castriel overtook me and raced forward. My head was somewhere else now. This was more important.

"Excuse me. Can you repeat that, Detective?"

"Izzy." He sighed. "During the holiday season, many office staff members are absent. That's why no one notified you sooner, but… He's free. He was granted parole and has been out for some time. I believe that despite the restraining order, he'll follow your trail. He'll be looking for you—"

"He can't find me."

"I know that, so my advice is that you move—"

"With all due respect, that's shitty advice. I changed my name, Detective. I changed my location, even the state. I reside in a location with a vast population. How could he track me down?" My voice went up several octaves. I didn't mean to be mean, but my anger was at its limit. The police had one damn job—to keep me safe away from him. They blew it.

"I know you're upset, but I'm trying to fix what the office screwed up. Maybe it would be better…"

I shook my head. He understood nothing. Running away wouldn't be any better. My father wanted to get me out of the place where I was. He wanted to make me feel like a rat.

"I'll think about it, Detective," I said, knowing it was a lie.

"Okay… Fine. Think about it and please call me."

"Thank you, Detective." With that, I hit the intercom button and hung up.

The monster, brought by the news, now coursed through my veins. It traveled throughout my body, poisoning everything in its path. Uncertainty, terror, powerlessness.

I knew that the day might come when I would have to face my past again. I had fed on the hope that this would never happen.

My whole life flashed before my eyes, and then crippling fear blocked my view of everything.

Run or fight?

I took a breath, but I felt it wasn't enough.

I needed to be in my house, in my apartment, in a dark corner as soon as possible. I wanted to hide and think about my next move in muted solitude.

The motorcycle whined underneath me as I added gas. I sped forward.

Castriel was standing at the starting line, the finish line, reminding me of the race. He held his removed helmet in his hand, dark hair disheveled. He stared at my approaching silhouette with a wry smile.

I lost. Oh my God! I lost the damn race!

The thought was unbearable.

The smile on Castriel's face vanished the moment he realized I wasn't slowing down at all. I sped past him. I didn't have time to chat. Talking to him would have to wait.

As if in a dream, I arrived at the building where I lived. Using the app to open the garage door, I pulled into the parking lot.

Castriel must have arrived at the last second before the gate closed, because before I even turned off the engine, he had parked his black Hayabusa right next to my green Blackbird.

I swiftly turned off the bike, dismounted, and removed my helmet. He did the same. He looked nervous and confused.

"What the hell are you doing?" I shouted at him. "You can't park here!"

"I want to know what you are doing! You don't know how to lose or what?" he demanded. His eyes shone and a nerve jerked on his clenched jaw.

"Castriel, get out of here. We'll talk about this another time."

As long as I'm still here.

"No, we'll talk now," he said.

"You have no right to demand explanations from me. This isn't a good time. Go home."

I walked past him and stood in front of the elevator. Just as I was about to press my floor button, someone's hand got in the way. I turned in a panic, thinking my father had already caught me. A muffled squeal escaped my mouth, and I reflexively took a step back.

Instead of him, a startled Castriel stood before me. His eyes scanned my face. He searched for answers to new questions that arose suddenly. Nothing escaped his attention.

I put on an indifferent expression, but it was too late.

"What... Why..." He tried to say something more, at the same time trying to piece together the puzzle of my behavior. "What happened on the way?"

"None of your business. I wish to be alone now, so you may kindly—"

"No, I may not. You're not acting like this because you lost, are you?"

Restlessly, I moved from foot to foot, unable to wait to shut the door and be by myself. His attention was the last thing I needed.

We reached my floor, and the door slid open silently. As I walked past him, I threw over my shoulder, "Go home," without waiting for his reply.

I opened the door to my apartment and when I closed it, I was met with resistance. Castriel's hand pushed it one way and then the other. A loud bang made me jump and drop my helmet on the floor.

It's the second time. It's like déjà vu again.

"Fuck! Castriel! What are you doing? You were supposed to leave me alone!"

"That's the point, don't you understand? I can't leave you alone! If possible, I would have done it a while back. And I have no idea why."

His brown eyes darkened. The muscle in his jaw continued to jump rhythmically. His breathing was deep and heavy, as if he had just run a marathon. He looked like an angry bull, ready to charge at any moment.

"Tough luck. Leave me out of this. You have a one-sided infatuation."

I measured him with an icy stare, and he responded with a smile. His head rose, and he looked at me from under half-closed eyelids. Throwing his helmet on the couch, he took a step toward me, then another and another.

In an instant, I felt insecure and backed away. His height made me feel even smaller. When my legs felt the table against the wall, I had nowhere to run from him. His towering frame awakened something in me.

Instead of fear, I felt excitement rising between my thighs. My face must have had surprise written all over it, because his smile grew even wider.

Castriel leaned over me, his palms flat on the tabletop. His head was right next to mine. He turned his face toward me; my eyelids dropped and I breathed quickly. A rush of excitement ran through my body.

Castriel's nose was right next to my ear, then it went higher and found itself between strands of my hair. As if through a haze, I heard him take in my scent.

"Hmm... green apple. You know this smell haunts me? Even in my dreams," he whispered.

I shivered again as his breath brushed across my sensitive ear. I bit my lip to keep a moan from escaping my throat.

Castriel's hand found its way to my waist and moved slowly upward. My brain fried.

"You're trying to distract me." My words sounded like something between a question and a statement. I let the air out.

"Is it working, baby?"

"Absolutely not..."

"What happened back there?"

Castriel's nose left my hair. Instead, I felt the tip of his tongue as it wandered along the spine of my neck. An involuntary moan escaped my throat, and I tilted my head to give him better access.

In a second, I completely forgot how I got here, why I came home, what was threatening me.

"Tell me, baby, and my tongue will reward you for everything."

His licking turned to kisses, and those turned to sucking and biting. My hands went to Castriel's shoulders. They wandered along the curves of every muscle. I still couldn't get enough, so I started unzipping his jacket to feel more.

"I... Oh, God..." I moaned as his thumbs cupped the sides of my breasts. "Your tongue can't be that good."

"Want to bet?"

"Yeah... no..."

"Little determined?"

"I don't want to talk about it now."

I pulled his jacket off and he took a step back. I opened my eyes to see his hot chocolate eyes. He grabbed the zipper of my jacket and pulled it down too. Much too slowly. For a chance at the big O with him, he needed to act fast.

I slipped the jacket off my shoulders as he said in a serious tone, "I'll be sorry if you don't agree, but I don't want you to do anything because you lost our race."

"What about the challenge?"

"I'm not the monster you think I am. I've never fucked a woman who didn't want me. I teased you, but I also had fun during the race. Except maybe for that one moment, but you'll get spanked for that thoughtlessness. If you want nothing to happen between us, tell me now. I won't hold it against you."

"And I won't be a coward in your eyes?"

"I've provoked you. Let me be clear. I want you. I fucking want you, but I'm not a rapist. Even if you lost, I want you to decide if you want me too. Then I'll be able to prove to you that you can get the big O in bed with a guy."

I didn't know why, but his words warmed my heart. I had a choice. I just had to admit out loud that I wanted him too.

"One time," I said after a moment. "Just once, we allow ourselves to be weak. You know I want you, but I want more to get rid of the wanting. So just one time. All or nothing."

A lazy and sinister smile appeared on his face, as if he knew something I had no idea about.

"All or nothing. If I get you to the big O, you can tell me what happened there today." He held out his hand as a sign of agreement.

I had no desire to tell him about my past, and I was sure he didn't have a magic wand between his legs.

Our hands met in the middle as I sealed the deal between us.

"Now give me your A-game and help me forget everything."

Chapter 16

IZZY

In a second, a beast entered Castriel that I had no intention of stopping. Maybe that should have been a red flag for me, but it only aroused me more.

He pulled his hand away, sealing our agreement, and let out a low growl. Before I knew it, I was standing in front of him in just my panties and T-shirt. When had all this happened? I didn't know. He must have helped me pull my pants down because I came to my senses as soon as he kneeled in front of me.

When he got up, he traced his hands down the back of my legs. I could see in his eyes the desire to torture me with his touch. Curiosity about what this man thought, knew, and could do bubbled up inside me. Who was Castriel Russell?

Before he could straighten up, Castriel's hands grabbed my butt and lifted me into the air. Instinctively, my legs wrapped around his waist. There would probably be traces of his fingers on my skin the next day, and I was happy about that. I wanted him to mark me as if I were his.

Our rapid breaths mingled. I looked at this man in confusion, and he didn't take his eyes off me. Excitement and arousal made me tremble. The tickling in my lower abdomen turned into spasms and my pussy clenched its walls. Never in my life had anyone brought me to such a state, and I hadn't even taken off my bra yet.

"Isabelle, you have no fucking idea what you're doing to me," he said in a throaty voice. "It's unreal. If I'm not careful, I'm going to lose what's left of my control."

His words did something to me. I let out a growl and with a movement of my hips, I rubbed against his hard cock. A hot sensation filled every cell in my body.

"Who said I wanted that? Maybe the lack of control is what we both want? What we both need?"

"You don't know what you're talking about. I don't want to hurt you. If I lose control, you won't be able to walk straight for a week, and my marks on your body won't leave you for much longer."

Surprised by his words, I looked for the truth in his eyes. What did it mean? Was he one of those men who liked to beat women? I had read about various extreme games like knives, fire, and humiliation in front of people. Did that turn him on?

"Stop it, Isabelle. Your thoughts are written all over your face. I'll never hurt you like that, but I'm a guy who likes to explore the limits of pain and pleasure. But not today. We'll talk about this another time."

I was about to correct him that this was just between us so there was no need for that, but something distracted me. Holding me with one hand as if I weighed nothing, he ran his other hand across the tabletop, knocking everything onto the floor.

Later, I would wonder if he had caused any damage and where I should send the bill.

He sat me down on the cool surface and I hissed. My inflamed skin didn't appreciate it at all.

Castriel took a step away from me. Staring into my eyes, he unbuttoned his pants, takes it off and tossed them aside.

During this time, my eyes couldn't stop wandering over his body. Castriel took care of himself. That much was clear. I wanted to run my tongue along his heavily sculpted arms, along every curve. The swollen veins on his body gave my pussy another spasm. This never excited me, but Castriel was different from everyone else in many ways.

My eyes traveled to his chest and then to his stomach. For the first time in my life, I saw with my own eyes that a man could have such toned abs. Muscle on muscle. My fingers tingled, wanting to touch each one.

My gaze dropped a little. Not that I didn't notice his well-built thighs, but I focused on his erection tucked into his black briefs. I opened my mouth and licked my lips.

Castriel's excitement was obvious. His hard cock formed a tent that was impossible to miss, even with poor eyesight. I remembered what I had thought about the magic wand moments before and was ready to eat my own words.

"Your eyesight and your tongue will get you into trouble one day," Castriel growled.

Castriel's hands found their way to my lap, and he spread my thighs apart to make room for himself. I felt the heat of his skin as he stood between them. Then the remains of my brain melted like ice in the sun, the last logical thought leaving my head.

I felt his fingers melt into my hair, wrap around one hand, and pull. So hard that my head snapped back, and I felt my scalp burn. My knees tightened against his thighs.

"You have no idea—"

Whatever Castriel was about to say, he interrupted his own words and threw himself against my lips. He didn't kiss me, he didn't press himself against them, he literally threw himself at them. That was the best way to describe it. An animalistic growl came from inside him as we devoured each other. I didn't have time to think about his taste. All that mattered was satisfying the need.

His tongue explored me greedily, and mine did exactly the same thing in his mouth. God, it was pure fire. When he bit my lip and then stroked it with his tongue, my hips moved, seeking even the slightest friction.

I wanted more. I needed more. Suddenly, I had too many clothes on, too little feeling of his skin against mine. I no longer knew who was moaning or who was growling. Everything blended together.

With my fingers, I explored his body, his chest, his abs. Castriel's skin was smooth and hot. He smelled of leather, something woody and marine at the same time. Whatever it was, that scent should be forbidden.

Finally, his lips moved lower and tasted my neck. His hand released my hair and roamed my body. The first touch of my breasts made me arch my back as if I wanted him to knead them harder. I may not have been aware of it, but he knew exactly what my body needed.

I still didn't have enough.

"Can you take off my shirt?" I urged him and in response, I heard soft laughter until his body shook.

Was he just laughing?

He was always so serious, focused, a little scary. He even treated words as an unnecessary invention until I asked him to use them. And now he was laughing...

"Impatient enough? Baby, we're going to have so much fun together..."

He pulled my T-shirt over my head with a deft motion and I immediately took a deep breath. His amused eyes found mine, only to darken in an instant as he looked at my breasts.

"Perfect," he whispered. "They're so fucking perfect. Never in my life... I've never seen a more beautiful creature. Every time I see you, it takes my breath away—"

"Castriel—"

"God made a mockery of my plans when he sent you to me."

I pressed him closer to me with my legs. I leaned forward and ran my tongue along his chest, then began to kiss and bite it.

I didn't know where that came from, because I had never been one to bite my partner in bed. Apparently, he was the one who had that effect on me.

Castriel unhooked my bra and, a moment later, pulled down my panties as well. His fingers squeezed and twisted my nipples to the limit until I squirmed in place like a trapped animal. And as his lips encircled one of my nipples, a loud moan filled the room.

"If you only knew what I want to do to you, how deeply I want to mark you as mine, you would run screaming."

His words should have been another red flag. They should have been, but they weren't. They aroused me even more, and I was ready to beg him to do just that.

Biting one nipple, then the other, he made me rub against him shamelessly.

"Castriel, a few more minutes in this agony and I'll come before you even touch my pussy. Will you do something about it?"

He raised his head and smiled mischievously.

Two can play this game. I smiled just as mischievously and touched his cock through his briefs. He immediately became serious and closed his eyes for a second.

He hissed through his teeth as I put my hand inside his briefs and squeezed. The skin of his cock was silky and pre-cum had collected at the tip. I moved my hand once, twice, three times. I massaged the tip with my thumb, pulled my hand out of his briefs, and put the same thumb in my mouth.

Castriel's eyes opened, and he watched me suck my thumb.

"Oh, baby, now you're in trouble."

A chill ran through my body. Before I even took my thumb out of my mouth, Castriel dropped to his knees in front of me and sucked on my clit. He didn't start with licking like most guys do. He went straight for it.

I screamed in surprise and disbelief. I threw my head back and hit the wall with a thud, when he was sucking hard and rhythmically. Non-stop. He didn't use his tongue, he just kept sucking. I was so intensely aroused that I knew I wouldn't last ten minutes.

I was wrong. I didn't even last five minutes. When he slid two fingers into my pussy without the slightest resistance and flexed them, I was lost. The orgasm was powerful. If I had been standing, I would have fallen like a tree in a hurricane. A wave of heat went through me from my legs to my head as I screamed with ecstasy. And Castriel sucked and sucked and massaged that one spot in my pussy.

When the last trace of orgasm left my body, Castriel's tongue emerged and licked me lazily. I looked at him as if enchanted. What he was doing to me gave him pleasure as well.

At one point, he opened his eyes and, without interrupting his feast, looked into mine. He was in a trance. Did he see me at all? Was he feasting like a starving prisoner?

Suddenly, he got up from his knees and pulled his fingers out of me. He kissed me greedily again. I loved his impatience. No man had ever behaved like that with me.

God, he will be my undoing...

In the background, I heard the tearing of a foil condom wrapper. I didn't know where it came from in his hands, but I didn't care. An urge bubbled up inside me again, the power of which was already equal to the previous one.

"Are you ready, baby?" he asked, breaking the kiss, and I longed for his lips. This was insane. "Look at me. Look into my eyes as I thrust into you."

So I did. I looked into his chocolate eyes, now almost black. I didn't have time to wonder if it was too intimate, too intense. I did what he wanted me to do.

My obedience pleased him and a second later, he entered me all the way. He looked at me and I didn't know what he was looking for. The only thing I was sure of was that he filled me completely.

I'd had several lovers in my life, but none of them had ever been the size of Castriel. He was the perfect size for me.

I could feel his heat and his pulsation even through the condom.

And then Castriel woke up and entered me again and again. Not fast, but hard and deep. I grabbed his shoulders for extra balance, because I was almost sure that the table underneath me wouldn't withstand the ride.

He played with my nipples with his hands. For the first time in my life, I forgot I was ashamed of anything and put my hands on his. Our hands worked together, massaging my breasts, kneading, pinching.

Castriel fucked me harder, faster. I could feel the orgasm growing inside me as I approached my climax. He slid one of his hands down and found my clit without direction, rubbed from side to side, applying pressure.

Impossible...

"Isabelle..."

And...

No, no, no... Please don't...

Suddenly, the peak I had been approaching with such speed receded. The walls closed in around me.

I had never been so close to overcoming this barrier and yet I was still defeated.

I felt my excitement drop dramatically. I felt shame. I felt broken.

What the hell is wrong with me?

Normally, at a time like this, I would decide to get out of the situation with my face and fake an orgasm. I faked it. I was faking it. Every single time.

I was partly responsible because I never came. When I didn't fake it, men were disappointed. Whether in themselves or in me, I didn't know. If I faked it and they didn't know it, I killed my chances of getting to the top. There was no winning in that situation.

I thought it would be different with Castriel, but I was wrong. The sight of an orgasm was slipping away.

But I couldn't force myself to pretend in front of him.

He was still moving hard and fast inside me, and I knew he was close. I felt pleasure, very much pleasure, but it was already too late for an orgasm.

I opened my eyes. What he saw in them made him open his mouth. Maybe he saw sadness in them, or maybe surrender. Maybe it was high time I came to terms with my defect.

"Come for me, baby," I said with a forced smile.

He leaned over me, kissed me, thrust into me a few more times, mouthed "fuck," and went quiet. I could feel his cock pulsing as he came, wave after wave. It made me proud.

I rubbed his sweaty temple with my hand. His breathing was deep and hard.

Before he even came out of me, he said, "Let's talk about this."

"Not now," I said with a shake of my head. "Let's not spoil this moment."

"You promised to tell me the truth when you orgasmed," he reminded me with a wry smile.

"But I didn't reach my orgasm."

"Yes, you did. You came. Not on my dick, but on my mouth. I promised, and I delivered."

So this is how we play now?

"Yes, so... I promised to answer the question, but I didn't say when I would answer it. I promised and I will deliver."

Castriel's laughter was deep and loud enough to be heard all over my floor.

***

That night, for the first time in a long time, I slept like a baby. I had no dreams. I didn't let my emotions run all over the house. I stopped thinking.

Not long after I kicked Castriel out of my apartment, I took a shower and fell face down on my pillow.

What was I supposed to do that night? What did he expect? That after great sex I would just spit out my guts? He should have known better, for he himself was a fortress of secrets.

I didn't need to be psychoanalyzed five minutes after sex.

I didn't need a cuddle.

I didn't need company.

So I kicked him out of my apartment before he even had time to open his sinful mouth to shower me with an avalanche of questions. Before he even had time to return to his usual self, or I never would have gotten rid of him.

The next morning, having rested like a baby, I jumped out of bed. I stretched and started my day.

The detective's call was a priority. If my father had been out for a while, he might be close by now. He might even know where to find me.

It was either run from him or face the situation. Where would I run to? For how long? I would spend the rest of my days afraid of shadows and looking over my shoulder. Was that what I wanted? Of course not, but the threat was real. Would I be able to defend myself against him? Probably not in a contact fight, but I always had a weapon with me.

This had to end sometime. I couldn't live in fear this anymore, no matter what the outcome.

This thought unlocked the peace in me. I smiled over my cup of morning coffee. It was a bit like coming to terms with death. Mine or his?

We'll see.

Not much later, I called the detective with the information that I had decided to fight for my future.

Burk wasn't happy with this decision and tried to convince me to move away, at least temporarily. For my sake. When I remained unmoved, he sighed heavily and promised to work something out with the New York Police Department.

We both knew these were empty promises, but neither of us admitted it.

With this determination to survive, I prepared for the photo shoot. I hoped the second session with Brad would be more successful.

I hadn't seen him since that photo shoot. I hadn't met him in the hallway. He hadn't knocked on my door. It was as if he had disappeared.

Or he was avoiding me. Well, if he wanted to act like a child, it was none of my business.

With renewed determination, I went to work. Just like the last time, everything went smoothly. Lyla helped me just like last time. She was wonderful at her job and we developed a bond of friendship.

I felt much more relaxed than the last time.

Miles had been fired, and no one had taken his place yet. Jason took care of his equipment, which he didn't want to part with for a second. Some other employees bustled about or whispered in corners. None of them dared to look me in the eye, which I found strange. The hustle and bustle of the previous photo shoot had turned into a graveyard silence.

Strange.

The lingerie I wore for the first time was more expensive than all my possessions. Well, okay, maybe that wasn't an accurate comparison because I didn't have many possessions. Anyway, I put on a pink bra. From the bottom of the cups to the top were four strips of diamonds that came together to form a strap. Four strips of fucking diamonds. Real diamonds.

I think I had a minor heart attack when I saw that. I trembled at the mere idea of touching it, let alone attempting to wear it.

The panties were a true masterpiece. The pink material covered the most intimate places. From there, rows of diamonds went to the next material, which was a garter belt. That's actually saying too much, because the belt consisted of four triangles. Successive rows of luminescence connected each of them. The right side was connected to the left side by three rows that went down the middle of my stomach. On the side, the straps went down to the stockings.

The previous lingerie had made me feel special. However, that impression paled compared to the current one.

I had often heard that Papilio's job was to make a woman feel special, majestic, magical. The power of the lingerie was divine. I felt attractive, energetic, and on top of the world.

I was ready. I put on the satin robe and went to see Jason. As I passed some women on the team, I smiled at them and they measured me with their eyes, smiled, and went back to whispering.

What the hell is going on?

"Hi again, Jason. How are you?" I greeted the photographer, standing next to him.

He raised his eyes from the camera and beamed at me. "Hi. Pretty good. And you?"

"Fine, thanks. Have you seen Brad?"

His eyes widened at my question as if he had seen an alien. "You don't know?"

"What don't I know, Jason?"

There was a minute of silence. The hairs on the back of my neck stood up. I knew we weren't alone.

How was it possible that I felt him before I even saw him? It was beyond me.

I turned on my heel and faced Castriel. He was close, too close. There was a small step between us.

The first thing I noticed were his smiling eyes, as if he was happy to see me. Or as if he had caught his prey in a trap. Satisfied with himself, he stood with his arms crossed, dressed as usual in a black suit and white shirt.

"Brad won't be your photo partner anymore," he replied, and his deep voice made my stomach tingle.

Not now, you slut! I'm trying to work here.

"Oh... I didn't know. What happened?"

"Apparently there wasn't the right chemistry between you two," Jason offered.

Castriel just shrugged.

I took a step back to get some distance between us. At least now I could see both men in front of me.

"So, who's my new partner now?"

"I am." Castriel's velvety voice was deadly not only to my body but also to my brain cells.

"Ha... What?"

"I'm your new partner."

"You can't... You're a CEO, not a model." He shrugged again, as if to say "so what?" Panic grew inside me. "Don't you have anything better to do?"

"I have a lot of things I would and should do right now. It is what it is."

Castriel had mentioned nothing about changes before. In fact, he didn't need to inform me. Had he planned it?

The panic in me grew; Castriel was dangerous to me for many reasons. I couldn't get rid of him, not even for a moment. He was in my work, he was in my home, in my thoughts, and he even haunted my sacred motorcycle rides.

"We can't work together," I growled, trying to swallow the lump in my throat.

"Can't we?"

"Come on, I'll show you something." said Jason, trying to smooth things over.

I followed him to a long desk against the wall. Before I did, I gave Castriel a stern look over my shoulder, but the asshole just smiled innocently. Another flip of my stomach...

On the table were several piles of photos in an enlarged format. Jason turned some of them over. Some showed me with Brad, others with Castriel. They were all from the earlier photo shoot. The ones with Brad were kind of bland, no expression, no message. But when I looked at the ones with Castriel, I froze.

Heat filled my cheeks and moved down. A chill ran through me and my breathing quickened.

I reached out my hand to touch one photo but pulled it back as if it would burn me. These photos radiated sex. They were bursting with energy, hot air saturated with desire. The lust was almost tangible.

"Now do you understand?" Jason asked.

"I don't remember you taking pictures back then. It was supposed to be a practice run."

"I convinced Jason that it was in your best interest," Castriel said. He was standing behind my back again. "In your mind was every person in the crew, every movement, every click of his camera. It blocked you out. I made it all disappear."

He was right.

"But you're not a model," I said weakly.

"We've concluded that there is no objection to Castriel accompanying you. It's not a conflict of interest. He has the looks of a model, that's for sure. And then there's the chemistry between you, the attraction..."

Jason's explanation made sense, but I had some doubts about the counter-orders. I could almost immediately come up with some arguments to the contrary. It wasn't a good idea. It wasn't a safe idea either.

There was a chance that I would forget myself and lose control. There was a chance that I would come in front of the entire team.

"What if I don't want him as a partner?"

"Tough luck, baby. We're doing it," Castriel murmured in my ear.

Just as I suspected, this session was a complete flop. By the time we finished, I was a bloody ball of nerves, all hot and bothered. Desire was seeping through my panties and dripping down my thighs. I couldn't control my breathing or my racing heart. I was trembling.

I was like clay in Castriel's hands. He did whatever he wanted with me. We assumed the poses he saw in his imagination. He touched me where he wanted.

The worst thing was that I didn't want him to stop.

Chapter 17

CASTRIEL

"Fuck off," I snapped into the phone, already losing my temper.

"Don't be like that, son. You know that your hostile attitude toward the world doesn't impress me in the least." Takashi's joking tone contained a seed of truth. I was hostile toward the world.

"Stop listening to damn rumors and get on with your life," I said.

"Are you telling me there are, or could be, rumors?"

I bit my cheek.

Asshole.

"All right, all right. I won't mock you, though I admit I like this turn of events. Who is she?"

"Who is who?" I dropped the question and played dumb.

"The woman who brought you to your knees, of course."

I closed my laptop harder than I had planned, because I was sure I wouldn't get anything done today anyway. I looked out the window of my office. Night had fallen over the entire city, and yet everything was lit up. That was New York. It was always alive, at any time of the day or night.

My thoughts returned to the woman who had supposedly brought me to my knees.

Takashi wasn't wrong. Isabelle was like my personal drug. I was already hooked on her—on her as a person, on her taste, on her smell. I noticed I started looking for ways to be in the same room with her, looking for ways to be close to her.

I didn't understand this at first. I was always the person who turned on my heel after sex. My pleasure was the priority. It was the women who were an addition to my person.

Until one day I realized that even if Isabelle didn't want to be, she was deep under my skin. She was the one who kicked me out of her apartment after sex, even though I didn't want to leave. It was her pleasure that was now my priority and mine had faded into the background. I was the addition of the most beautiful woman I had ever met in my entire life.

Of course, she brought me to my knees. I had no objection. A king may kneel before his queen. But only to his queen.

"Who told you such nonsense, Takashi? Have you ever seen me on my knees?"

"Not yet... But every man eventually meets such a woman in his life." Was he speaking from personal experience? Perhaps.

"And let me tell you something, son. When you're ready, grab her with all your strength and never let her out of your arms."

Once again, my thoughts flew to the red-haired beauty. The photo session with her had been both a nightmare and the most beautiful dream.

She understood the difference between Brad and me. She didn't question them not clicking, and it was completely clear in the photos.

When she turned her back on Jason and me, I nodded at him. He knew what to do beforehand. He was to have the camera ready and muted. My

Isabelle let herself be carried away by my touch, my closeness, as long as she wasn't aware of her surroundings.

I threw off my jacket and caught up with her in two steps. I grabbed her shoulders and turned her toward me, clutching the waistband of her robe. Her eyes found mine, pupils dilated.

I know how you feel, baby.

Releasing the knot in her belt, I ran my flat hands up her body. I didn't miss her swollen breasts and erect nipples, nor the skin where goose bumps appeared. I grabbed the robe and slid it from her shoulders to the floor.

Then I began a dance for which only we knew the steps. I took a step forward as she stepped back. Then a second and a third. We were standing in front of the green backdrop. She tried to walk away from me but as she turned, my hand landed on the silky skin of her belly, holding her in place.

I heard a soft moan and knew I was on the right track. I grabbed her wrist with my left hand and lifted it up, placing her hand on the back of my neck. Oh God, how I needed to feel her hands on my body...

My fingertips rolled gently down her forearm, shoulder, groin, and the entire side of her torso. Her head fell back and rested on my chest.

It only got worse after that. Or better. I tortured us both with closeness, with touch. Several times, I kissed her collarbone, her neck.

"Isabelle," I whispered as memories flooded my mind, of pushing her body against the wall, sliding the diamond strap of her bra, of me on my knees with her foot on my chest.

The atmosphere was so thick that the entire crew was looking at us, stunned and probably excited. Everyone must have felt electricity coming of us.

As our fun ended and Jason announced that he had all the shots he need-ed for the day, Isabelle snapped awake. She looked at everyone gathered around her and her cheeks turned scarlet. She lowered her eyes and walked off the set to the dressing room without a word.

Even though I had the fucking urge to go after her and finish what we started, I couldn't fuck her in front of so many witnesses. I had to let her go.

"Excuse me?" Takashi asked, bringing me back to reality.

I shook my head. "Her name is Isabelle."

"I know, Castriel. Thank you for telling me her name. I spoke to your assistant earlier. She was being cryptic, yet I somehow forced some information out of her." There was a smile and happiness in his voice.

"Please remind me to fire my assistant first thing Monday morning for gossiping," I growled at him.

"You will do no such thing. Meghan didn't want to tell me anything, but as I said, I forced it out of her. She told me she had instructed HR to send out an email to everyone in the building. The email was to state that, under internal policy, the company disapproves of any behavior that has the hallmarks of or leads to gossip. This includes, but is not limited to, talking offensively about absent employees, expressing negative opinions, creating a negative image, etc."

My eyes widened in surprise. "Meghan did all this without consulting me?"

"She wanted to protect your image and Isabelle's as well. People can be cruel. I, for one, am grateful to her for taking such steps before people started spreading rumors about you forever."

Maybe Takashi was right. Maybe I was exaggerating and should praise Meghan's caution instead of blaming her. Knowing myself, I would make her aware of both sides of the issue.

"We have a billboard ready," I said, changing the subject. "In a little while, there will be a TV commercial as well. We're starting a war for our piece of land."

"Good, good. I'm thrilled and proud of you."

His fatherly attitude was nothing new, but most of the time, I found it embarrassing.

"Yeah, yeah... We'll be in touch."

I heard Takashi laugh and hung up without saying goodbye.

***

Before I left the office, I thought about calling Emma and asking her about Isabelle. But I dismissed the idea. What on earth would I tell her? That my infatuation with her friend was turning into an insatiable obsession?

All I wanted to know was what I could learn from her alone. My inquisitive nature would tell me everything I needed and wanted to know in time.

I also doubted that Emma would help me find a workaround for Isabelle's defense system. So, she was useless to me for the moment.

My thoughts continued to revolve around my girl, and I knew once again that I wouldn't be able to do any more work today. I sighed as I gathered myself to leave.

As I exited the elevator through my reverie, I didn't even notice a woman before I bumped into her. She wobbled on her high heels and probably would have fallen backward if I hadn't grabbed her arm.

I didn't know her, that was for sure. Her straight black hair flowed down to her shoulders, and she was very tanned. Gray eyes were surrounded by black false eyelashes. Enlarged lips, enlarged breasts, and who knows what else.

Despite all that, I had to admit that she was a beautiful woman. Truly beautiful. But that wasn't what struck me the most.

I noticed that my dick didn't even rise an inch. It rested calmly between my legs. This was nothing abnormal. I wasn't a pervert who got hard at the sight of a woman. But it always reacted at least with interest at the sight of such a beauty.

A few months ago, I would have struck up a conversation with her. I would have immediately expressed my intentions and within the next hour, I would have fucked her.

Just a few months ago... Now I looked at this woman, let go of her arm, and felt absolutely nothing. I didn't want her. I didn't want any woman other than Isabelle. This thought hit me like a tsunami.

"Thank you for your help," the woman's voice interrupted my thoughts. She smiled broadly, and I saw the proverbial heart in her eyes.

"You're welcome. I'm sorry."

"Don't apologize. I'm not sorry at all that you ran into me."

I also realized that the few words I had said were too much. I didn't feel like talking to many, many people. It was Isabelle who gave me the pleasure of communicating with her. But for the others, nothing changed. I still preferred to be silent.

I'm cursed.

Without saying a word, I walked around the woman and headed for the exit. Rude? Probably. Did I care? Absolutely not.

I got on my bike, intending to go home. As I rode through the streets of the city, I couldn't get the image of Isabelle's face out of my head as she came screaming. Again and again, her face.

Before I knew what was happening, I was standing at the door of her apartment, knocking frantically. I knocked and knocked as if my life depended on it.

It was late, but not so late that she would be asleep. Maybe she wasn't home? The thought that she might have met someone, might have a date right now, caused a wave of heat that melted my insides. Everything inside me trembled.

What the hell is happening right now?

Finally, I heard a small question from the other side of the door. "Who's there?"

"Isabelle…" I gasped out her name. I gripped the door frame with my hands until I heard the lock being turned.

The door swung open slightly and dim light streamed into the hallway. In front of me stood the woman who had possessed me, though she didn't know it yet. I rolled my eyes at her silhouette. She was wearing a T-shirt that came down to her mid-thighs. Just that piece of fucking white material. Nothing else.

"Holy shit," I whispered.

"Castriel? What happened?"

"You. You happened."

I lowered my hands, took a step toward her apartment, and grabbed her ass. Her arms caught my neck and her creamy legs instinctively wrapped around my waist. They should have been there the whole time anyway.

Isabelle's green eyes widened in surprise as she felt how hard I was.

Apparently only for you, baby.

With a kick, I closed the door behind us. Pulling my hand away from her for a moment, I turned the lock. Whatever was going on with my Isabelle, she needed a sense of security. I could feel it.

She froze in my arms and stared at me. She opened her mouth slightly and licked her dry lips as if she felt the same hunger I did. Whatever she saw in my face, she breathed faster and a blush filled her cheeks.

I leaned my face in and fell into her kissable lips. I was hungry. So fucking hungry for her.

I moved deeper into the apartment without breaking our kiss. The last time, we hadn't even reached the bedroom, but it wasn't complicated. One door was open and out of the corner of my eye, I saw the shower. The other door was closed, and that's where I went.

We plopped down on the bed and only then did I stop kissing her for a moment. It quickly became clear that this was one of the few things in the world that I liked. And most of them were related to the woman lying beneath me.

I looked at her and pushed a strand of hair away from her face.

"Castriel... It was only supposed to be once," she gushed.

"Not enough."

As if those two words explained everything, I bent my head down to her neck. I started licking and biting it. It was the first time I noticed how much she enjoyed having my teeth mark her skin.

She tilted her head to give me more access. My hand found the hem of her T-shirt and slid underneath.

Her breast became swollen, heavy, and hot. The hard nipple begged for my attention. When I ran my rough hand over its surface for the first time, Isabelle gasped and hissed. I massaged her with my full palm, squeezing, showing her the limits of pain and pleasure.

I didn't know if Isabelle was aware of it, but she enjoyed the balance of pain. I only wondered how far her limits went.

This woman is perfect for me.

I pulled away from her and got off the bed. I had to get rid of all the barriers that separated us, so the clothes had to go.

In a flash, I was naked in front of her. She stared at me like a hawk. I loved the way she looked at me. Her attention was always one hundred percent on me. Isabelle's look made you feel as if you were the only person in the room, despite the crowd.

I pulled some condoms out of my pants and threw them on the bed. Then I took my cock in my hand and squeezed it. I felt a rush of pleasure and moved my hand up and down a few times.

Pre-cum was already everywhere, including my hand.

I was about to pounce on her again when she surprised me.

She raised herself to a sitting position first. When she pulled her T-shirt over her head in one motion, she was only wearing her white cotton panties. Somehow, by some fucking miracle, this plain piece of cotton aroused me more than the entire Papilio collection put together. I couldn't wait to put my lips on it.

When she got up from the bed and sank to her knees on the soft carpet, I was lost. She placed her hands on my knees and pulled them up to my stomach. There her fingers flexed, and she deliberately dragged her nails across my skin, moving down.

I licked my lips as I smiled.

"Feed me with it."

Feed me with it.

Feed me with it.

Those words would haunt me for the rest of my life.

I grabbed the back of her head with my left hand and pushed her closer.

"Open your mouth, baby. Nice and wide," I croaked.

Her mouth opened, and I slid my cock halfway into her velvety heaven. A soft sound escaped my throat.

When I looked into her eyes, I saw the truth. My girl didn't want it nice and slow. She wanted me to possess her.

I slid out a little, then pushed in a little deeper. She let out a murmur that went straight to my balls.

Holding her head, I began to fuck her mouth, going a little deeper. Tears appeared in her eyes and began to run down her cheeks. Still, she let out another murmur of satisfaction, as if she was finally relieved.

I wiped the tears from her face with my fingers. She wasn't wearing an ounce of makeup, so only an invisible trace remained. But I knew they were there.

"You're taking it so well." I stroked her face in a gesture of praise. "Too bad you can't see yourself now. You look like a masterpiece. You're so beautiful."

My girl liked the praise. One of her hands massaged her breast as the other found its way between her thighs. I saw her massage her clit in a circular motion.

Her throat tightened, her nostrils flaring with each breath. Another wave of tears ran down her chin.

I could feel my orgasm beginning to build, the current running from my balls to my brain. I knew all I needed was a few more deep thrusts and I would come. But it wasn't my time yet.

I pulled my hips back and left her mouth completely. Grabbing her under her arms, I lifted her up and threw her on the bed. Startled, Isabelle made a screeching sound.

Before she could take another breath, I was on top of her and my tongue entered her mouth. She tasted of the sweetest sin. She tasted like my girl. She tasted like home.

Her hips immediately rubbed against me in search of relief. I could feel the wetness of her excitement. Goose bumps covered her skin.

I broke the kiss and kneeled between her thighs. Looking straight into her eyes, I put on a condom and tossed the wrapper somewhere on the floor. All that mattered was the here and now.

I kissed her breasts. Her nipples were the trigger. Isabelle bent her body toward me and asked for more. She wanted more. She needed more.

"So good," she hissed into the room.

I grabbed one of her knees, threw my leg over her shoulder, and entered her without warning.

The more I thought about it, the more certain I was of what it would take for Isabelle to finally find her way to orgasm during sex. I had an excuse on the tip of my tongue, because today she wouldn't experience that satisfaction. At least not with penetration. I simply had to test my theory.

Isabelle immediately moaned, arching under me. Automatically, she moved her hips to meet my every thrust. My pubic hair continued to tease her clit, stimulating her even more.

Her head turned left and right. With her eyes closed, she fought her weakness, her sense of being broken by her inability to have an orgasm.

"Look at me, Isabelle," I ordered. When she did, I asked, "What do you need, baby? Tell me and I'll give it to you."

"It's wonderful. Don't stop, Castriel. Fuck me harder!"

I almost told her that fucking harder wouldn't do any good, but I did exactly what she asked. I rammed my cock into her like a wild animal, hard and deep. I was so focused on her that my growing pleasure frightened me with its presence. The tingle in my balls grew, and I drew closer.

I grabbed Isabelle's neck and squeezed. Not too hard, as I only wanted to test her reaction to my control.

At first, her eyes widened and after a few seconds, they became misty. She closed them and turned her head to the side as if to hide from me.

Still, her moans grew louder. I wished I had the third hand I so desperately needed at that moment.

At one point, Isabelle went stiff all over. This could mean that she was about to come in a few minutes or that she had just reached the point where she would turn around quickly on her way to the edge. She sighed and clenched her teeth as hard as she could.

Isabelle was losing the rush of orgasm. I was sure that in a moment guilt would overwhelm her, anger at herself, failure.

I had little time to save the situation, so I let go of her neck, pulled out of her, and pealed the condom off my cock. I grabbed it firmly in my hand and squeezed her clit with the thumb of my other hand. I massaged her again and again without changing the rhythm or direction.

After a few minutes, her breathing became labored and her moans more intense. She was almost at her limit.

I squeezed my cock and fucked my hand hard. The sight of Isabelle on the verge drove me crazy. I squirted right onto her pubic mound, onto her clit, while my other hand massaged my cum into that swollen button. The sight was simply insane.

As I looked at her, she was also staring at what I was doing to her body. Our eyes met, and she threw her head back and came with the most beautiful scream I had ever heard.

***

There was something special about that night. After the fantastic sex, Isabelle wanted to kick me out of her apartment like before, but I turned her around, put my arms around her, and told her to get some rest. Not much later, her breathing calmed down. She fell asleep with her head on my shoulder, and for the first time in my life, I spent the night cuddling with a woman. I was happy, like a fucking teenager, that it was with her I had experienced this for the first time.

I woke up before six in the morning. Not wanting to wake her, I reluctantly crawled out of bed. I left a brief note on the kitchen counter telling her I had to go to work, that the night had been wonderful, and that I hoped to hear from her as soon as she got up.

I had softened, and she had me wrapped around her little finger. I was proud of that.

But Isabelle didn't call for the next few hours. I was losing my patience when I saw her name on the phone's display.

I smiled to myself.

"Hi—"

"What have you done, Castriel?" She interrupted me.

CHAPTER 18

IZZY

I couldn't believe it was actually happening. Life is like a roller coaster. When you're at the top, there is no way you can go any higher. You have to go down. Sometimes you just hope you don't hit the ground and go *splat*.

That night with Castriel was the best night of my life. Not only because of the sex. Afterward, he refused to be kicked out of my apartment and out of my bed. He just flat out refused. He made himself comfortable, hugged me, cuddled me. That's how much I remember before sleep overcame me.

I woke up in a great mood, even overlooking the fact that Castriel was no longer with me. The feeling of security he had given me during the night was still with me.

I wanted to call him, but at the same moment, the phone lit up with Em's name.

"Hello, my dear pregnant friend. How are you?"

There was such a high-pitched squeal I had to move the phone away from my ear.

What the fuck?

A half minute later, there was finally silence. I put the phone back to my ear and giggled, "Holy Jesus, what has gotten into you? What happened?"

"My best friend is a supermodel! We should celebrate today. I can't get drunk with you, but I can join you in this shameful state. Isn't it wonderful? Are you excited?"

"Slow down, Em. I thought I was your best friend, but since you relegated me to second, at least introduce me to this supermodel."

"It's you I'm talking about, silly," Em said between giggles. "So, what are we doing tonight? Hit the most extravagant clubs? There might be a problem with Mason, because he'd rather nail the door shut than let me go to a club. Maybe I can convince him to come with us..."

"What? God, Em, stop it. Hormones make you crazy at the highest level. Take three deep breaths." A smile appeared on my face as I heard her obey my command.

"Now what?"

"Now tell me from the beginning. What do I have to be so excited about?"

"Well, the supermodel job, of course."

"Hardly. It's just a job like any other. What in the world are we supposed to celebrate?"

"What do you mean what? You're going to be a runway superstar! You're so beautiful and sexy in those pictures, it makes me ache all over."

"Em, what pictures are you talking about? Where have you seen my pictures?"

"Me and half the continent. Okay, I exaggerated a bit about the continent. I guess. Or maybe not? I don't know because my best friend hasn't told me anything lately."

"Focus, Emma," I growled, feeling remorse at the same time. "Sorry. It's the stress. Where did you see my picture?"

"I heard from a few people about different places in the city, but in person I saw you in Times Square. Times Square, Izzy! Do you know how much half a minute of advertising costs there? Over two million bucks. Do you understand, Izzy? Oh my God, New York is going to go crazy for you. I saw you in the picture and I felt myself getting wet. My water didn't break, nothing like that. I'm not into women either, but that photo was, like, super hot. Full of lust and sex. I was jealous, I admit..."

It was a good thing I was standing by the couch, because when my legs gave way under me, at least I landed softly. Shivers ran down my spine and my stomach tightened painfully.

A billboard in Times Square?

Em talked and talked until she finally fell silent, followed by another deafening screech.

"Em! What's going on?"

"Oh God, oh God, oh God! You didn't tell me about the commercial on national TV. God, how you and Castriel look together!"

Then my world stopped forever.

A commercial on national television...

"Fuck me. I'm fucked."

"Fuck me too!" she shouted.

"I'll call you back because someone's knocking on the door, okay? Bye!"

I felt sick at my fake sweet tone.

This wasn't really happening. This couldn't be happening!

I unlocked my phone and dialed a contact.

"Hi—"

"What have you done, Castriel?" I cut him off.

"Morning to you too, baby. It's almost noon, but still..."

"I'll be at your office in half an hour. We need to talk."

Without waiting for an answer, I hung up. I had to fix this whole mess before my life got any more complicated.

***

"Come in." I heard the answer as I knocked on the door of Castriel's office. His smiling assistant had announced me earlier, but culture demanded it anyway.

I hurried in, slammed the door behind me, and took a vague look around. The style of his office was modern; simple, yet elegant and masculine. Castriel was just coming out from behind his desk, dressed in black as usual.

For a moment, I forgot why I was angry with him. There was a spark in his eyes that went right between my thighs. I clenched them and a smile appeared on his face. He knew exactly how he was affecting me.

"Castriel, I won't beat around the bush because this is a serious matter. You need to take down Times Square billboard and TV commercial," I said, immediately attacking him.

He stopped halfway across the office. Looking at me closely, he noticed my hands clenched into fists. Then he tilted his head back.

"Come here, Isabelle," he said in a serious tone.

"This isn't funny. Did you hear what I said?"

There was silence. He didn't answer me, just stared, unimpressed by my behavior. One of his eyebrows rose, as if to say, "What are you waiting for?"

I shook my head and sighed. "Castriel, we don't have time for this."

"All the more reason for you to be here already."

I put my hands on my hips, annoyed that he was making fun of me, and then I did what he wanted. I stood half a step away from him.

"What happened, Isabelle?"

"You need to take down that billboard."

"I understand what you're asking me to do, but I asked you what happened?"

Nervously, I stretched my fingers and played with my rings. Right and left. Right and left...

"I can't tell you," I said after a moment. "But it's really important. Trust me."

"It's not about trust, Isabelle. What's wrong with that billboard?"

"Nothing. Everything is fine. I mean, I haven't even seen it, but that's not the point."

"Then what is the point?"

"Well, I can't tell you." I rubbed my face with my hand, heartbroken because I knew exactly how it looked to him.

"Baby, I can't do it." Castriel's face was stony as he said it. He was calm and serious.

"I have to go."

"What? First, Isabelle, have you even read your contract? You have absolutely no say in where and how your photos are used for the brand. Whether it's a billboard or a mug with your picture on it, it doesn't matter. You're the face of the brand, for God's sake."

"I know..." A groan escaped my throat. "But something has changed. I told you I wasn't ready for fame, that I didn't want it. It's not for me."

"Second, darling, the machine is already in motion. You're the image that just graced the whole city—"

"Then there's the TV commercial."

"Exactly. There are still commercials on TV. The company spent a lot of money to get this thing going. I can't just stand in front of the board and say we have to take two steps back because that's what you want, because that's what you're afraid of. That they can't turn a blind eye to the money that is being thrown down the drain. We're not talking thousands of dollars here, we're talking millions. This isn't the Chicken Little League!" Castriel yelled the last sentence.

I didn't blame him. The whole situation was fucked up, and he had a right to be upset. I had put him in a very embarrassing situation.

What could I have done differently? How could I protect myself?

The frustration reached its peak and the first tears fell from my eyes.

"Please, Castriel... Please..."

His eyes grew sad, and he shook his head. "I can't take it back, Isabelle. I'm sorry."

I nodded. He couldn't do that, not even for me. I even understood that.

I wanted to fight when the time came, but in the face of tangible danger, fear took over.

The tears flowed faster.

Castriel's hands rested on my cheeks and wiped away the salty drops one by one. "Tell me, baby." His whisper wrapped around my face. "Tell me what this is about."

"He'll find me," I groaned as the truth flowed from my mouth.

"Who will find you?"

"I can't— I have to go—"

Within a second, I was in this strange man's arms as he carried me bride-style to a couch. He sat down and placed me on his lap.

"You're not going anywhere. Trust me. Please. I won't let anything happen to you. Who will find you?"

Then the ugly truth poured out of me.

"He... My father... My name isn't Isabelle Knox. My real name is Hansen. My father is Michael Hansen." I looked Castriel straight in the eye, but it was obvious he didn't know who I was talking about. "Michael

Hansen is a serial killer. He murdered at least a dozen girls around the age of eighteen. That's all the police have been able to link to him. I'm the killer's daughter."

"Go on."

I took a deep breath. "We were a happy family. He, my mother and I. We had a beautiful home in the suburbs of Oakdale, Louisiana. You would never in your life say there was anything wrong with that picture. He was a good father, a loving husband... He wasn't very social, but that's not unusual. He worked as an auto mechanic. Liked by co-workers, recommended by customers. Anyway, one day my mother got the idea to surprise my father. He had mentioned more than once that he needed to build a small gym at home because he wasn't getting any younger and he wanted to be in shape. So my mom secretly prepared this gym for him in our basement.

When he went to work, she would roll up her sleeves and paint this room. While painting one of the walls, she noticed that a brick was moving. She obviously wanted to fix it somehow, patch it up, but when she turned around, she accidentally hit the wall with her elbow and two more bricks fell out of the wall. She was persistent and decided to fix that as well. When she looked in the gap, she saw a hidden place behind the wall. The hiding place where my father was hiding something. He cut the little fingers off each of his victims and kept them in small jars with some kind of liquid. These were his trophies. He took pictures of his victims, at each stage of the end of their lives—"

"Jesus..." Castriel groaned, hugging me tighter.

"It was like a sport to him, and this was his wall of fame. Literally. He must have returned from work earlier that day than my mother expected, because he found her in the basement. As we found out later, he used duct tape to seal her mouth and bind her arms and legs. He threw her in the trunk of his car like a bag of garbage. He drove her to some place and left her locked in the basement. And then he came to pick me up from school. He picked me up with a smile on his face, as if nothing had happened. I was surprised, but he told me he was preparing a surprise for my mom for their wedding anniversary. He wanted us to spend the day together as a family. As I got into the car, he told me about a wooden house in the middle of a beautiful forest. He talked and talked and it took us more than an hour to get to that house. He said it was the house of a friend from work and that he had lent us the keys."

Tears streamed down my face. I didn't feel Castriel's arms trying to comfort me or his hand stroking my head. I was there again. With *him*. In that cabin. I could smell it.

"We left the car at the edge of the forest and continued on foot. I was happy as a child. I was excited. We arrived at the place, but the old wooden house somehow didn't reflect my stupid fantasies. It was dirty, stinking, and made my skin crawl. For a moment, I thought it smelled like death. Under the pretext of showing me something in the basement, he took me there. That stench cannot be described in words. I was afraid to throw up when he closed the door behind us. And when he turned on the light, I saw my mother lying on the floor, curled up like a baby. I wanted to run to her to save her when my father pushed me. I fell down the stairs. For a moment, everything went dark, and I realized my father wasn't with us. It wasn't my father, it was some kind of monster. For the first time, I was afraid for my life. As he stood over me, his face was twisted with a grimace. I saw hatred in it, but I didn't understand why. After all, I was his favorite daughter. At the first kick to my stomach, I ran out of air in my lungs. The second kick hit my ribs and broke two of them. I don't know what happened with the next ones, but I started spitting blood out of my mouth."

"Fuck, baby..."

"Before I could gather my strength and fight back, I was hit again. With his feet, with his fists… It didn't matter. Hit after hit. In the face, in the back, in the stomach…"

"How did you get out?"

"He left us alone for a while. He went away, and I crawled over to my mother. I used a piece of glass to cut the tape on her hands and mouth. She told me everything, every detail. I begged her to try to escape, but when we heard his footsteps upstairs, we both knew it was too late. Mom told me to go back to my place, and she lay down in the position she'd been in before. He came downstairs and walked in my direction. Apparently, my father was in such a state that he'd completely forgotten about her. Or maybe he was just sure that he'd already killed her. While he was standing over me with a knife in his hand, my mother found a crowbar in the corner. I don't know what he needed it for, but that damn crowbar saved my life.

"Mom hit him again and again, as hard as she could. The knife flew out of his hand and rolled somewhere. They started fighting, struggling. He hit her with his fist and started lunging at her. This was my only chance. It gave me a moment to gather my strength. I climbed up the stairs as quietly as I could. I don't know why I didn't help her when she was still down there. God, I don't know…"

"It's not your fault, Isabelle." Castriel shook his head.

"Not mine? Then whose? Standing on the last step, I watched him point the crowbar at Mama's neck. I watched him stab her through with this fucking crowbar! I watched him kill her, and I did nothing…"

"Fuck! You couldn't do anything when you were hurt, beaten. You were just a child."

"I locked him in there. When he killed her, I locked him in there. I locked the bolt. Then I ran as far as I could through the woods. Somehow, he got out. I had an advantage that was diminishing by the moment. He was after me. He wanted to kill me and bury me in the damn cabin. In my moments of greatest doubt, when I fell to my knees, I heard my mother's voice telling me to keep running. I finally made it to the street. A man driving by stopped and took me to the nearest police station. I was sure my father would run away. And you know what he did? He drove to our house. The police stopped him in the shower. None of his trophies were found in the basement. He never revealed where all those girls were buried, and the bodies... None of them were ever found. Michael Hansen denied everything."

"Jesus Christ!"

"The only thing the police could pin on him was the murder of my mother. I was a witness against him. He could have gotten the death penalty or life imprisonment for killing all those people. He got twenty-five years for the murder of my mother. His lawyer made up a story about an alleged argument between the two of them and defended him by lying about what really happened."

"It hasn't been twenty-five years yet."

"No, it hasn't, but my father is already free. He knows my phone number—"

"Deaf phone calls—" he interrupted, nodding slowly. He put the pieces together.

"Yes. The only thing he doesn't know is what I look like now and where I live. I don't think he knows that. When he sees my pictures, he'll know me. He'll find me. It's just a matter of time. And then—"

"Isabelle! Don't even think that," Castriel growled. He wiped his face with his hand. "I'm sorry. I'm sorry, baby. I can't turn back time. I can't stop it. But I can promise you I'll do everything in my power to keep you safe. I won't let him hurt you again."

I looked at him and wanted to believe him, but part of me was afraid he wouldn't be able to keep his word.

"I'm sorry this happened to you. I'm sorry you lost your beloved mother to that bastard. I'm sorry that such tragedy happened to you."

"Now you know my dark secret. I'm afraid," I confessed.

Castriel put his arms around me and pulled me close. Now and then, he kissed the top of my head. I shivered—not from cold, but from emotion. I shivered despite the warmth radiating from his body.

"I'll never let him hurt you. I promise. You're mine to protect, Isabelle. You're mine..."

Chapter 19

CASTRIEL

"Have you lost your mind?" Suspicion flared in Isabelle's eyes. She looked me over from top to bottom as if I were about to dance the Cancan. Naked. If I had told her I was a messenger from hell, she would have found it less ridiculous.

"Do I look like I have?"

"Well, if you're asking—"

"No. I know exactly what I'm saying to you."

"Then why on earth are you telling me to pack up now?"

After our conversation in the office, when Isabelle had calmed down, she wanted to go home. Even before we left the four walls of my office, a new plan was forming in my mind, piece by piece.

On my way out, I told Meghan that I wouldn't be available for the rest of the day. She looked with sympathy at my girl, then sternly at me, as if her tears were my fault. She nodded and went back to her duties.

If Meghan noticed anything strange about my behavior, she kept it to herself. Since we started working together, I had never left work at this hour. Not for personal matters anyway.

"Meghan, two more things. If you go behind my back again, you can pack your shit. I appreciate the intentions, but the decisions here are mine. Second, decide quickly whether you work for me or Takashi. I will not tolerate information being slipped under his nose, even if he's God. If you do, not only can you pack your shit, but you can be sure you'll never find a similar job in this town again. I'll pay you a lot of money for the loyalty written into your duties. Do we understand each other?"

There was a moment of silence, but my words got to the point, as her eyes looked scared.

"Yes, sir. It won't happen again," she apologized.

I nodded to her, grabbed my girl's hand, and headed for the elevator.

The gesture of taking her hand felt so natural. The warmth of her skin, the intimacy of that simple gesture, made my fingers tingle. In my life, I had never held a woman's hand except as a gesture of greeting or to hold her in bed. I was surprised to find that I enjoyed it more than I would have thought possible.

So we stood in her small living room and Isabelle looked at me as if I were crazy.

"Why are you standing there? Pack your things," I ordered her as if she were a little child.

With her arms crossed over her chest and a pout on her face, she had no intention of moving.

"Shall I do it for you, Isabelle?"

"No! Can you answer my question?"

I rubbed my face with my hands and sighed. I wasn't good at expressing feelings or anything like that. How was I going to explain to her what was going on in my head?

"Baby, you're going to live with me. Please pack your things."

"What?"

I gritted my teeth. After all, I had made myself clear. Even my tone was soft, as if I was talking to a wounded animal.

"I told you I would do anything to keep you safe. This is me doing just that."

"This is messed up. I can't do it." She turned away to leave, but I grabbed her hand.

"It doesn't have to be this way. I'm really trying to be polite here and let you make the right decision. Pack your bags."

"Or what? Do you hear yourself?"

That's it!

In the blink of an eye, I grabbed her hips, lifted her into the air, and Isabelle squealed. She wrapped her legs around my hips, and I moved into her bedroom.

"What are you doing?" she whined in a husky voice.

We entered the bedroom and collapsed together on her bed. I lifted my body slightly and propped myself up on my forearms. I loved it when she found herself underneath me.

"Or what? Or I'll fuck you so hard that I teach you to be submissive. And until you beg me to give you a break. Spoiler, you won't know my mercy until you understand what's good for you."

"You mean?" she whispered, moving underneath me.

"I mean me. Listen, at first that thought seemed strange to me too. I can't remember the last time I shared my personal space with anyone. I've always been an action-oriented person, not one to play house with a woman. The more I think about it, the more perfect and comfortable this thought seems to be. I mean, you, in my apartment, in my bed. Plus, of course, the security I can give you. And I *will* provide for you."

"It was only supposed to be once," she said weakly.

"It was supposed to be, but it is what it is." I leaned over and nibbled at the skin of her neck with my teeth. She responded by moving her hips, trying to soothe her growing desire. "The chemistry between us hasn't diminished at all, has it? The certainty that you were like all the others was crap. When I first entered you..."

Her breath became rapid.

"When I first entered you, I knew it was all a lie. That you were special, and one time wasn't enough. You felt it, didn't you?"

I was now openly kissing her skin just above her breasts while moving my hips so she would know what she was doing to me.

She rewarded me with a moan. "God, yes..."

"Agreed, Isabelle."

"Why do you keep saying my name?"

"I love the taste of your name on my tongue."

"Stop distracting me."

I slid the tip of my tongue inside her bra and pulled on her hard nipple. She bent over, wanting more. I was ready to tear her apart, but I had something else in mind with this game. My animal instincts had to wait until we were in my apartment.

"Are you going to pack your things like a good girl?"

"God, yes..."

"I love it when you call me your God. Now get to it."

I got off the bed and pulled her toward me. Once she was standing, I gave her a quick kiss, a light slap on her ass, and turned on my heel.

"Wait, what?" I noticed her confusion out of the corner of my eye. "Cas—"

"Pack your things, baby. We're going home."

***

One phone call was all it took to get Shadow for Isabelle. From now on, her every move outside the apartment would be monitored by an invisible man. Invisible to her, that is.

I wasn't going to risk anything happening to her. Her shadow's life depended on it. Literally.

Fifteen minutes later, my girlfriend came out of the bedroom with puffy cheeks but a bag in her hand.

"This is weird. I can stay at Emma and Mason's for a while. I'm sure they won't mind."

"Absolutely not!" My voice was sharper than I expected. "Mason spends most of his time at Media Linc and Emma is pregnant. Which one of them is going to defend you? I'm not going to put your security in someone else's hands. I'm a motherfucker who doesn't trust anyone by nature, and even less so when it comes to people who are important to me."

The sound of a crash filled the entire apartment as the bag fell from her hand. Isabelle opened her mouth to say something, only to close it a moment later, defeated. "Am I important to you?"

I knew women loved that kind of crap. Verbal declarations, confessions, grand gestures... Words... How could I explain it to this woman?

Before I could answer, there was a knock at the door. I looked at Isabelle with raised eyebrows, but she just shrugged. She wasn't expecting visitors, that much was clear.

In three steps, I was at the door and opened it.

On the other side was none other than Brad. Surprised by my presence in Isabelle's apartment, he froze.

"What are you doing here?" I crossed my arms and stared at the fucker.

"Um... I hope I'm not interrupting anything. Is Izzy home?"

"You're actually interrupting. Isabelle is very busy at the moment. Thanks for stopping by." I grabbed the door, dreaming of slamming it in his face, but Isabelle's hand was on mine.

I measured her with my gaze and she rolled her eyes.

"Hi, Brad," she greeted him with a smile, standing next to me.

Instinctively, my hand found its way to her waist. Not to mention that I didn't like the smile on her face. I felt a ball rise in my chest. I didn't like her smiling at him. At the mere thought of her smiling at any man, the urge to kill became hard to tame.

"Hi, Izzy." His nervous gaze jumped from her face to my hand on her hip, then to my face. "I just wanted to see how you were doing."

"Everything's fine. Thank you, Brad... Stop it, Castriel." Her elbow found its target in my ribs. "All is well. How about you?"

"Fine, fine..."

Enough of this bullshit.

I went back for the bag Isabelle had left in the living room and grabbed the keys from the glass bowl placed on a table in the hallway.

"We have to go now, baby," I said, pushing her out of the apartment and past Brad. I closed the door, grabbed her hand, and headed for the elevator.

She didn't put up much of a fight, thank God. Otherwise I would have had to throw her over my shoulder. That's how high my irritation had reached.

"Are you going somewhere?"

The bastard's question was already at the top of the list. I pressed the elevator call button and answered again for her, "She's not going anywhere. She's moving in with me."

The shock on his face was worth it. What a wonderful feeling. I was almost sure Isabelle would be angry with me for this, but there was a smile on her face that grew with every second.

"Izzy, don't do that," Brad growled at her. "He's not... You can't... He's a bad person!"

Fortunately, the elevator doors opened, and we went inside. I was expecting an argument from my girl, but she just kept smiling at me while ignoring Brad.

I liked that.

No, I fucking loved it!

Before the door closed, I looked at him and vowed that if I ever saw him near my Isabelle again, I would beat the bastard to a pulp.

"You were jealous," she whispered, still staring at me with a smile.

"No."

"Correction, you *are* jealous."

"Shut up."

"You're insanely, freakin' jealous of me."

"Of course I'm jealous! You're my girl."

I was grateful when she stopped pursuing the subject. Eventually, she stopped looking at me and looked at the door. On the one hand, I was happy, on the other hand I wasn't at all. The smile didn't leave her face for a long moment.

***

I wasn't proud of my outburst earlier, but I couldn't help it. Only when we were in my apartment could I take a deep breath.

I showed Isabelle around. She insisted on claiming one of the guest rooms, but she didn't stand a chance against my stubbornness. As far as I was concerned, she could have as much freedom and space as she wanted, as long as she found her way to me and my bed every night. It wasn't just about sex, although that was something I wanted to explore with her to her own limits. I wanted her close to me.

To her surprise, I found a place for her things in my organized walk-in closet within seconds. In fact, half of the closet was immediately hers. When she finished unpacking and I saw her clothes next to mine, I felt a strange peace in my soul. It was as if something had jumped into place.

I was grateful that since the incident in the elevator, Isabelle had stopped fighting me on every detail. It wasn't in her nature, and I was sure my lioness would soon reappear but I was grateful, nonetheless.

Her person had already changed so much in my life, but I felt a peace that I couldn't find for most of it.

After the lunch I had prepared for us, I decided my girl needed a moment to relax after today. I handed her a glass of red wine and turned on the television. I sat down next to her and pulled her to my side. Such gestures were new to me, but they were damn satisfying.

"Go back to the previous channel," she said as I jumped from channel to channel.

The screen showed the latest news.

"From what we have been able to gather, the man found is Maverick Johnson, a former employee of the governor's office. The motives for this murder are unknown to us. Was it politically motivated? We are currently interviewing the victim's relatives. We have determined that the cause of death was more than a dozen stab wounds. About more..."

A photo of the man appeared on the screen. At first glance, he wasn't much younger than I was. A groan brought my attention back to Isabelle.

She was pale. Her mouth was open and a fresh wave of tears was streaming from her eyes.

"What happened, baby?"

When she turned her eyes in my direction, I saw pain and fear in them.

"It's him... It's definitely him... Castriel—"

"Who, Isabelle? Do you know this man?"

"Yes... I knew him from school. Same thing with Leo, the previous victim. It must be him."

"Him? Do you think this was your father's fault?"

"It's my fault. It's me. While Leo may have been a random victim, the other person I knew lost his life, and I don't believe in the same coincidence."

For the second time that day, Isabelle cried over the bastard. It broke my heart to see what she was going through. It was all so messed up.

I felt like wiping all those terrible moments from her memory, like my fingers wiping the tears from her flawless skin. I wanted to take all that pain and turn it into dust.

"Come here." I hugged her tighter and wrapped my arms around her. She trembled and cried against my chest as I stroked her like a child.

At some point, her cell phone vibrated on the coffee table. I saw an unknown number calling. If it was her father, I would love to talk to the bastard.

I nuzzled her away just enough to grab the phone. She didn't protest when I took the call and turned on the speaker.

"Hello?" Isabelle's voice was weak.

There was silence. No one spoke, but I had a feeling he was there.

"Isa." A deep voice rang out just after she repeated "hello" a second time.

Isabelle held her breath, and I knew for sure it was him.

"What do you want?" She snarled in disgust.

"My little princess..."

"I'm not your princess anymore! Forget about me. I died for you that day in the forest. And it would have been better for you to die there too."

"My blood." He laughed softly, as if fascinated.

I couldn't bear it. "Shut up!"

"Castriel... I wasn't expecting you, but it's nice to meet you."

I looked at her with raised eyebrows. He knew about me, which meant he was closer than we expected. He was two steps ahead of us, and it was driving me crazy.

"Listen to me, you motherfucker, and you better listen good. This is your last call. If I find you even a few miles away from Isabelle, I will kill you. That's not a threat; that's a promise!"

"Not if I have something that my Isa wants..."

"She wants nothing from you."

"Not even to know where all the girls are?"

"I've changed my mind. I'm going to kill you one way or another. See you, Michael." I ended the call.

CHAPTER 20

IZZY

Several days passed since that fucked-up evening. I had calmed down enough to think logically. Meeting my father was inevitable. I knew he wouldn't let go. In order to finish what he started, he would try to find me.

He had already found me. He knew who I was with that day, and that meant he was closer than I thought. His knowledge exceeded my comfort level. No one could help me. Not the police, not Detective Burk. The police said they couldn't trace the call, let alone determine that it was definitely my father. They refused to take my case. Detective Burk was very concerned, but all he could do was once again advise me to leave town.

I was left alone with the problem. Alone with Castriel. I was comforted by the thought that the nightmare I had been living for so many years would end. How fucked up was it? Terrible.

Castriel and I fell into a sort of routine. Every morning, he would make me coffee and breakfast while I got ready for work. We would eat breakfast and then go to work together. When I returned to his apartment after work, I would prepare dinner and we would eat together. He would come home from work a while before it was ready. We spent our evenings in different ways. Sometimes we watched something on TV together, sometimes we read in bed, sometimes we sipped wine and looked at the city below our feet. We always ended up in his bed, without exception. Never, without exception, did he take my panties off.

I felt my need for his body grow more and more each day. I felt a frustration that tormented me. Once I even tried to touch him suggestively first, but he caught my hand and said, "It's not that time yet." I wanted to scream at him, my claws wanting to mark his tempting skin.

What did that even mean? I didn't know. Then he turned us over so that his chest enveloped my back and told me to go to sleep. That was the last thing I wanted to do.

He gave me the distance I didn't want. Maybe in his mind, that was what I needed? But I was sure that if he didn't fuck me today, I would either explode or do it myself.

That day, Castriel had to stay late at the office. I prepared dinner and waited for him—until the lights went out in the apartment.

Paralyzing fear gripped me. I closed my eyelids for a second and my breath caught in my lungs. My heart pounded in my chest and my blood rushed in my ears.

I turned on my heel and looked around, eyes wide with fear.

Was this the moment my father would catch me? Now that Castriel wasn't with me? Was he waiting for when I would be alone?

My eyes fell on the phone on the coffee table. On shaky legs, I approached it from the corner of my eye, watching my surroundings as if a monster were about to jump out from around the corner. I touched the screen, but the phone didn't blink. Nothing.

The battery must be dead.

Seriously? Isn't there a better time?

I threw the phone on the couch and slowly made my way to the kitchen, my heart pounding. I felt like its beating was drowning out everything else.

I walked over to the light switch and flipped it a few times. Nothing happened. The light didn't flicker on. A great relief washed through my body as I touched the handle of the kitchen knife lying on the counter. I gripped it tightly when I heard a thud deep in the apartment.

I felt like I was going to pass out.

My gun was put away in the dresser drawer in the bedroom. Too far away to get to it.

"Who's there?" I called out.

I was met with silence.

"I'm armed, so you better get out before I hurt you!"

I left the kitchen as quietly as I could. I was barefoot, so it wasn't too difficult.

I looked around the living room again, and then I heard another knock coming from the hallway leading to the bedroom.

"Castriel?"

Silence.

"Fuck this," I whispered to myself.

Although my first thought was to fight, I immediately thought of running. What if running was the only thing that could save my life?

Fuck.

As I passed the corridor, I thought I heard a noise and looked around with panic in my heart.

It couldn't end like this.

I looked at the front door only a few steps away and again into the darkened hallway. Nothing. Total darkness. I decided and moved toward the door.

I grabbed the doorknob and my heart rejoiced when, suddenly, everything changed.

I didn't even hear a rustling sound; instead, I felt someone's hand land on my neck, pushing me against the apartment door. To counteract the impact on my face, my hands involuntarily dropped to the wooden surface. The blade of the knife made a rattling sound, and the attacker's other hand grabbed my wrist. I felt the warmth of someone's body much too close to me.

For a second, I expected pain that would kill me, and then I fought for my life.

My uninhibited left hand shot back, and I felt my elbow strike something very solid. I took satisfaction in the gasp I heard behind me.

Taking advantage of my attacker's surprise, I lifted my right leg and hit his foot with my heel as hard as I could. This had a surprisingly good effect, as the man let go of my wrist holding the knife.

Wasting not one precious second, I swung my hand, hoping to hit his thigh, but he expected my move. He jumped back with his lower body, but his hand still held my throat. His right hand grabbed my wrist again, this time bending my arm back and palm up.

My breathing quickened as I frantically tried to figure out my next move. I had to get free somehow.

"Drop your weapon!" I heard an unfamiliar, deep voice.

"No," I groaned.

The hand holding my wrist rose even higher. I felt pain in my shoulder, and if my face hadn't been resting on the surface of the door, I probably would have snapped in half.

"Drop. Your. Weapon."

"Fuck. You!"

"With pleasure."

At once, I felt a kick to my right ankle until my leg swung to the side. "Spread your legs," my attacker growled. Immediately, he kicked the other ankle. My spread legs gave him room, and he took advantage.

He stood between my spread thighs and I felt his warmth through the fabric of my clothes. I felt his firm stance and semi-hard erection thrusting along my lower back.

This isn't my father!

I didn't know if I was thrilled that it wasn't him or more worried that it wasn't. I didn't recognize this voice, and that meant someone else was a threat to me.

I bit my lip to keep from moaning.

"Where's your hero now, huh?"

I grabbed his thigh with my left hand and dug my nails into it. It was the only place my hand could go. The pain I inflicted made him laugh softly. His chest vibrated and his hips pressed into me even more.

This time, my lip slipped from between my teeth and a strange sound came from inside me. Shame immediately clouded my logical thinking.

The attacker let go of my neck and grabbed my thigh with his free hand. I hoped my fingernails had drawn at least some of his blood. Before my hand was also behind my back, I looked at him.

The attacker was wearing a mask that I had sometimes seen on social media. A bright green "X" was scrawled on the dark mask where the eyes should have been, and vertical lines crossed the outlined mouth. I knew the design so well...

I had to do something, and fast, because my situation was getting worse by the minute.

I was on the verge of tilting my head back to hit him right in the face with the back of my head when he predicted my actions again.

His hands were so big that he grabbed both my wrists, while his right hand easily pulled the blade out of my hand.

"Fuck!" I screamed in frustration.

The hand with the knife moved, and I felt the metal on my throat. I froze. I stopped breathing. Only the beating of my heart in my ears told me I was alive.

The man leaned into my ear. "Nah-ah... I think you were a very, very bad girl. Did you think it was funny with a knife like that? Hmm?"

"What do you want from me? Soon my friend will be here and he will kill you."

He laughed and then his lips landed on my neck. I felt his teeth bite into my skin and then his tongue tried to soothe the burning spot.

I closed my eyes, unable to believe this was happening. I had never thought that I could be a potential rape victim. I also felt something else.

"What if I'm the one who kills him and then fucks you in a pool of his blood? How about that?"

"You're sick. What you say is sick."

"Oh yeah?"

The blade of the knife descended from my throat, across my breasts, down my stomach to my pubic area.

One, two, three heartbeats... I felt the metal blade leave the sensitive spot and then I heard it fall to the floor somewhere else. I opened my eyes in surprise.

The attacker placed his now free hand on my throat and squeezed lightly. Then he spread his fingers. He ran his flat hand over my rhythmically rising breasts, down my stomach, down to the elastic band of my yoga pants.

I struggled in a desperate attempt to break free. This couldn't be happening. And yet it was happening! With every move I made, his erection got bigger and bigger. He was already so hard that he could fuck me without even using his hands.

Fuck!

"In that case, why don't you let me check how sick you think it is?" His warm fingers slipped under the elastic of my pants and found their way into my panties without hesitation. And then deeper...

I knew what he was looking for and what he would find.

"So? You want to know my thoughts?" He laughed darkly. "Because as far as I'm concerned, you're just as sick as I am. You're soaked. Your panties are ruined." Two of his fingers found my entrance. He fucked me hard with them. "Your pussy is so wet that you welcomed me without the slightest resistance. We're going to have a lot of fun together before your boyfriend gets back."

His lips found their way back to my neck. He kissed me to mark me, to caress me with his tongue. At the same time, he fucked me with two and then three fingers. I felt sick, but he was a lot stronger than me and I tilted my head back.

My hips moved in their own rhythm, occasionally rubbing against his cock. A moan escaped my throat.

"Don't you dare come on my fingers. You'll come if I let you. You'll come on my cock like a good girl so I can look your man in the face later, smile and shake his hand. Isn't that fun?"

"No, it's not, you fucked-up pervert. Fuck off!"

Before the last words were out of my mouth, I was on the floor. I got up on all fours, intending to run away, but he grabbed me by the ankles and I collapsed forward. I had no intention of giving up, though, so I kept fighting.

I felt his presence behind me and his fingers digging into my waist.

"Stop fighting or it will hurt!"

"Over my dead body!"

Once again, I tried to get away from him on all fours as he grabbed my pants and, with a flick, they were around my knees. The sound of the panty material ripping filled the room. I felt the cool air reach the most sensitive parts of my body. It was such a contrast to the moisture that had accumulated between my legs.

I didn't even want to think about my body's reaction. *If I survive this, then I'll wonder what's wrong with me.*

His muffled laughter reached my ears as I felt a hard slap land on my bare bottom. I yelped in shock and received a second, third, and fourth spanking.

"When you wrestle with me like this, you turn me on even more, you know? I need to be inside you. You're safe with me, sweetheart."

I didn't hear the zipper of his pants or the tearing of the condom foil, but instead I felt the head of his cock begin to push into me.

"No!" I growled.

"Yes," he moaned.

He put his hand between my shoulder blades and pushed down so that my chest touched the floor. With one thrust, he entered me completely and I let out a muffled moan. He filled me all over. He was big, really big. Even though I was wet, I could feel his cock rubbing against my walls.

When he pulled out almost completely, he was immediately back inside me with a thrust. He fucked me hard. The rhythm changed from time to time. Sometimes he went in hard and deep, sometimes fast and shallow.

"You are fucking delicious. I'll make use of you in a way that no one before me has ever dared."

His words rippled through my bloodstream. My body responded and something powerful built inside me.

Sweat covered every inch of my body. The grip of his hand on my waist tightened. He let out a growl unlike anything I had ever heard in my life.

"No... no... no..." I repeated, feeling like my head was about to explode.

He didn't stop. My refusal seemed to encourage him to continue because his movements were even deeper. This was impossible, but my head didn't understand.

"No... no..."

"Fuck yes! Yes, come for me!"

"Oh fuck, oh fuck... Castriel!"

The words ripped out of me as I felt the stars explode in my head. Paralyzing pleasure moved in slow motion from my head, through my heart, my stomach, my pussy, my toes. I wasn't sure if I screamed long and hard, but I wouldn't be surprised if the police were on their way.

Three motions later, he stopped while he was completely inside me and came with my name on his lips.

I had no idea when the first tear rolled down my cheek. As the dizzying sensation slowly left my body, I felt a headache. I collapsed to the floor, exhausted.

The man's body rolled away from me and fell beside me with a thud.

***

That evening, I didn't move from the floor for hours. I lay naked on the blanket as Castriel's fingertips lazily ran over my skin.

"What's wrong with me?" I asked neither him nor myself.

"Nothing, Isabelle. There is nothing wrong with you."

"How can you say that, Castriel? That was the first time I came during sex. And that was when you pretended to rape me."

"Baby, that's not at all unusual for women. It's just a fantasy I was playing out for you. And fantasies are there to be fulfilled, to play with their limits, to learn about yourself."

"But rape?" I asked, disgusted. "You think it has something to do with a feeling of fear? An attempt to escape? That it has something to do with—"

"Don't even go there. It has nothing to do with the things that happened. You have never been completely honest with yourself. Your body needed it. It turned you on. Consensual sex has a thousand faces and none of them bad. Have you had such fantasies? Have you told anyone about them?"

"Yes and no. How could I tell anyone that I like it when a guy puts his hand around my neck? How could I say that I like it when a man takes me, even when he hears 'no'? It's—"

"Isabelle, there's nothing wrong with that. I'm glad that you have fantasies we can fulfill together. I fantasize about you too. I don't think there's anything wrong with that."

I nodded, although I wasn't convinced that he was right. "But rape?"

"Not rape, just attempted rape, if not attempted assault. I've suspected for some time that you're not a person who likes to be fucked in the dark, under the covers. You like to be fucked hard, you like to feel power over you, you like rough play.

"But you recently rejected me in bed."

"I'm sorry, but I saw the tension building up inside you. I've seen you need sex, and the desire in you was growing every day. For you to finally unlock yourself and reach orgasm while fucking, you had to stop feeling and thinking about your limits."

I shook my head and then laughed.

"When did you realize I was the one behind the mask?"

"I didn't know at first. Your hands seemed familiar, but adrenaline dulled my common sense. Then I felt your erection and became suspicious. I gained certainty when you dropped the knife. By the way, I might have killed you. That wasn't very smart."

"I had everything under control, baby."

We lay in silence for a long moment, snuggled together. Then I realized something important.

"Cas," I began, "I need to tell you something. I realize you're becoming more important to me every day."

"Mm-hmm…"

"If it's something you don't want to hear, then tell me now. I don't want you to feel any pressure, but I also don't want to fool myself that the situation might change one day."

"Isabelle, stop, baby. You're not alone in this. I feel it too. I feel so much that sometimes I can't put a name to it. But I have to be honest because I've never been in a relationship. I never want to hurt you, but I can't promise that it won't happen. Still, I'm all in."

"I'm all in too," I whispered and kissed his lips.

We were all in this together.

CHAPTER 21

"You're the one who killed Maverick!"

"Nah... it wasn't me."

"You're lying! You're the murderer. It was you who killed him!"

I rolled my eyes at his childish persistence. "I'm telling you, I didn't kill him. It was a fucking accident. He killed himself."

"What do you mean, it was an accident? He accidentally stabbed himself thirteen times?"

"So much drama. He accidentally stabbed himself once. The next twelve times, I made sure he did it right."

"You're fucked up," he spat.

Almost an hour ago, I had felt bored. Now I was bored to the point of exhaustion. My new friend's whimpering and screaming was just pissing me off.

"Do you know what it used to be called? It was 'bloody eagle.' History says this kind of torture came from the Vikings."

Connor didn't say a word; just kept moaning. At least he had stopped crying some time ago, so I was sure we were getting better. "There are two versions of why it was called that. The first is that the Vikings would tie up the person being tortured with their arms outstretched and then cut the skin between the ribs to resemble wings. The victim's lungs were then pulled out."

I laughed and nodded. I walked around Connor and looked at his back. "Funny, isn't it? And how stupid at the same time. It would be medically impossible. The victim wouldn't have survived to the end of his torture, as the legends say. The second version mentioned in the story you've already learned on your own."

I was getting closer to the person I was looking for, which gave me an extra shot of adrenaline.

"So, the second version says that the tied up victim had his wings cut out of his back and then the wounds were rubbed with salt. Simple but effective, if you ask me. Isn't it?"

I turned to face Connor again, wrinkling my nose at the fresh stench wafting through the air. My new colleague was peeing in pain, as his soaked jeans showed.

"Connor," I growled. "How could you? You ruined all the fun." Once again, I raised the photo so that it was right in front of his face. "Where is this person?"

"I... I don't..."

"Don't fucking lie!" The shout echoed through the bunker. "Answer the question before the 'bloody wings' are not only on your back, but on your chest."

A former athlete, Connor was quite well built. Still, his muscular arms couldn't support him after the last few hours, so he hung limply from a rope.

Sweat dripped from his bald head, down his forehead, face, neck, and lower body. I looked into the dark eyes of the man about to die.

"Look again. More carefully this time. Do you know this person?"

After several seconds, Connor squirmed and finally nodded.

"Where does he live?"

This time, Connor shook his head.

"Use your words, motherfucker."

"I... I don't know... It's true... I don't know."

"How about we start at the beginning, my friend? What's his name then?" My smile got bigger and bigger with every word that came out of his mouth.

Finally. After years, I felt closer to my goal.

CHAPTER 22

IZZY

I woke up to find myself trapped in my dream. My heart was pounding like crazy. My hands shook as I rubbed my face.

In this nightmare, my father had thrown me into a maze with no way out. Its stone walls rose so high that the sun was barely visible. At first, full of energy, I ran ahead, wanting to get out. But as each corridor turned into another and another... I knew I was fucked.

His laughter was audible from up there. I didn't know how he could see me down here, but he did.

At one point, the wall behind me moved toward me, making a horrible grating sound. Scared, I looked at it, unable to believe that this was really happening.

So I ran forward, but the wall in front of me also moved.

My eyes moved from right to left and back again. Both walls were moving lazily without stopping for a second.

I panicked and tried to climb, but the wet stones weren't my ally. There was no rescue for me.

When both walls were a few steps away from me, I woke up shaking. Drops of sweat adorned my forehead. The nightshirt clung to my back.

God, what a nightmare.

My eyes landed on the clock placed on the bedside table. It said it was past four in the morning.

Wanting to snuggle up and go back to sleep, I turned to Castriel.

I blinked twice to confirm I was fully awake.

Castriel wasn't in bed. From the moment we acted out the attack scene the other day, everything had changed. I felt that we were looking at each other as if we were holding a secret together. But he was right about everything.

This situation helped me unlock something inside me that was preventing me from having an orgasm. No man before him had ever succeeded. It wasn't all their fault, but none of them had tried to understand my body. Was it their own selfishness? Laziness? Or my own failure to understand my needs? It didn't matter anymore.

This one night didn't change everything and I could orgasm every time. That's not how it works in real life. This situation showed me the way to understand my body better. I learned that my body would reward me if I treat it right.

With Castriel, I didn't have to pretend to anyone or anything. He seemed to enjoy walking this path with me.

The acceptance was liberating.

Every night we tried new things. I found I loved it when he licked my clit and I came hard on his tongue, but it made it harder for me to come when he fucked me right after. His tongue skills could bring me to multiple orgasms.

Riding him didn't give me as much pleasure as feeling his power over me in bed.

I stopped being a fan of toys; instead, tying me up and fucking my face without mercy was another dimension.

Every night we slept together, and Castriel helped me explore my desires.

When I woke up this night from my nightmare, turned to him and found he wasn't in bed, I freaked out. I immediately sat up, wide awake. My hand touched the black sheet where he had been in bed only a few hours before, but it was cold.

I threw the covers aside and stood. I knocked on the bathroom door, but silence answered me. He wasn't here. So I made my way to the second bedroom door.

Once I opened it, I listened. Silence...

Is Castriel trying to experiment again? Could it be that he wants to frighten me again?

If so, he was doing a good job. My pulse quickened, and I swallowed saliva.

On shaky legs, I walked out into the hall. After two steps, I heard a faint sound like a door closing.

"Castriel?"

Déjà vu hit me. The situation repeated itself. Only this time I was far away from the kitchen and the sharp objects.

On tiptoe, I glided slowly and when I stood at the doorstep of the living room, I saw a figure. Standing by the window, in the background of the illuminated city, was Castriel. He was staring at something outside the window, lost in his own thoughts.

He appeared dressed as if he had just returned from the gym, wearing sweatpants and an undershirt.

His bare feet were spread wide apart, arms crossed.

"Cas?" I asked again.

Wherever he was now, he was far away.

Not wanting to startle him, I walked over and gently placed my hand on his biceps. He didn't turn around immediately, and that worried me.

"Castriel, sweetheart. What's wrong?"

In slow motion, Castriel blinked twice, closed his eyelids for a moment, and sighed. When he opened them, he gave me his full attention.

There was a battle going on inside him I had no idea about.

"I woke up, and you weren't here. Can you tell me where you were?"

My man's silence made my stomach turn.

Why doesn't he speak?

I watched, waiting for him to come out of this strange trance.

"Baby, say something. You're scaring me."

These words brought my man back to reality. He shook his head as if he couldn't believe it.

Then I noticed something else. As he shook his head, I noticed a mark on his neck. I reached my hand to the spot and removed the drop with my finger.

Castriel looked into my eyes and then at my outstretched finger. He stared at it like a hawk, so I did the same.

My eyebrows furrowed in confusion at what the hell was going on, and then I turned to the window. The lights from the surrounding buildings fell directly on my finger. Then I realized what I was looking at. It was a drop of blood. I rubbed my index finger and thumb together, and when I pulled them apart, I saw a dark red trail.

Slowly, I turned to face the man who crawled into my mind. He looked at me expectantly, with resignation in his eyes. Or perhaps it was a decision...

"Oh God, Castriel, that is blood. Are you all right? Are you hurt? Should I call a doctor? What—"

"Breathe, baby. I'm okay." When he said those words, relief washed over me.

"You scared me. What happened? Where have you been?"

"We need to talk," he announced in a serious tone. "But first I want you to meet someone."

"Okay. We'll do it first thing in the morning."

"No... We should go now."

"Now?" I didn't hide my surprise. "It's not even five in the morning. Where are we going at this hour?"

"I just want to introduce you to someone. It's important."

The whole situation was strange, to say the least. But I knew Castriel well enough to know that he wouldn't waste time on something meaningless. If he said it was important, it was.

"Okay, sweetheart. If it's important, I'll get dressed."

"Okay. I'll take a shower in the meantime and we'll be on our way in a minute."

Castriel turned on his heel and headed for our bedroom. He didn't wait for me, didn't say another word, didn't turn around. For the past few days, he hadn't walked away from me without giving me a peck on the lips first.

My heart knew something was wrong.

I rushed to the bedroom, put on my jeans and sweater, and returned to the living room.

A few minutes later, Castriel found me in the same spot by the window.

"Are you ready?" he asked with a small smile on his face.

He looked much better than he had a moment ago. Dressed in jeans and a black sweater, he looked alluring. Different, but seductive.

"Sure. We can go." It was time to put on my big girl pants and face what was so important to my man.

Moments later, Castriel pulled up in front of a large red brick building. The building looked old, but well kept. The surrounding lawn had been mowed, the flower beds cleaned, and the benches for passersby repainted.

A sign with the name of the place hung on the stone fence at the entrance, but enchanted by the view of the building, I paid little attention to it.

"What is this place?" I asked as Castriel parked the car.

He turned off the ignition, looked at the building, but remained silent. Just like all the way here.

My gaze landed at the building again. It resembled a hotel somehow, but was hardly one. Most of the windows were dark; only a few had lights on.

"Let's go, Isabelle."

We got out of the car and walked to the double front doors.

Just before entering, I felt the warmth of Castriel's hand wrap around mine. He intertwined our fingers, lifted my hand, and kissed it.

We walked inside and to my left, I noticed a woman sitting behind a large desk. With her glasses on the tip of her nose, she was staring at a book on the table. A knock on the door distracted her, and she looked at us. She was more than unimpressed.

"Mr. Russell. Nice to see you again," she said.

I almost rolled my eyes but stopped myself at the last moment.

"Hello, Greta. This is Isabelle, my friend."

"Good morning," I greeted her, and she replied with the same.

"Please continue, Greta. I won't be long. I just wanted to introduce my lady to him."

Him?

Greta nodded, and only when we were moving on did she start reading again.

Castriel led me deeper into the complex. Walking through the maze of corridors, I wouldn't know how to find the exit on my own. It was like a real labyrinth.

Finally, we stopped in front of a door at the end of one of the corridors. The oak door had the gilded number twenty-two decoration. Castriel stopped, looked me in the eye, and pressed the handle.

He led me into the room and closed the door behind us. The room looked a little like a hospital room. A bed was in the middle of the room, surrounded by various machines. In the corner was a table with two chairs. A wardrobe and a bookshelf stood next to each other against the wall.

My eyes fell on the wooden bed on which a man lay. He was sleeping.

"Isabelle," Castriel whispered. "This is Isaac."

Chapter 23

IZZY

The man lying on the bed seemed to be about my age, maybe a little older. A few strands of blond hair fell on his forehead. There was fresh stubble on his cheeks, unshaven for a day or two. But a light stubble suited him. His face was regular and looked young. I was sure that if he smiled now, he would look even younger. Certainly his smile would be charming. His closed eyes couldn't tell me anything.

He was asleep. Or rather, he was unconscious. The lower part of his body was covered with a sheet and a blanket. Under his white shirt were some tubes and wires. Perhaps they belonged to the device that controlled his vital signs. A tube was attached to his face, which hid in his mouth. The man was intubated. And that meant he wasn't breathing on his own at the moment. Both hands were on the bedding. A catheter was taped to one of them.

What was most alarming was the appearance of his skin. It was pale, grayish, and it seemed thin, almost translucent.

Castriel pulled my hand and, without taking my eyes off the man lying there, I took a few steps. He fixed a chair beside the bed. I looked at him, but once again, his face said nothing.

I sat on the chair as he came over from the other side. He leaned over the man and kissed him on the forehead. Then he brought another chair and sat down in front of me.

"Little I., please meet the woman who stole my heart. This is Isabelle."

I looked at the man and then back at Castriel. He looked at the man in the bed with love in his eyes and spoke to him as if he were standing in front of him.

"Isn't she the most beautiful woman you've ever seen?" Castriel continued. "I know she is, and I know I've told you this before, but it's the truth. If it occurred to you to steal her from me, I would have to beat you to a pulp."

I shuddered at his words. Was it appropriate to talk like that to a person who couldn't even breathe on his own? This sight alone caused pain in my heart.

"We've never fought for anything but for her, I would fight like a lion. She's my girl, who will be your sister-in-law one day... so it's not appropriate for you to have naughty thoughts..."

Castriel laughed and my breath caught in my throat. Not only had he said he was thinking about marriage, he said it to his... brother.

God...

Castriel's hand fell to Isaac's palm. He shook it firmly and didn't let go for the rest of our visit.

His gaze turned sad, as if he realized Isaac wasn't going to answer him.

I felt tears gathering at the back of my eyes and blinked several times.

I didn't know the man, but I did exactly what Castriel had done. I grabbed Isaac's other hand, if only to give him the feeling that someone was by his side.

Castriel noticed my gesture at once. His eyes rested on my embrace for a moment. Then he raised them, and I saw undisguised gratitude in them. He nodded at me and looked back at his brother.

Silence filled the room, and I had no intention of rushing anything. This was their moment.

Eventually Castriel spoke, this time to me.

"Isaac is my younger brother. My only brother. My mother left us first. I was eight years old. One day she decided that two children and a husband who worked from dawn to dusk were not the height of her dreams. She left us without ever looking back. As far as I know, she's living in Oklahoma with some drunken bastard. If those were her dreams, I'm glad she got to live them. She left us like we meant nothing to her and we never saw her again.

"Dad was all we had left. He was a good father; he took care of us, he tried to make up for what we lacked from our mother. He was diligent. I grew from a child to an adult overnight. Not because he wanted me to, but because my family needed it. While he worked, I learned to cook for us. While he made sure we had food on our plates, I cleaned and took care of my brother. I couldn't replace a woman at home for him, but I could take care of them as best I could, and I would..."

The first tears streamed down my cheeks. I knew so little about this man and there was so much to discover. Underneath that heavy armor, there was someone truly special.

"When she left, Isaac was less than two years old. It happened during the summer break. The problem came when I had to go back to school. Dad had to work. Who would take care of my little brother? Gina, our

217

neighbor, saw our problems and offered to help us. At first, Dad wanted to be proud, but it soon became clear that this wouldn't help us at all. So he gave in and gratefully accepted her offer. Gina worked shifts at the grocery store. When she worked the afternoon shift in the morning, she would take care of Isaac while I went to school. If she had the morning shift and there was no way for her to change, I would stay home. Gina lived alone with her mother. Her husband had been killed in the war. I had no idea how she had such a big heart, but I thanked her every chance I got for being with us. It wasn't all easy.

Soon my absences from school became a problem. My grades were low. The school started calling my father because they suspected I was skipping class. I don't know any eight-year-olds who skip school, but... We had another problem. My father arranged for fake medical documents to certify that I had kidney disease, and whenever my health required it, dialysis was necessary for me to survive. I have no idea how he arranged this. I never asked out of fear. It could have caused him so much trouble, and a father in prison was the last thing we needed. But I was afraid every day that it would come out and someone would knock on our door. Anyway, the document did the trick and the school let me out. If I had to stay home, they excused me without a problem. All I had to do was keep up my attendance as best I could and improve my grades. That's what I did. During the day, I took care of my brother, and at night I caught up on my schoolwork."

I rubbed my cheeks with my free hand. I really wanted to come up and hug my hero, tell him how much I loved him, what an amazing person he was, but I didn't want to interrupt him. So I stayed in my seat and listened to his life story.

"For a long time, we did the best we could to keep our heads above water. Isaac started kindergarten at four. We all greeted that time with a deep breath. Gina finally had time to rest and only helped when Isaac got

218

sick. I miraculously healed and started going to school like before. Dad became calmer about our lives. After school, I would pick up Isaac from kindergarten and we would go home together. At first, Gina came to pick us up because they didn't want to let my brother out with me, but later the kindergarten teachers gave us a break.

"Because of all this, I didn't grow up like a normal kid. While they were playing on the playground, I was playing at home. When my peers were partying and drinking beer in the corners, I was helping my brother study. I was grateful for the life we had and never complained. I was different, yes, but no one ever told me that to my face. Soon my body gained weight. I was taller than most of my classmates. No one wanted to mess with me. Besides, I was a loner, so this mysterious aura scared most kids.

"Our lives changed again when Dad got sick. Cancer. I was an adult by then. I started working wherever I could, took out a loan, and went to college. But the cancer attacked Dad's lungs aggressively. He didn't have a chance when we found out. As unfortunate as it sounds, I'm grateful that he didn't suffer very long. In the end, cancer took him and we were left alone. I was of age, so I took care of everything and got legal permission to take care of my brother. He was in a period of rebellion. He was angry all the time, at everything—at me, at our father, at our mother, at the world around him, even at himself.

"He did some stupid things and was threatened with legal consequences. To show off to his friends, he stole something from a store. Then he damaged property by smashing a storefront. I had school, work, and more problems on my mind. I was barely getting by. That's when I met Takashi Saurii. He saw potential in me that I didn't know I had. He helped my brother and me. All he wanted in return was a promise that when I graduated, I would apply for a job with him. And that's what happened."

Castriel looked at his brother without blinking an eye. He was here in body, but he was reliving these moments with his entire self.

"Isaac finally wised up, calmed down. When he was a senior in high school, I spoke to Takashi again. I was almost ready to repay my debt of gratitude. If he was surprised that I remembered, he didn't show it. But he did something I hadn't expected: he paid off the rest of my student loans. So, I took out another loan so Isaac could start college. A month after he started college, I packed my bags and flew to Japan to see Takashi.

"Things were going well again. Within a few months of working for Takashi, I'd paid off my debt. I was learning a new language, a new culture... I craved knowledge like another breath. I returned to see my brother whenever life and work allowed. Until tragedy struck.

"At the end of my sophomore year, Isaac went to a party..."

Tears streamed down Castriel's face. My heart was beating so hard it felt like it wanted to jump out of my chest. Everything hurt, but my heart hurt the most. It was breaking into a million pieces.

"At that party... Isaac was being bullied by some people at school, which I found out much, much later. These bastards had a great idea... That day, they apologized to him for their actions and then got him drunk. He also had some drugs in his blood, so one of them slipped him something. Or maybe he took it voluntarily. It doesn't matter anymore. One of them had an excellent idea for a game. This game is called Russian Roulette...

"Where did the old gun come from? Who had it? I don't know.

"So they sat down in a room in the house where the party was. All four of them and my brother..."

I froze.

That's when I knew.

"They all had fun, but I found out much later that Isaac didn't want to go. So they used group pressure and started taunting him. I don't know why he agreed. The game had simple rules. If the gun doesn't fire, you drink a round. When it was my brother's turn... he wasn't as lucky as the others. The fucking gun went off. He shot himself in the head."

A sob came out of my throat that I couldn't stop. I covered my mouth with my hand.

"And they ran away... They left him there. They left him to certain death. It was impossible not to hear a gunshot, so the people at the party began to run. One person found Isaac in a pool of blood, called 911... She stayed by his side until the paramedics took him to the hospital. She held his hand..."

Castriel's eyes found mine, though I couldn't see him clearly through the veil of tears.

"When they called me from the hospital, my brother was still alive. I returned as quickly as I could. The bullet had damaged his brain, but he survived. That is almost impossible, and yet... This time, I was left alone. Isaac never woke up after the surgery. The doctors couldn't tell how much damage he had suffered. They claimed that anything could happen when he woke up, but it never happened. He never raised his eyelids. I already had money that could help him. I moved heaven and earth to wake him up. I brought the most famous specialists in the world to America. No one could help us. Isaac has been sleeping ever since. The only thing keeping him alive is that damn machine."

"Surely something can be done," I whispered.

"No, Isabelle. There is nothing more to be done. Really nothing.

"I found the best center for Isaac that would take care of him day and night. I wanted to come back here permanently, but I had to finish some things first. I wanted to take him with me, but it was too risky for him. He might not have survived the transport. I returned to Japan with a heavy heart. Then Takashi got sick and I couldn't leave him alone. I owe him more than I can admit. His battle with cancer was terrible, and all I could do for him at that time was to take the burden of his company off his back. That company is his entire world, so I did what I could. On the ground, I did what I could for Takashi, while making sure from afar that Little I. didn't miss a thing. I always called him that: Little I.

"Such hatred consumed me that I couldn't recognize myself. Witnesses at the party pointed out four boys who had been partying with my brother that night. None of them admitted what really happened. None of them. In the end, the case was dropped because my brother had pulled the trigger himself. But I didn't forget it for a second. I've lived that moment for the past ten years of my life. I lived with that hatred and that desire for revenge. I only cared about what would happen to me after that. Until I met you."

"Castriel... What are you talking about, sweetheart?" I asked, frightened.

His eyes bored into my soul. I saw a pain in them that couldn't be described in words. He closed his eyes for a second and breathed. And when he opened them, the truth struck me straight in the heart.

"I was going to tell you the other day. I really wanted to, but I wasn't ready. It wasn't because of you that those guys died. It wasn't because of you..."

Suddenly, I understood what he meant.

It wasn't about me. It wasn't about my father.

"Thanks to them, you learned so many details."

Castriel nodded at my assumption.

"You were there then..."

Another nod.

"You only found two, so—"

"No. I found three. The media haven't found out yet."

I should have felt disapproval for what he had done. I should have felt disgust, want to report it to the police, want justice. But the police had failed, so he had to get justice himself. And I would keep his secret.

"I should let him go. I know I should. It's been ten years. His chances of survival are slim to none. I wanted him to live to see when justice would be served. I wanted to tell him I avenged the wrong done to him. I know he's there, trapped in his body. I promised myself that I would let him find peace afterward."

A fresh stream of tears ran down my face.

"And Isabelle... Thank you. Thank you for not abandoning my brother then and for holding his hand..."

CHAPTER 24

CASTRIEL

That evening, as I stood in the shower, the scene from the facility I took Isaac to before I even moved to New York, played out before my eyes once again.

When Isabelle realized I knew who had saved my brother's life that day, her eyes almost popped out of her head. At first she had no words, then she blushed and lowered her eyes.

"You don't know how grateful I am. If it wasn't for you... I wouldn't have the chance to sit by his side now."

"I'm sorry I couldn't do more. When did you find out I'd found him?"

"Just a few days ago. Connor told me who found Isaac. I couldn't believe it. How is that even possible?"

"Connor? Connor Blackwood?"

She lifted her eyes to mine and I nodded, waiting for her to say more.

"I remember him... Like through a mist, but I remember. He and his classmates were among the privileged students. I'm talking about the kind with buckets of money and connections on speed dial. That wasn't my crowd. But all the students knew about them. I avoided other people's attention, and by extension, theirs. Until that evening...

"One of my friends had a birthday and insisted that we go to the party. I didn't want to, but in the end I let her persuade me. I thought since my father was in prison, I would allow myself to live a normal student life for once. That's how I found myself there. It turned out that my girlfriend had peculiar tastes in fun. She was more interested in a threesome with a boyfriend and another friend, right after I turned her down. Then she decided and disappeared with them behind one of the doors on the first floor. I stood in the corner and pretended to be drinking and having a good time, even though I'd been holding a full cup for an hour. Anyway, I had to go to the bathroom, but there was a line downstairs, so I decided to try my luck upstairs. I was at the bottom of the stairs when I heard a shot..."

Isabelle's eyes went to my brother.

"There was complete chaos. People were running in panic. The music wasn't playing very loud, but at that moment it went completely silent. I don't know why I didn't run away like everyone else. Halfway down the stairs, the birthday girl walked past me and didn't even notice me.

"It was already quiet upstairs. No one was there. Most of the doors were wide open and only one was closed. Something pushed me into the room. I know how that sounds, Castriel, but I wasn't crazy. I felt I had to go in there, and when I did...

"I couldn't leave him when I called 911. I grabbed a T-shirt and balled it up and pressed it to his head. Like an idiot, I talked to him. I introduced myself, told him about myself as if he was sitting next to me and listening. I remember telling him that since I'd survived a fucked up psychopathic father, he would come out of it too. God..."

"They wouldn't let me go with him in the ambulance, so I took a cab to the hospital. I waited in the hall for hours and the doctor wouldn't tell me anything. I knew he'd survived, and that was a lot. I went back to the hospital the next day, and the next, and the next, but each time I heard they couldn't tell me anything. They would tell me that his brother was with him, and then I could breathe easier, knowing that he was no longer alone. The last day I was there, I learned he'd been moved to another hospital.

"As time went on, I realized that the money had spoken. After the interrogation, there was no trial. No one sat on the defendant's bench.

"I just realized that you're the brother who took care of him. I really didn't know before."

"I know, baby. I know. It's just so hard to believe that fate has brought us together again."

"I'm so sorry this happened to you and Isaac."

She looked as if she suddenly understood something. After a moment, she said, "I'm in love with you, Castriel…"

I smiled, and she had a wry look on her face.

"I love you too, Isabelle. For a long time. When I fell in love, I fell hard for you," I confessed.

"I'm sorry. I shouldn't say this now."

"You should. I know what you were trying to tell me."

The shower door swung open, and I felt Isabelle's presence behind me. I didn't lift my head from the rain of drops. I stood there, leaning against the wall, my mind full of memories.

For a moment, there was complete silence. I longed to feel her hands on me. I longed to kiss her, but for the last time in my life, I had to give her a way out.

"I've told you the story of my life because I want you to know who I really am, what kind of person I am, what terrible things I can do. But I'm still able to sleep peacefully. I didn't want and don't want your mercy. My soul is damned, and I will never receive absolution again."

I felt her hand on my shoulder. The warmth emanating from it brought relaxation, although I wasn't aware of how tense I was. Isabelle was like a balm to my soul.

"You're not a monster, Castriel," she whispered. "These people hurt your little brother for fun. Because of them, Isaac will never come back. He won't have the chance to live the life given to him. Like cowards, they left him and went on living as if nothing had happened. They should be punished, and I'm sorry the system failed them. You're not a monster, Cas, and if I were you, I'd do the same thing."

I felt my body shake. Her hands stroked my back.

"In the hospital, I said I was in love with you. I don't know how or when it happened. But I know you mean more to me than I can put into words. I won't tell anyone what I know—"

I turned to her and held her close, my face falling to the hollow of her neck. The damn smell of green apple... Her arms wrapped around my waist.

"I'm not worried about you telling anyone what I did. You don't have to vouch for me. My actions cannot be fully justified. I take someone's son from this world. I kill someone's husband, friend, and maybe even father. I'm not a good person, but I'm not afraid of being punished for it either."

"You're mistaken. Not everything is black and white. There are a thousand shades of gray."

"I love you, Isabelle. I know that it all happened quickly, that neither of us were even looking for love in our lives. I also know that I can't imagine a day without talking to you and a night without the warmth of your body beside me. I used to never look at the same woman twice, and now I can't see anyone but you. He feels the same way." I moved my hips to indicate who I meant. "You've spoiled him for others, and we're both happy about it."

Isabelle tilted her head and laughed.

"I was telling the truth to Isaac when I said you would be my wife. Not now, but one day it will happen."

I looked at her pink, tantalizing lips. When her tongue slipped from between her lips and she licked them, I felt myself harden. I leaned in and followed the same trail with my tongue. She tasted of something sweet and strawberry.

My new favorite taste.

I kissed her slowly. The rough sex with her was the best I'd ever had in my life. Gently caressing her, kissing her. That was something new for us.

Her back was against the wall when I turned her over. I kicked her legs apart and found myself between her thighs.

Home...

I grabbed her cheek with one hand and tilted her head to make it easier to reach her mouth while my other hand was on her breast. I teased her nipple with my palm, which hardened to the touch.

I loved the way this woman responded to me and I to her.

I took my hand off her cheek and attacked both breasts at once. I massaged them harder, then more softly. Isabelle's breathing became faster and shallower, then she finally rewarded me with a soft moan.

I made a few circles with my hips. The head of my cock teased the entrance to her hot pussy. Her nails dug into the skin of my arms. As I continued to kiss her, I hissed through my teeth, and she smiled in response.

My lioness.

I took a step back. Emerald eyes filled with wonder. Swollen lips lifted, begging for more. I rolled my eyes all over her body. She loved it when I looked at her like that. Goose bumps appeared on her skin as proof.

"On your knees," I growled, licking my lips.

She didn't obey my command at first. I had already noticed that she liked to resist, and she liked it even more when she was spanked for it. Watching her explore her sexual possibilities, limits, and lack thereof was like opening a gift layer by layer.

"For every hesitation you have, you're giving me something precious. I won't tell you what it is now. You'll find out soon enough. So what will it be, baby?"

In the blink of an eye, Isabelle dropped to her knees, though I could see intrigue and impatience in her eyes.

I took a step forward and stood right in front of her. She looked at my cock for a moment, licked her lips again, then returned to my eyes.

"You like what you see, don't you? Isabelle... You're made for me. Now close your eyes." She blinked again and again, but only obeyed my command when I added, "This is your second hesitation."

I took my cock in my hand and brought it to her lips, drawing it along with the perfect shape of her lips. She looked so beautiful, so tantalizing, that I wanted to mark her for the rest of her life.

"Open up and don't you dare touch yourself between your legs."

Isabelle obeyed, and I entered her throat. She immediately choked. She grabbed my thighs with her hands and tried to push me away, but to no avail. The first tear dripped from the corner of her eye.

"Swallow it all down," I said in a deep, lustful voice.

When she did just that, I could enter her deeper than before.

"Breathe through your nose. Swallow me again. I'm almost inside you."

A moan of protest came from inside her and I felt a vibration in my balls. I let her breathe and pushed forward. She swallowed me with difficulty, but I realized that it was her bonds that were talking, not her.

I slid in and out. Slowly, I fucked her throat. At the same time, I stroked her head. I turned the rain shower on her, but despite the warm water, she was shivering. She was shivering from desire, from excitement, not from the cold.

I stroked her wet hair and when she opened her eyes, I saw joy in them. From time to time, I complimented her on how well she was doing, how perfectly she was taking care of me. She liked it. She enjoyed being mine.

As I felt the orgasm building inside me, coming closer and closer, I thrust into her throat a few more times and then pulled out.

Isabelle kneeled down, shaking.

"Stand up and put your hands on the wall," I told her.

I helped her to stand slowly as her legs were like jelly. As she straightened up, a wry smile filled her mouth and her rebellious eyes sparkled.

"That's three." My hand came down on her bottom with a loud smack.

Isabelle jumped to her feet, turning her back to me. A second later, her hands were on the wall. This time, I didn't have to help her. She spread her legs wide and let me know what she needed from me.

"Are you ready?" I asked.

"God, yes."

I grabbed her sweet ass and pulled her hips toward me. Her back arched.

My taut cock was hard and ready, and I didn't need to tell him which way to go.

I entered her with one deep thrust. Isabelle screamed like a horny wild animal. She put her head on my chest.

Without stopping my movements in and out of her, I played with her nipples. Twisting my fingers left and right, I drove her crazy.

I began to move to my rhythm. Her beautiful ass met my every stroke. We slowly approached the moment when...

"Please, Castriel... Please... Oh, God... Don't stop!"

It doesn't matter.

I couldn't stop fucking her even if a fucking earthquake started.

I took the shower head off the handle, turned the knob from rain shower to pulsating shower. Isabelle, in her oblivion, didn't even notice what I was doing.

When the first wave of water hit her clit, her scream echoed throughout the bathroom. She immediately trembled like a little bird as wave after wave brought her new sensations.

I felt the walls of her pussy smother my cock with each thrust. She was already close.

"Oh, fuck! Cas!"

I entered her hard and stopped as Isabelle went over the edge with another scream. I felt her orgasm take her breath away as her legs refused to obey.

I let go of her hips to wrap my arms around her waist and support her. I moved the headset away from her sensitive pussy and let her quietly ride out the last wave of orgasm.

I waited a moment, and when her breathing settled, I leaned into her ear. "One down, two to go."

Tired, she turned her face to mine, not understanding what I meant. Then, without a shred of mercy, I brought the showerhead to her clit for a second time and moved inside her.

"What are you doing?" Isabelle whimpered.

"Giving you a multiple orgasm."

"You're kidding me—" A moan that escaped her lips cut her words short.

I wasn't kidding at all. Not about my girl. Not about her or her orgasms.

If I didn't focus completely on her, her moans alone would bring me to my climax. I wanted to feel every one of her orgasms on my cock, so I had to be patient.

We didn't have to wait long for the second orgasm. She was so sensitive after the first one that the second one built up at a rapid pace. As she came, she slapped her hand against the wet tiles on the wall. She moaned and bent over backward, my name on her lips.

The shower handle went sideways.

Pride filled me. I was the only man who could satisfy this woman. I would be the only one to have that privilege.

"That's two, baby. There's one left."

"Castriel, I can't do it anymore. I can't do it anymore. Please don't..."

"Shhh... You can do it, Isabelle."

A fresh wave of water hit her pussy.

This time we came together. I kissed her bare back while she screamed. The last orgasm took away any remaining strength. I carried her, still wet, from the shower to the bedroom. As we sank onto the bed together and she cuddled up to me, I don't know if five minutes passed before soft snoring filled our bedroom.

Chapter 25

IZZY

With her round belly, Emma looked like the most delicious muffin. She was beautiful, alluring, and sweet.

Life had been so messed up lately... Em also had her own errands and responsibilities, so meeting her was a miracle. But this time it worked.

We arranged for her to pick me up at Media Linc at noon. She walked proudly out of the entrance, with rosy cheeks and a bright aura around her, smiling from ear to ear. Dressed in a flowing dress that accentuated her curvy stomach, her blond hair seemed to stand out even more.

"Izzy Knox! My famous best friend. Godmother and aunt to my unborn daughter Aurora! I missed you!" she shouted across the hall before she even reached my desk.

Her voice pulled me away from the document on my desk. I felt a huge smile appear on my face. I squealed with excitement and ran to greet her. I jumped out from behind the desk and in two steps, I was standing in front of her with my arms open.

I hugged her tightly, spun her around, and hugged her again.

"You look wonderful, Em. The blessed state suits you."

"What doesn't suit you is being a stranger. Even though you look beautiful, you've lost weight and you look sleep deprived, like someone kept you awake half the night." She chuckled and winked at me.

You have no idea, girl.

I let her out of my arms, grabbed my purse from the cabinet under the desk, and we were off.

Instead of finding a place to have lunch, we ended up at our favorite coffee shop. Unable to decide, Em opted for juice and two kinds of muffins, while I ordered coffee and strawberry cheesecake.

We sat in silence for a while, just looking at each other.

"I can do this all day, you know? I have tons of patience now," she said with a giggle.

"Oh, shut up. Your threats don't affect me. Tell me how my niece feels."

"We'll both feel better when she pops out of my belly."

"Are you okay? I'm such a shitty friend that I didn't even ask first."

Emma answered about all the things I had missed lately. She was happy as Mason's wife and a mother-to-be, and I was happy that her life had turned out that way.

"So, how's the foundation going?" I asked.

"It's a lot of work. I didn't even realize it. I organized three major centers that will raise money. A TV station will broadcast the event in one day. We'll have an online auction with donors like movie stars, singers, and athletes. I want to gather as many local volunteers as possible."

"That sounds wonderful. How can I help?"

"So far, nothing. I want to do as much as I can before the baby arrives, and then free time will be a luxury. Anyway, I'm already working on online platforms, gathering people by introducing them to my idea of helping. The awareness that everyone can help is growing. Social media has picked up speed as people follow my every move in this cause. Things are really coming together."

"I'm happy for you," I said with a smile.

"You'd better tell me what's going on with you."

Two weeks had passed since Castriel and I had been with Isaac. That time was quiet. My father hadn't contacted me again. Another photo shoot was behind us. Twice during this time, I woke up alone in the middle of the night. Each time, I was afraid that something would happen to him.

Despite my questions, he refused to tell me the identity of the last person to hurt his brother. He would look at me strangely but would never answer. Then something restless would creep under the surface of my skin.

Those two weeks were also filled to the brim with sex. Castriel was insatiable, and I was no better. I still couldn't get enough of his taste, his smell, his skin under my fingers.

"It's all good, Em," I said.

"Don't even try to float me with something like that. You haven't said anything to me in a while. You're closed up tight like a tin of sardines. I don't like it. I feel you're pushing me away. What is this all about?"

"A lot has been going on lately. I really didn't mean to push you away. On the one hand, the photo shoots, on the other, still working for your husband. The whole move to Castriel—"

My friend's squeal filled the cafe. Several people looked at us like we were crazy.

"What did you say? Moving to Castriel's?"

Huh...

Living with my man had become so natural to me that I forgot I hadn't told her about it.

"Shh..."

"What the hell? Why don't I know anything?" Her radiant face changed to an offended one.

God, I really suck as a friend. How am I going to explain all this to her now?

"I'm sorry, Em, that I didn't tell you before. Castriel has a phobia about my safety, so one day he told me to pack my things and... He sort of moved me into his apartment. And that's basically how it's been so far."

Her brow furrowed, as if she were thinking about a difficult math problem. "So you live as roommates?"

"Not exactly... We were kind of close before that. There's no way around what I'm about to say, so I'll just say it. I fell in love with him."

"What the fuck? When did all this happen? And where was I? Was I abducted by a UFO or something?"

I wiped my face with my hand. She was right. I had kept her out of the loop for too long.

"It all started practically before the first photo shoot..." I told her my and Castriel's story from the beginning.

At the news that I had finally found the big O in bed, she started bouncing up and down in her chair. She was even happier that I was.

"Wait, wait, wait... You said that Castriel has a phobia about your safety. What does that mean?"

Fuck. Did I say that? I must have, since she picked it up.

I sighed and looked at her. I didn't want to do this. I didn't want to drag her into this.

"Em, I don't want you to get upset in your condition," I said.

"Do you think I can turn off my emotions just because I'm pregnant?" she asked. "It doesn't work that way. You not wanting to upset me makes me upset."

"Promise me you'll take it easy."

She nodded eagerly.

I knew it was time to tell her the truth about me. As gently as I could, I told her everything. Everything about my relationship with my father.

"I... God, Izzy, I don't know what to say," she whimpered, a horrified look on her face.

"You promised me you wouldn't get upset. For the baby's sake, take a few deep breaths."

"You tell me that my best friend is in mortal danger, that her psychopathic father could strike at any moment, and you expect me to take deep breaths?"

"Therefore, I didn't want to tell you now," I muttered. "You're in an advanced stage of pregnancy. You shouldn't—"

"Don't tell me what I should or shouldn't do!" Her snarl froze the atmosphere. "I'm sorry. I'm sorry, honey. It's just—"

"I know, Em. You don't have to apologize. I just want the best for you and the baby."

"That's why Castriel wanted you to live with him. He knows everything. He knew everything before your best friend? Where is your feminine honor?"

"If it helps, I didn't want to involve anyone. He's so damn perceptive it scares me sometimes. He saw the details of this puzzle and kept at it until he knew and put it all together. I'm sorry you didn't find out first, but by the time my past caught up with me, you were already pregnant. The last thing I wanted to do was spoil this wonderful time for you. And yes, that's why we moved in together. Before I knew it, we were a couple in love up to our ears."

"I'm thrilled for you. You deserve someone who will put you first. I had mixed feelings about him, but if he brings you happiness, that's all I can ask for. But never keep such details from me again."

"Em, this is all for your safety. Please understand me."

"I understand. I also remember how you kept me safe last year. You followed me at night when I went to the park to meet Dusk. You dragged the whole cavalry behind me to George's house. I love you, but don't protect me from the truth, please."

"You're pregnant. That's a different situation."

"I realize that. I'm not saying I'm going to pick up a gun and go to open war with your father. I can protect you in other ways."

It was almost impossible to win an argument with her. Maybe she was right. Maybe not.

"I love you too," I countered, and Emma replied with a smile.

Despite the heavy topics, it was wonderful to spend this time with my best friend. As we parted in front of the office building, tears streamed down her face. Emotions and hormones had done their work.

***

I finished work later than usual that day. As I left work, dusk was falling. The crowd on the street had thinned out. I wanted to get home as quickly as possible. I saved a little bit of the street by walking through the park.

That's when I first felt something was wrong, but I told myself it was just my imagination.

The blood in my veins grew colder. I rushed through the trees. The street was lit by lanterns, but I felt that someone was behind me. I looked over my shoulder but saw no one.

Was it just my paranoia? Maybe talking to Emma had brought it on.

The muscles of my entire body tensed as I heard a deafening thud behind me. I stood still in the middle of the alley and turned around. My alarmed eyes scanned my surroundings. No one was there, nothing was moving. I was alone.

I started walking again but took out my cell phone and punched in numbers.

One, two, three beeps and nothing. The voice mail came on, but I hung up and dialed again. Again, nothing.

In the background, I heard a branch breaking. I sped up and hit "Redial." I didn't want to panic and get paranoid. I knew I would calm down as soon as I heard his voice.

"Hello? Are you okay, baby?" I was right. Castriel's voice had that effect on me. I took a deep breath and looked back.

"I'm heading home. I had a strange feeling, as if someone was following me. I heard something behind me. I got a little scared."

"Where are you?"

"I'm almost out of the park. Don't ask me why I went this way. I made a mistake, but I was tired and wanted to see you as soon as possible."

"I have to take care of something right now, but everything is fine. You're safe. You have Shadow."

"I have what?"

"A shadow. A person who protects you from the shadows. He's probably the one you heard behind you. We'll talk about it later, okay?"

"Okay, okay, I'll see you later."

"Bye."

Beep, beep, beep...

Castriel hung up. I didn't know who this shadow was, although Castriel's words reassured me. If his job was to keep me safe, then perhaps it was indeed his presence I felt behind me.

I put the phone in my pocket and shook off my paranoid thoughts.

I took a few steps and finally saw the streetlight through a thicket of trees. That's when I heard another thud, as if something metal had hit the path. I stood as if struck and my lungs held their breath. In an instant, all the birds broke from the trees and took to the sky. There weren't many, but still…

I turned back in the direction I had come. There was silence. I didn't see anyone. My intuition told me that something was wrong.

I took out my cell phone and hit Castriel's number again. After a few slow signals, the voice mail continued.

"Baby," I whispered. "I have a feeling something is terribly wrong. I can feel it, Cas. I can't see your Shadow. There doesn't seem to be anyone here with me. God, I'm getting paranoid… I turned on the GPS locator on my phone, just in case. I'll probably be home by the time you call back. We can laugh about this later. I love you—"

"Hang up."

Something cool touched the back of my head. A gun… And that voice… I knew that voice. It haunted me in my nightmares.

My heart pounded as if possessed. A chill ran through my entire body.

For a moment, I stood paralyzed, still holding the phone to my ear.

"Now," he growled again.

I slowly pulled the phone away from my ear and pressed the red button.

If my life was going to end here, I couldn't let him shoot me in the back. I wouldn't die like a coward. If it was going to happen, he had to look me in the eye first.

I turned to him. There he was: my father. I hadn't seen him in many years, but he hadn't changed much since the last time I saw him. His dark hair was streaked with silver. The once gentle eyes were now hard as steel. A few wrinkles had appeared on his face, but his athletic figure hadn't changed at all.

I was now facing the person who had killed my mother and caused me a lifetime of fear. I hated him more than I had ever hated anyone in the world. I wanted him dead; I wanted him to free me from himself. A quick death would have been a pardon for him. He deserved much, much more.

He took a step back without stopping, aiming at my face.

Not bad, Daddy.

"Drop the phone on the ground. In my direction."

I didn't want to do that. God, how else was Castriel going to know where I was?

"Drop it, I said!"

I did as he told me. I threw it under his feet and, almost in slow motion, I saw my father raise his leg and smash his heel down on the screen. I blinked, feeling like I was on my own.

Aiming at me, he bent down, picked up the broken phone, and put it in his pocket.

"You have changed, daughter. You have become a beautiful woman. Your mother would be proud." His deep voice sent shivers down my entire body.

"Never mention my mother again," I said with undisguised hatred. "You killed her, you motherfucker."

"Yeah... I did. Don't forget that you carry me in your genes, daughter."

"I don't have a single bone in my body that came from you. I'm not your daughter anymore, and you're not my father. You're nobody to me."

"Yet. Your opinion has little to do with reality. Go on..." He pointed the way out of the park.

"I'm not going anywhere with you."

"You'll come with me voluntarily, or I'll be forced to do you harm here. But I thought you wanted to know the truth about my life. Besides, this park gives me the creeps. Go ahead."

I still didn't want to stand with my back to him, but again, I had no choice. If I wanted to survive, I had to play by his rules. Only now I was on my own; Castriel wouldn't be able to track me.

I would have to kill him myself...

I walked past him, heading for the exit. I had gone only a few steps when I felt a pinch in my shoulder, as if a mosquito had bitten me. Immediately, I felt the heat covering my body. My legs became so heavy that they couldn't hold my body upright. I fell backward as my father's hands caught me behind my back and below my knees. I lifted my increasingly heavy eyelids. As if through a haze, I saw his eyes.

"Good night, princess."

CHAPTER 26

CASTRIEL

I had been watching this bastard for several days. For my taste, I already knew him too well. Still, I deepened my knowledge of his schedule and his life.

I had already planned everything, every day, every hour. Something inside me wouldn't let me rest.

Before noon, I couldn't stand it any longer and made a phone call.

"Hello," came the voice in the receiver after the second beep, as if he had been waiting for my call.

I didn't say a word because I didn't know what to say. Why was I calling? What was I expecting?

I thought of Isabelle. My heart beat faster. *When she finds out, it will be too late. Will she look at me differently? Will she hate me?*

Would I be able to give up my plan for her?

"I'm here, son. Whatever you need, I'm here. Even if you need silence in company."

"I'm close."

"I know, I can feel it. Has doubt gotten to you?"

Takashi was the only man on the planet who knew about my plans. He had helped me so much in my life that I could never repay him. He also never judged me.

"It's not really a doubt. I don't really know what it is myself," I replied, closing my eyes for a moment. In my mind, I saw the image of Isabelle sleeping peacefully in my bed.

"It's about a woman," he guessed. "Isabelle, is that right?"

"Yes, Isabelle..."

"She's close to you."

"Very close," I confirmed.

"She already knows everything?"

"Yes. She's the one who saved my brother that night. I found out that she was at the fraternity house and found Isaac. She was the one who held his hand while he waited for the ambulance."

"Fate has an interesting way of putting two people in its path. Doesn't it?"

I thought about his words. He was right; what were the chances that we would meet after so many years, in a completely different place, and I would pass her by a hair? I could have passed her in the hallway, in the doorway; we could have taken the elevator together... And I wouldn't have even known that it was her I should be thanking.

Would I have given her my attention? Probably, if I had been aware of the world around me at all.

"Are you afraid of losing her?" Takashi asked again.

"That is a possibility. She could have made better choices in her life. She could have someone good at her side."

Takashi's soft laughter reached my ears. "There are two types of good people: those who have died and those who haven't yet been born."

There was truth in his words. I recalled Isabelle's words about the thousand shades of gray. But now it was a little different.

"I've waited for this for so many years. Do you have any more Japanese wisdom for me?"

"Yes, I do," he replied. "A man of honor takes revenge even after ten years. You have bided your time, my son. It's up to you whether you end it with revenge in your heart or free yourself and your brother from the ghosts of the past."

Honor... Was I a man of honor? I promised my brother I was. His wrongs would feed on the wrongs of his persecutors. He deserved peace...

"Takashi—"

"You don't have to say anything, son. You're welcome. After all is done, give me a video call so I can meet this wonderful woman."

"I will," I vowed, and the line went silent.

***

Sometimes the simplest plan is the best plan.

It was dusk when I knocked. I heard footsteps coming from the apartment and the door swung open and I was face to face with my target.

"Mr. Russell," he greeted me with a nod. "Please come in."

Without forcing myself to be polite, I crossed the threshold, walked past him, and stood in the middle of his living room. I hadn't come here to admire his designer tastes, but I had to admit that he had set himself up stylishly.

I turned to him as he stood a few steps away from me. Face to face. I stared at him, unable to believe that I had been so close to the bastard all this damn time.

I should have killed him a long time ago. But then I would have done it for completely different reasons.

"I'll be honest. Your call surprised me, but it also intrigued me." He shifted from foot to foot, just to show how uncomfortable the encounter was for him.

"Bradley Donovan..." I said his name slowly. It tasted like poison on my tongue and was the sweetest thing under the sun at the same time.

"You know me. How can I help you?"

"Before I get to that, I want to talk to you a little. Has life been good to you after college?"

"I can't complain, thank you. You could say I was born under a lucky star. When I set a goal in life, I achieved it. If I encountered obstacles along the way, I crushed them." His joke seemed funny to him. Destroying my brother and then silencing the issue had been one such obstacle to his bright future.

"So you became a model, made a lot of money, created the future you dreamed of..."

"Maybe not exactly, but mostly, yes. For a while after college, I worked with my father in his company. But corporate life wasn't for me."

"Didn't you enjoy the privileged life under Daddy's thumb?"

My question surprised him. He scratched his neck in embarrassment. "I'm not saying there weren't benefits..."

"Benefits... I want you to be completely honest with me. Is there anyone, anything that could negatively affect your image or the image of the company? Maybe some past events? Wrongs?"

He paced again, looking around the room.

BINGO, motherfucker!

"No. Nothing I know of can bite me in the ass."

This time I laughed. "Appropriate choice of words."

Just then, my phone started vibrating in my pocket. I pulled it out and saw Isabelle's name on the screen. I ended the call and hid it. Almost immediately, it started vibrating again. I muted it, but my girl was persistent.

"Excuse me for a second," I said, taking a few steps away for privacy. "Hello? Are you okay, baby?"

"I'm heading home. I had a strange feeling, like someone was following me. I heard something behind me. I got a little scared."

I heard a hint of panic in her voice. "Where are you?"

"I'm almost out of the park. Don't ask me why I went this way. I made a mistake, but I was tired and wanted to see you as soon as possible."

My heart beat harder. I loved this woman madly. She had no idea how much. Her words of how much she missed me brought a smile to my face.

I glanced over my shoulder at Brad. He was standing motionless in the same spot, looking at his phone. "I have to take care of something urgent right now, but everything is fine. You're safe. You have Shadow."

"I have what?" she asked in confusion, sucking in air loudly.

"A Shadow. A person who protects you from the shadows. He's probably the one you heard behind you. We'll talk about it later, okay?" I said in a hushed voice.

"Okay, okay, then I'll see you later."

"Bye."

I ended the call and turned back to Brad.

"Where were we? Uh, you were about to tell me about the ghosts from your past."

"I was just telling you there aren't any—"

The phone vibrated again. This time I didn't mute it, didn't reject it, just let the call go to voicemail.

Brad looked at me expectantly.

Suddenly, an icy shiver ran through my body. A feeling came over me that something was very, very wrong. I felt like my whole body was paralyzed. I couldn't get my voice out; I couldn't move. I felt like my heart had stopped. I concentrated on feeling my heartbeat, but to no avail.

A headache started, as if someone was drilling through my skull. I closed my eyes and saw my girl's smiling face.

At first, I couldn't understand what was wrong until I saw her face.

I opened my eyes and took my cell phone out of my pocket. On the screen was an alert with a new voice message. I pressed the receiver to listen to it.

"*Baby,*" Isabelle's voice said. "*I feel something is terribly wrong. I can feel it, Cas. I can't see your shadow. There doesn't seem to be anyone here with me. God, I'm getting paranoid... I turned on the locator on my phone, just in case. I'll probably be home by the time you call back. We can laugh about this later. I love you—*"

"*Hang up.*"

The voice that said that belonged to a man. It wasn't very loud, but clear enough for me to understand the words. After these words, there was silence and the message ended.

With a glance at Brad, I entered the app that tracked her phone. Isabelle had come up with the idea a few weeks ago.

The location showed that she was heading north. She wasn't home at all.

I dialed her number, but it went to voicemail. Her phone was off.

Another wave chilled my body.

Isabelle...

FUCK!

I promised her... I promised her I would protect her from that motherfucker, that she was in no danger.

I stared at the moving point on the map.

No!

I punched in the number for Shadow, but only got his voicemail.

I raised my eyes to Brad, who was watching me like a hawk. Something told me something was wrong with this man.

I didn't know if he saw the fear in my eyes or something else, but a small smile appeared on his face.

What the fuck? Get a grip on yourself!

Easier said than done.

My hands were shaking. I had to go after Isabelle. I couldn't let her father finish the job from years ago. I couldn't let him hurt my baby! There was no way that bastard was going to take her away from me.

The phone showed the location, so I had no time to waste.

Brad's smile grew wider. I wanted to kill him right there and then, but I couldn't. Not after all these years of waiting for a moment of fun with him.

I faced a choice: Isabelle or Brad. The decision was more than easy, but I wouldn't leave the idiot behind.

I ran my hands over my jacket as if to iron out invisible wrinkles. I tucked one hand into my pocket and forced a smile. I approached him just enough to keep us a step apart.

"Brad, my friend. Unfortunately, circumstances are forcing me to postpone the problem I came here to solve."

I pulled my left hand out of my pocket and before he knew what was happening, I jabbed the needle into his shoulder. Seconds later, the contents of the syringe were already in his bloodstream.

I pulled it back as he grabbed his arm in shock.

"What the fuck? What did you inject me with?"

"It's nothing, my friend. You'll feel better soon. We're going to get some air."

"Really? I love rides!" Overjoyed, he clapped his hands. The drug was already working.

I looked down at the phone impatiently. I was wasting my time!

"Let's go. If we meet anyone, remember that we're best buddies. Aren't we?"

"Of course we are! You're my best friend, Cas!"

I gritted my teeth at the diminutive of my name. What an idiot.

Riding down in the elevator, I came up with a new plan of action. In the car, I would have to give him another dose to knock him out. Fortunately, he would now cooperate like a sheep going to slaughter.

Pushing him, I guided him to my car. I opened the trunk first. I was reaching into my pocket for another dose to knock him out when his words caught my attention.

"He won't hurt her," he told me in a hushed voice, as if confessing a secret. "He promised me that." He nodded several times for emphasis.

I saw red! Knowing that I had just reached the limit of my patience, I placed the cap on the needle. My hands clenched themselves into a fist as I swung and struck him with all my might. He fell cold to the ground, immediately unconscious.

I spat on him, wishing I could do it a second time right now. It felt good.

I looked around the underground garage where I had parked using the app Isabelle had given me. Scanning the iris was a breeze, since all I had to do was attach a photo of it to the reader in the right approximation. It was embarrassing.

I grabbed Brad by the shoulders and dragged him to the passenger door. Another change of plans. Sleeping Beauty could still be useful to me when he woke up. I threw him in the seat and slammed the door. Then I closed the trunk and got in.

Moments later, I was speeding through the city with my foot on the gas. Now and then, I looked down at my phone to check Isabelle's location.

Where the hell is he taking her?

I hoped she was okay. In my mind, I asked God not to take her away from me. I hadn't been a believer for many, many years, but at that moment, God seemed to be the only one who could hear my pleas.

Take care of yourself, baby. I'm on my way to get you!

It took me at least an hour to catch up. The car wasn't in perfect shape and it wasn't sporty. If my ass was on a motorcycle right now, I would have caught them a lot faster, but it was what it was.

We had no idea that Brad was part of the puzzle.

I had been driving for a good half hour when the distance between us suddenly closed.

"What the..."

The dot on the screen stood still and didn't move for a few minutes.

"No, no, no... Hang on, baby."

Brad moaned something unintelligible. I looked at him out of the corner of my eye. His head leaned against the side window and saliva was dripping from the corner of his mouth. I knew the drug I had given him had relaxed his muscles to some extent. I hoped he wouldn't pee in the car.

We continued to approach the spot where Isabelle was.

"What? Where are we... we're..." Brad opened his heavy eyes and looked around.

"Sit still. It's not far now."

"Cas... my best friend. Have I told you I love you?"

If I could throw up without stopping right now, I would do it with undisguised pleasure.

"Yeah, yeah..." I rasped.

"What's wrong? My cheek hurts... And my nose... And my head all over..."

"You fell down. I had to help you into the car."

"Really? Thank you."

"I have an idea. Let's play a game. I'll ask you a question and you answer the truth. A fun game?" A conversation like a therapy session.

"Oh, that's just fun. Go ahead."

I checked the card and started. "You said he promised you he wouldn't hurt her. Who promised you that?"

"Well, he did. Duh." He rolled his eyes for effect.

"Who won't he hurt?"

"My Izzy, you know? I fell in love."

"You're doing great. Why are you helping him?"

Brad fell silent and pursed his lips like a three-year-old, then shook his head. "You'll be mad if I tell you, so I won't," he said.

"Friends don't keep secrets. Remember?"

"I know. I just wanted Izzy all to myself. I was supposed to help him get to talk to his daughter and in return, he was supposed to take care of you so you wouldn't get in my way with Izzy. You shouldn't steal your friend's girlfriend. It's not nice."

My nerves might not be able to take this, crossed my mind. The upside was that all the pieces of this puzzle were slowly falling into place.

"I know. Do you know where he took her?"

"To a quiet place. But that's a secret too."

"A secret like the Russian Roulette with Isaac?"

Brad gasped. "I wasn't supposed to tell anyone, but I can trust you. Now you're going to carry this secret with you. It's strange that I told you about it, because we were never supposed to talk about it again. How did the game go for me?"

"You're unbeatable at it," I complimented him. My indifference was met with his happy squeal.

Hang on, baby. It isn't far now.

With maybe a few miles to go, I was almost at my destination. When the navigation announced that I had arrived, I braked and pulled over to the side of the road.

I looked around. We were sitting on the side of the road in the middle of a soggy forest. Thick trees towered over us. Just the road and the trees. No sign of cars or people.

"There's nothing here," I said, concluding that this was where the range broke off.

"Of course there's nothing here, silly, because it's farther away."

I turned toward Brad so fast my neck hurt.

He smiled dully at me.

"What did you say?"

"That it's farther. There's the road to the bunker."

To the bunker?

"Will you show me where it is?"

"Of course! What do you have friends for?"

I stepped on the gas and slowly pulled away from the side of the road. After a few yards, Brad held out his hand and pointed to a side road that led into the deep. I turned into it and indeed, a few yards away, in the shade of trees and bushes, I saw a black pickup truck. It wasn't visible from the highway. I would never have noticed it if I hadn't had Brad as a guide.

.

CHAPTER 27

CASTRIEL

Taking advantage of Brad's distraction, I retrieved my Glock and a small flashlight from the safe compartment under the seat. I had a second gun, and a hunting knife tucked under my pant leg.

We left the car in the same spot as Hansen's pickup. It occurred to me to slash his tires. But I was wasting my time, and I suspected it wouldn't be easy to move with a stoned Brad at my side.

I was damn right, because now and then he would admire a plant, a crooked tree, or a bird that shit right next to him. I should have killed him and gotten it over with, but there was too much risk that I wouldn't find the damn bunker on my own.

"Focus, Brad. Where is the bunker?"

"Not far, bro. I've only come across it twice here. I don't remember exactly."

I turned on my heel and grabbed him by the shirt. "Listen to me, bro. If we don't make it, he's going to kill Isabelle, do you understand? Move faster or no one will get out of that fucking bunker alive!"

"No, he won't hurt her. He promised me that…"

I rolled my eyes and let him go. I would rather deal with a four-year-old than him in this state.

"Don't you miss her? Don't you want to see her as soon as possible? If you love her so much, we should hurry."

"You're right. You're right."

He nodded for better effect, but at least he felt motivated as he moved forward, almost running.

After a few minutes, he pointed with his finger. "There, see that tree lying down? It's over there!"

Of course I saw that tree, like many others we had passed on the way. At first glance, I wouldn't have thought there could be anything there. But when we got close enough, I saw that under the broken tree was a small hill with a dark hollow.

I let Brad lead the way as we walked inside. The brick walls smelled musty and gave off a chill. Something smelled like it had died here a long time ago.

There was complete silence inside.

What if this is some kind of trap?

I pulled the gun out of my waistband and held it to Brad's back. He immediately became quiet but, I suspected, more because his brain hadn't yet processed what was happening than out of fear.

With my other hand, I grabbed the flashlight. I didn't want to be surprised in this bunker.

"What are you—"

"Shut up!" A low growl escaped my throat. "Shut up from now on and lead me to this bastard."

"My friend—"

I clicked off the safety on the gun.

"I'm going, I'm going."

Brad led me down the brick stairs. The stench in here was so intense it made me sick. He led us down another hallway until we reached what looked like a room.

I lit up the room with a flashlight and looked around every corner. There was nothing but piles of junk and crumbling newspapers.

Then I heard a rustling in the background, as if someone was moving something, and then a voice, very indistinct. My eyes found an alcove leading to another corridor.

"Don't squeal, or I'll kill you," I warned Brad.

We walked slowly, as quietly as possible.

The closer we got, the clearer the voice became. It was a man's voice. Brad was right; I would find Michael here.

I turned off the flashlight.

The hallway led into another room with the glow of lanterns on the floor. Standing on the threshold before we emerged from the shadows, I whispered, "Stop. Not another step, not another word."

Brad was shaking all over. For a moment, I thought it was my words that scared him, but it wasn't that. What scared him was what he saw inside.

There were three tables and several chairs scattered across the floor. One of these chairs was placed in the middle of the room—and Isabelle sat on it. Her white dress was now stained dark with dirt. Beautiful red curls covered her face as her head hung limply. Just as he had done with her ankles, her arms were folded back and likely tied to the chair.

I held my breath as I watched her. I was looking for the slightest movement, even a rise in her chest, as proof that she was alive. My heart was pounding like it was about to jump out of my chest, blood boiling inside me. My fingers clenched into fists. Only when she made a brief movement of her head could I breathe again. She was alive.

I looked in Hansen's direction. He looked similar to the photos I had found online, maybe a little older. He was dressed in dark jeans, a black T-shirt, a black jacket, and combat boots. His face was clean shaven, with the first signs of aging in his dark hair. All that stood out were his eyes.

He looked at my Isabelle with dark eyes, hungry for revenge and blood. I had seen that look more than once. I had seen it when I looked in the mirror.

When Isabelle moved her head again, Michael's hand slipped forward, and only then did I notice that he was holding a gun in it. Everything froze for me.

CHAPTER 28

IZZY

The first thing I thought was that I was in hell. Pain pulsed in every cell of my body. I groaned when I moved my head, feeling like something was trying to rip my skull from the inside out.

My hands were bent backward. I tried to move them, but I was still too weak. I also tried to move my legs, but to no avail.

What's happening?

My head hung like that of a broken doll. I had no strength to lift it.

Memories came back to me.

I was at work...

I was walking through a forest... No, it wasn't a forest... It was a park.

I called out to Castriel.

The memory of my father's eyes came back to me. Oh, God...

I struggled to raise my head, but the throbbing pain wouldn't let up. My muscles protested as if they had run a marathon. My mouth was dry as paper. I felt cold pouring over me, followed by heat.

Finally, on the third try, I tilted my head back. I moved my fingers, and some sensation returned. This was a good sign.

My eyelids opened with some difficulty. Yellow light illuminated the room, and I was grateful it wasn't too bright.

"Wake up, my little princess." My father's voice seemed closer than I would have liked. "It's time to get up and talk to Daddy."

"Fuck you," I said weakly, straightening my head.

To my left, I saw his face. He was standing a few steps away from me, holding a gun.

I didn't have the strength to care. For a moment, I was indifferent to what would happen next, and then I saw Castriel's face before my eyes. Would he mourn me? Would he want revenge? Would he miss me?

I shook my head.

Cas...

"What do you want from me?" My vision became sharper, so I could see everything around me more and more clearly. I was in some sort of old building. The cold bounced off the walls. I looked over the scattered furniture, the corners full of litter. There wasn't a single window in the room.

Either that was intentional or I was in some kind of basement.

"You're a lot like your mother, you know."

"If I remember correctly, you weren't supposed to talk about her."

"We were very young when we met," he continued, as if he hadn't heard me. "I fell in love with her in the first five minutes. By the third date, I knew she was going to be my wife. That happened a year later. Two more years and you were born. We were the happiest parents in the world..."

I shook my head and snorted. "Even such a great love has its limits, doesn't it?"

"There was a 'but.' As I grew up, I realized I was different from my peers. I saw more, felt more, suffered more. Every teenager suffers at some point. My suffering turned into a dangerous interest in human anatomy, psyche, emotions. I don't even know when the sight of blood became so fascinating to me—"

"Where are the girls?"

My father looked at me like a wayward child before continuing, "For a certain period of my life with your mother, all my eccentricities and fascinations quieted down. I stopped hearing other people's thoughts in my head and finally heard my own."

"Why are you telling me all this?"

"Because you need to know the truth. I loved you and your mother with a love that cannot be described. As the years passed, the voices grew louder again. I heard the thoughts of all the people I passed on the street. Good and bad, wonderful and monstrous; they all filled me. The first was Chloe, a girl passing through Louisiana. She gazed at me with a lingering look as she licked her lips. I could hear exactly what she was thinking. She had a darkness in her that was calling out to me. She started it all—"

"How could you! How could you kill all those girls?"

"You don't know what they were thinking. If you knew, you would have wanted to kill them yourself."

"I'm not you!" I yelled, jerking at the tape on my hands. "I would never enjoy torturing innocent girls!"

My father burst into a thunderous laugh that echoed off the walls. "Don't be naive, Isa! They were anything but innocent! Every one of them!"

"Where are they? Where did you hide them?"

By this time, I was completely sober from the drug of whatever he had injected into me in the park. However, I had to think of something to get free. My phone was destroyed, so no help from Castriel would come. I had to find a way out of this sick situation on my own.

Distracting my father with conversation, I bent my hands to loosen my bonds. I felt no effect, but I couldn't give up.

A chill ran down my spine and drops of cold sweat appeared on my forehead. My throat scratched from the dryness, my heart pounding harder and harder.

"Where are they buried?" I shouted.

"Patience. I'll tell you just in time before I kill you." There was silence, his heavy breathing the only sound. My father looked at me with hatred in his eyes.

"You're sick. How could you kill a woman who did everything to make you happy? She loved you more than anything." The first tear proved to be stronger than my reserve and slowly ran down my cheek.

"When I found her in the cellar that day, I saw something in her eyes. Partly it was contempt. Partly disbelief at the kind of man she'd married. I heard in my head how she'd decided to turn me in to the police and I thought—"

"What have you done with your trophies? Where are all the pictures and the fingers you cut off? Why did you have them in our house?"

"I didn't think it was fair! She looked at me... Both of you looked at me like I was some kind of fucking monster when I had done this world a favor. I couldn't stand the sight of the two of you. They were evil. You were evil people with no values, no loyalty, no morals, no holiness at all!" My father pulled at the ends of his hair in frustration. He looked down at the gun in his hand, then tapped the barrel several times on his temple. "I burned the pictures. And I flushed the fingers down the toilet. The day you got away from me, I knew you would come after me with the police. Just like I knew that one day I would come after you."

My father raised his gun and pointed it at my head. I held my breath, realizing that I didn't have as much time to get away as I had originally thought. But before I could get anything out of my system, I heard a scream.

"Stop! What are you doing, Michael? This doesn't seem like a simple conversation to me."

My head followed the sound. A few steps away from me, just outside the entrance to the room, stood Brad, followed by Castriel, with a gun pointed at the back of Brad's head.

I blinked several times, but the scene didn't disappear. I hadn't imagined it.

"Brad? What are you doing here?" I gasped.

"Don't worry, Izzy, my love. Everything will be fine," he replied, then turned his face to my father. "Stop aiming at her, for God's sake."

My eyes found Castriel. He stared at me, inspecting every inch of my body as far as the distance between us would allow.

You won't find the bloodiest wounds on my body...

How did he get here? Never mind, the important thing is that he's here with me.

"Michael..." Brad growled at my father, which caught my attention.

Brad's behavior was strange, as if he were a big kid.

"Drop the gun, Michael," Castriel ordered.

"How long have you two known each other?" I asked my father.

"Well... Bradley kind of helped me get to know you. I came across your track some time ago, but the commercial was like a scent that drew me to you. When I saw you on the TV screen, I knew you were my daughter. Then one night I met Brad in a bar. It was true destiny. He told me about the redheaded beauty who had turned his life upside down. At first, I thought it was just a coincidence. But as I listened to him, I became more and more suspicious. Then he showed me your picture, and the rest, as they say, was history."

"What is this all about? Brad, what do you stand to gain from this deal?"

"I... I just wanted Michael to get Castriel out of our way. Um, sorry, my friend."

What the hell?

Since when are they friends? They hate each other like two dogs in a dark street.

Castriel rolled his eyes but said nothing.

"Jesus. Do you know what you just asked him?" Pissed off at Brad, I started struggling again.

"Stop squirming, little princess," my father said.

"I asked him for help," Brad replied with satisfaction. "This is all for you, Izzy."

"For me? For me?! You wanted my father to kill the man I love, and it's all for me?"

Brad made a sour face. He seemed much more sober now than he had been a moment ago. So he was either faking it or whatever was in his body was leaving him.

"I love you, Izzy," he growled, as if that explained everything. "I just wanted us to have our chance. Michael said he only wanted to talk to you."

The laughter I let out surprised everyone. "Talk? You're talking about my father, a person who killed for pleasure. A person who killed my mother because she discovered him. A man who almost killed me! He's not here to talk. He's here to finish what he started years ago!"

I looked at my father, who was watching me with a small smile.

"Stop pointing at her and untie her, Michael," Brad demanded.

"I'm afraid I can't do that. In my defense, when I got out of prison, all I really wanted to do was talk to you. The way you hid from me, the way you moved thousands of miles away from home... It just pissed me off."

"I don't understand. You could have been a free man and yet you hunted me down like some kind of animal. What's the point? All those phone calls, all this masquerade. Why all this?"

"When I finally found you, you didn't stay alone for a moment. And then you moved in with him. Brad was supposed to get you away from him, but he screwed up even that. He was useless. You had a guy watching you from a distance, a bodyguard or something. I had to take matters into my own hands. Isa, I lost all those years in prison because of you! You did this to your own father, to your own blood! That's not fucking forgivable!"

I saw in his eyes how he had crossed the line of patience, no longer hiding his hatred for me. This was the face of the father I used to love and consider my hero, whom I now hated.

Resigned, I looked at the gun he was pointing at me, his hand shaking slightly.

I lowered my head and saw my mother's face. She was smiling at me, standing in our kitchen, the home of my childhood. I missed her so much.

I raised my head and looked around. We were at a dead end. My father pointed at me. Brad looked at my father and then at me with pleading eyes. Castriel watched, still pointing his gun at Brad.

I found the chocolate eyes I loved so much. I knew something bad was coming.

"I love you, Cas," I confessed, and the tears that had dried up a moment ago flowed again.

"And I love you, baby."

"I have a secret I want to share with you, my dear daughter," my father said seconds later.

My attention was drawn back to him. He first pointed the gun at Brad by switching it to his other hand. He was ambidextrous, so his left hand was just as threatening as his right. He leaned toward me when both Brad and Castriel growled, "Don't go near her."

"Easy, boys. I just want to say something in her ear," he replied with a smile.

I started to struggle again, but my hands were so tightly wrapped in tape that it was impossible.

The closer my father's face got to me, the stronger I felt that something evil was coming toward us. Panic grew in me with each passing second. "No, no, no…"

"I just want to tell you something," my father reassured me.

Finally, his face was right next to mine. Watching Castriel and Brad closely, he confessed the truth. I closed my eyelids, remembering his words.

This is the end.

"I promised to tell you where all the bodies are. Do you remember when I took you to that cave as a child? You called it the Cave of the Moon because it had an opening at the top through which you could see the moon. They went there as well, but they didn't deserve to see your moon ever."

I shook my head in grief and sadness as more tears flowed from my eyes. My whole body was shaking and my breathing was fast and shallow.

My father moved away from me, but I didn't open my eyes again. Before I could say anything, the room was filled with gunfire.

CHAPTER 29

CASTRIEL

When he leaned toward her to confess his long-buried secret, I knew it all came down to this moment. I remembered what he had said just before I entered the room.

"I'll tell you just in time before I kill you."

As Michael whispered his secret in her ear, I had seconds to decide how to play it next. I felt a shudder of fear as he pulled away from her.

So I grabbed Brad with my left hand and yanked him aside with all my strength. I heard his body fall to the ground, but that didn't matter now. I pointed my outstretched hand at Michael and shot right into his chest.

He didn't see it coming because he didn't have time to pull the trigger. I couldn't risk him making good on his threat to her.

Isabelle, with her head bowed, whimpered. Only after a moment did she realize that someone's gun had discharged. Her eyes opened, so round, full of fear in my direction. Then relief and new tears appeared in them.

Brad moaned somewhere off to the side.

I ignored him. It wasn't his time yet.

Michael didn't move, but I cautiously approached his body on the ground. Blood seeped through his shirt, forming a puddle beneath him. His face was motionless. I had no qualms about pulling the trigger again. "This is for Isabelle's mother." And again. And again... "This is for all the damage you've done to her and the others. And this is for daring to dream that you would take her from me."

I shot him a total of four times, none of which moved the body an inch. And yet I felt a sense of satisfaction.

I turned my eyes back to Isabelle. She was now gaping at her father's body, shaking like a leaf in the wind.

I secured my gun and slowly approached her. I knelt in front of her, blocking her view of the body. I placed both hands on her cheeks, drawing her attention to me.

"Hey, look at me. You're safe now, baby. You're safe. Do you hear me?"

Glassy emerald eyes looked up at me.

"Everything's going to be okay now," I reassured her. I leaned forward and for a moment, our lips met. I kissed her lips, her nose, her eyes, her forehead... "Baby, now turn your head the other way, okay? Do it for me. Don't look. I'm going to untie you, okay?"

Isabelle didn't say a word, but when she turned her head the other way, I knew she heard me. I reached for the knife hidden under my trousers and cut through the tape that bound her. I started with her legs and then did the same with her hands. Once she was free, she moved her hands forward and rubbed her sore wrists.

I stood up and held out my hand to her and when she grabbed it, I helped her up as well. My arms surrounded her. Hugging her was the best reward. Holding her felt like holding the most precious thing in the world. The relief in my heart was indescribable.

A muffled sob escaped from her throat, as if she had just realized what had really happened. I glanced over her shoulder and saw Brad sitting on the floor, looking at us with resignation on his face.

I kissed the top of her head and stroked her back reassuringly. After a moment, she calmed down.

Brad, meanwhile, crawled up from the floor.

"How did you find me, Cas?"

"Thanks to the tracking device you turned on."

"But my dad smashed my phone."

"The screen may have broken, but the phone still sent out a signal. You're safe, baby," I said, nuzzling her away. "Go to the exit now. I'll be right behind you. Okay?"

"No. Why? Let's go from here together."

"I still have to do something." I looked at Brad, who was standing with his hands clasped and looking at us.

"What?" Confused, she looked at Brad and back at me. "No."

"I have to finish this. For Isaac..."

Isabelle suddenly understood what I meant. She turned to Brad with a look of disbelief on her face.

"You? You played Russian Roulette with his brother?"

The now completely sober Brad finally understood. "Who are you?" His eyes fell on me.

"I'm the brother of the man who, because of you, cannot get up to this day. I'm the brother of the man whose life was just a game to you. I'm the brother of Issac Russell, upon whom you and your friends committed an unforgivable crime. A crime that was covered up."

"You killed the others, didn't you?"

"I carried out the justice you avoided all those years ago, hiding behind your money and your fathers' backs. You left him for dead and then went on with your lives as if nothing had happened—"

"We thought he was dead already! What could we do? Has anyone ever survived Russian Roulette?"

"Yes. They have. It happened."

Brad lowered his head and shook it. "What happened changed all of us. I'm not the same person. We were young jerks!"

"You were his tormentors!" I shouted. "You were executioners, born in this society. Murderers!"

"You're no better than us," he growled. "You killed Leo and Maverick—"

"I killed Connor too! And I don't feel sorry for any of you motherfuckers!" I looked at Isabelle again. "Go on, baby. I'll see you soon. I promise."

"No. Don't make me go there alone. Don't—"

"Please."

"I want to stay here with you," she pleaded.

"It will change you too, Isabelle. I don't want you to see it."

One look into my girl's eyes and I already knew that whatever happened, we were in this together. For better or for worse. God, how I loved that woman...

"So what? Are you going to shoot me?" Brad threw back in anger. "Is that why you came to see me?"

A bitter laugh came from me. "No, my friend. We're going to have some fun. We're going to play Russian Roulette."

"What?" Isabelle shrieked and Brad tilted his head to the side, wondering if I was joking.

"Set up one table and two chairs."

Brad looked at me like I had lost my mind. I pulled out my gun, unlocked it, and handed it to Isabelle. "If he tries to cheat, shoot him. For Isaac. Do it. I want a fair game."

"Cas—"

"Do it, Isabelle."

Isabelle's chest began to rise and fall rapidly. Her eyes glazed over again.

I whispered, "I love you."

She opened her mouth to argue with me further, but I turned back to Brad.

"How can I be sure you won't shoot me if I win?" He shrugged.

"You don't. And you don't have a choice. Set the damn table up!"

Brad turned and grabbed one of the overturned tables from the corner and set it up, then did the same with the two chairs. In keeping with tradition, he placed them facing each other.

I walked over and sat down, and he did the same.

I pulled out a second gun from the holster beneath my pant leg.

"Do you recognize this, Brad?" I raised my eyebrows and his eyes fell on the gun.

"Where did you get that?"

"Yeah, it's the same gun you used to play with my brother. It took me some time and resources to get it out of the police evidence room, but it was worth it."

I opened the cylinder, and a bullet fell out. I showed it to Brad by holding it between two fingers, then put it back in the cylinder, turned it, and closed it.

"Would you like to start?" I asked, but Brad shook his head.

"Oh, God," Isabelle cried.

"An eye for an eye." I put the muzzle to my chin and pulled the trigger without waiting a moment.

Isabelle's screams grew louder.

I swallowed my saliva.

"A moment of maximum danger is a moment of minimum fear, you know? Unless you put yourself in danger," I said. "Your turn."

I put the gun on the table and slid it toward Brad. The man caught it as he looked me in the eye.

He was shaking.

"Have some fucking balls, Brad. You had them so many years ago and now you're afraid to lose?"

He slowly raised the gun and pressed it to his head.

"A tooth for a tooth." I said as the first tear dripped from his eye.

He took a deep breath, closed his eyes, and squeezed the trigger. Nothing happened.

He let the air out with a swish of undisguised relief. He opened his eyes, put the gun down with shaking hands, and pushed it toward me.

I caught it and, once again, the cool metal touched my skin. "Blood for blood," I growled and squeezed the trigger.

"Castriel, please," Isabelle screamed between sobs.

I knew that if I looked at her now, I could never finish what I had started. Her sobs tore at my heart.

The air was thick. Brad knew that with each pull of the trigger, his chances of survival approached zero.

The revolver was back in his hand.

When it was at his neck, he looked me in the eye.

"We're all going to die," I said.

To this day, I don't know if he felt the end of his life approaching or if fear clouded everything. "I'm sorry," he whispered and pulled the trigger.

BANG!

The sound was mixed with Isabelle's scream.

CHAPTER 30

IZZY

When I woke up that day, I felt everything was heavy. I dreaded the day and knew it was going to be one of the worst ones of my life.

I felt nauseous just thinking about it, so I didn't swallow a single bite of breakfast.

I was almost ready and just waiting for Castriel when my phone buzzed. I rolled my eyes at the screen but answered it.

"Hello, Detective Burk. How can I help you?" It had been over two months since I had last heard from him and less than two since I had last seen my father.

"Hi, Izzy. I wanted to fill you in on something before you found out everything from the TV."

"Okay. What happened?"

"All the girls, all of Michael Hansen's victims, have been found. I mean, it's unconfirmed so far, but in one cave in Louisiana, they found the remains of numerous people. It looked like a mass grave. I have in front of me a document confirming the identity of one girl, a girl named Chloe

Charlson. We believe that the results of the others will be confirmed within the next few days and that they belong to your father's other victims."

I didn't say a word.

"Izzy, are you there?"

"Yes, I am. I thought this wasn't your area of expertise, Detective."

"I keep up with your case all the time."

"That's good. And it's good that you found them. I hope their families get the peace they deserve."

"Yes. The lab investigated the letter that was sent with information on where to look for the bodies. It was an anonymous letter sent from a small town in Mexico. Untraceable."

"That's strange, isn't it?" I asked him, looking at myself in the mirror. "But the important thing is that they were found."

Where is Castriel?

"True. Both of them. But you know what's even stranger, Izzy?"

"What's that, Detective?"

"That your father is missing. Literally, Izzy. You don't know what could have happened to him?"

"Of course not." I put on my lipstick and pressed my lips together. "Lord knows, Detective, he was the last person on this planet I ever wanted to see again."

Alive...

The detective laughed. "Anyway, no one has seen him, and I hope he never crawls out from whatever rock he's hiding under. I'm glad you're safe. You're in no danger."

"I think that's how it will be. Thank you for calling me with this information. I appreciate you wanting to tell me in person."

"No problem. Take care, Izzy."

"You too, Detective."

I put the phone down on the table. I stared at my reflection. Intuition told me the detective suspected I had something to do with my father's disappearance. Even if that was the case, there was no way he could find a speck of dust to incriminate me. I was sure that many people could breathe again after his disappearance.

As for Brad, the news reported that the poor man committed suicide. He was found in the woods, in a bunker. They found a gun on him. Of course, it was unregistered. His family didn't want any publicity, so the case was closed very quickly.

Maybe they were afraid that the media would link him to the Isaac case again. I could only guess.

I smiled as I saw Castriel in the reflection in the mirror. He came up to me, put his arms around me, and kissed the top of my head.

"Ready?" I asked him.

"As ready as I can be."

I turned in his arms and kissed him.

"Let's go," he whispered.

He took my hand, and we walked out of the apartment.

***

Castriel parked in the first available spot. For a moment, he sat motionless, like a statue, just breathing. His eyes were fixed on something far away, probably the past.

I had no intention of rushing him. I knew how much this was costing him.

When he looked at me after a while, he said, "I don't know if I'm strong enough to go in there."

I nodded sadly. "If you don't feel—"

"No. I have to give him his freedom sometime. But... He's my little brother... How can I say goodbye to him?"

"Cas, all I can say is that I'm here for you. I'm here for you and for him. You never say goodbye to someone you love. He lives and will live with you. His body dies, but he never dies. Never him."

Castriel nodded. The pain reflected in his eyes pierced my heart.

Slowly, Castriel leaned forward and planted a subtle kiss on my lips. "Thank you for being here for us," he said.

"Always."

We got out of the car and walked slowly to the building. Nodding, we greeted the older woman at the reception desk. We stopped at the door of Isaac's room, where the doctor was waiting for us.

"Mr. Russell, Ms. Knox. All formalities have been completed. You may enter Isaac's room now. Please let us know when you are ready."

"Doctor," I began. "And... And the pain?"

"He will feel no pain, I guarantee you that."

"Thank you."

Castriel sighed and pushed the door open. We stepped inside and sat facing each other, just like last time. We each took one of Isaac's hands.

"Hello, little brother..." Castriel's words were barely audible. He swallowed loudly and tried to smile. "Little I... I don't know what to say. For the first time, I don't know what to say. Lately I often think about our childhood, you know? I loved you from the first second you were born. I was always willing to do anything for you. As an older brother, I thought it was my duty to protect you, to take care of you, to teach you. I'm sorry. I failed you in so many ways—"

The first tears ran down Castriel's face, and mine too, but neither of us tried to hide them.

"We were still small, and life was already hard for us. But we had each other. Sometimes I wanted to curl up and cry all night. Then I thought of you. You were my rock, my strength that motivated me to fight. And I fought—for you, for us.

"Do you remember when you were in second grade and you had to recite a poem you'd written in front of the entire school? I remember we were standing behind the stage and you were panting all over the place. You said you couldn't do it. You were scared to the bone, paralyzed by fear. I remember the tears in your eyes. I had to make you feel invincible. I had to make you overcome your fear. I took out a stone out of my pocket I'd found in front of our house that afternoon. This stone was almost transparent, but when the sun shone on it, it shimmered with different colors. It was magical, just like you. All you had to do was believe in your magic.

"I gave you the stone. I closed it in your hand and said, *'You are unshakable like this stone, your strength comes from within, there is nothing in this world that can defeat you. Don't be afraid of anything. There's nothing stronger than you.'* You grasped the stone and believed in its magic. You believed in yourself, you overcame your fear. You walked out onto that stage and gave it your all. You didn't win that contest, but you won something far more precious. I was so damn proud of you. We celebrated over pizza that night."

I sniffed as Castriel reached into his pocket and pulled out the little stone. I couldn't stop crying.

"I have it, Little I. I have our magical stone. Every time one of us doubted ourselves, was afraid, we held this stone until the fear and doubt disappeared." Castriel let go of Isaac's hand, opened it, placed the stone in the center, and rested his own back on it.

"We'll keep it together, okay? Its magic has never faded. Its strength has never waned. Don't be afraid, little brother...

"I know it's time for me to let you go. I have avenged your harm on every one of your tormentors. I love you so much that there are no words in this world to express it. And I will always love you. I'm honored to be your brother. There's nothing that can separate us, not even death. So finally be free, little brother... Be free... Have no fear... Be unshakable like a stone... And when we meet again, we will celebrate together over pizza."

Castriel rose from his chair. Looking into Isaac's face, he leaned forward and kissed him on the forehead. For a long moment, he didn't take his lips off, as if giving him a blessing.

Before sitting back down in the chair, he pressed the button to call the medical staff.

I wanted to say something, anything, but I had trouble finding the words. I didn't know Isaac, and yet he was so close to me.

When the doctor entered the room, neither of us took our eyes off Isaac. Tears silently streamed down our faces. Our hands rested on his palms. Castriel's other hand rested on his leg, and when I took it, we intertwined our fingers. For a moment, he looked at me with gratitude mixed with pain. Not only our eyes, but our hearts and souls were crying.

"We're ready, Mr. Russell," the doctor whispered.

Castriel just nodded. His eyes never left his brother's for a second.

"Would you like to leave the room?" the nurse asked.

I hadn't even noticed when she appeared. Castriel shook his head as a sign that we weren't leaving.

"Good night, Brother. Until next time," Castriel whispered.

"Good night, Isaac. Until next time," I repeated.

Moments later, the machine that kept Isaac alive went silent. His heart was still beating on the monitor.

Isaac looked peaceful, as if he were asleep. If that was the case, I hoped he was dreaming the best of dreams.

I shook the two hands I held. The three of us were now one.

The doctor verified Isaac's vital signs or rather, lack thereof. "Time of death 12:41. I'm very sorry. Please accept my deepest condolences," he said in a low voice.

Puzzled, I looked at the monitor where I had just seen his heart beating. Now it showed a flat line.

Isaac was dead.

I blinked as fresh streams of tears flowed from my eyes.

Just seconds ago, he was here with us.

A man thinks of what will be in the future, lives years ahead, when meanwhile one second here and now changes the course of everything.

The power of a second is underestimated.

Isaac wasn't with us anymore.

Epilogue CASTRIEL

Standing in the church, I felt my brother's presence beside me. He was there for both the unpleasant and beautiful moments.

We buried his body, but he was always with us, as Isabelle told me that day.

"*We die from the moment we are born,*" says Japanese wisdom. It's true.

A part of me died with my brother, but another part was born. That part is eternal.

So, as I stood, surrounded by my brother's presence, I looked around at the handful of people gathered.

In the front was Mason. He held their one-year-old daughter in his arms. This blonde angel would one day break all the boys' hearts. I suppose she would be a devil too, but who was I to judge? I wanted to laugh at their naivete that this wouldn't be the case.

"Ready?"

I glanced over my shoulder at Takashi. He couldn't miss such an important day for us. He was a second father to me, a guardian angel, and a lifelong friend.

"I'm always ready. I've been ready ever since I met this woman."

Takashi laughed at my words.

"Do you remember what I told you when you came here to create Papilio? There's a time for everything. There's a time for work. There's a time for play. There's a time for being alone, and there's a time for love."

"Don't spoil the mood, old man," I replied, smiling. Of course, I remembered.

"You laughed then. Don't deny it. I was right about that love, wasn't I?"

"All right, all right. You were right. Satisfied?"

"You don't know how much, son. I'm glad you found her. I'm happy for you."

"You're my best man, Takashi. It's your job to say things like that."

The Papilio brand had conquered the American market. My six-month plan was completed in eight months. This was because new priorities had emerged in my life.

The organist began to play a melody, but I didn't hear a single note, because at the end of the aisle, on the white carpet, she appeared.

My bride.

My love.

My...

Dressed in a snow-white wedding gown, she looked phenomenal. The lace top of the dress shimmered with tiny pearls that ended above her breasts. Her shoulders were bare and around her neck hung a heart-shaped diamond pendant that I had given her as a gift when I asked her to marry me. She wore small diamond earrings. The bottom of the dress was satin, straight and slightly flared. Isabelle's red curls were let down her back; only the front ones were pinned back.

She did that for me, I was sure of it. She knew how crazy I was about her loose hair.

In her hand, Isabelle held a bouquet of white and pale pink peonies.

The sight etched itself into my memory and will always be remembered. She was the most beautiful creature I had ever seen. The most beautiful and mine.

"You're drooling," I heard Takashi whisper.

"And you're surprised?" I replied.

I didn't take my eyes off her for a second as she walked toward me, proud, straight, happy. I was a lucky man, and I would prove it to her to the end of my days.

When she reached the altar, she handed the bouquet to Emma, who was standing behind her. Emma was her maid of honor. Then she turned to me and smiled.

I was so focused on the woman standing next to me that everything else faded into the background.

"I, Isabelle, take you, Castriel, to be my husband. I promise to be faithful to you in good times and in bad, in sickness and in health, to love and to cherish you all the days of my life."

"I, Castriel, take you, Isabelle, to be my wife. I promise to be faithful to you in good times and in bad, in sickness and in health, to love and to cherish you all the days of my life."

Those were the most beautiful words I had ever spoken in my life. It was the beginning of our life together, sealed with a sensual kiss.

Acknowledgements

As always, the biggest thank you goes to *YOU*, my friend. For taking a chance on this book. I hope you enjoyed this story. If you cried along the way, know that I did too. Thank you for being so supportive. This means everything to me.

Aneta, my friend. Thank you for being with me every step of the way on this writing journey. I'm grateful and happy to have you with me. Thank you for everything you do.

Finally, I want to thank my son, who is my strength. Without you, this would never have been possible. I love you. To the moon and back.

Viola

"Game We Play" series

Game Plan
Roulette of Redemption

***

Please Review This Book!

Reviews help me, as an author, more than you might think. If you enjoyed this book, please consider leaving a review on Amazon and Goodreads. I would greatly appreciate it.

***

Say Hello!

You can connect with me in a number of places. Go to your favorite platform, and let's meet there. Your support is extremely important to me.

Facebook @ViolaHermanAuthor

Instagram @violahermanauthor

TikTok @viola.herman.author

Website https://violaherman.com

You can also send me an email violahermanauthor@gmail.com. I will always answer you personally.

9 788397 025257